Praise for ~~Jess~~
and the Lucky Lovers of London series

"Everlee crafts a scorching affair...
Their romance is a combustible one."

—*Entertainment Weekly* on *The Gentleman's Book of Vices*

"This is a joyful, spicy romance; but with an emotional upheaval
of pain and trauma you feel for both of the lovers."

—*Buzzfeed* on *The Gentleman's Book of Vices*

"Everlee creates an intriguing cast of found family for
Charlie and truly thorny obstacles for the lovers to overcome.
Fans of Cat Sebastian and Olivia Waite will enjoy
this queer Victorian romance."

—*Library Journal* on *The Gentleman's Book of Vices*

"Everlee's fabulous second Lucky Lovers of London Victorian
romance (after *The Gentleman's Book of Vices*) takes the series
to new heights... Equally sweet and steamy, this will delight
Everlee's fans while enticing many new ones."

—*Publishers Weekly*, starred review,
on *A Rulebook for Restless Rogues*

"After wowing readers with *A Gentleman's Book of Vices* (2022),
the first in her Victorian-era Lucky Lovers of London series,
Everlee returns with a stunningly romantic, superbly
sensual friends-to-lovers story that brilliantly
makes use of the book's thoughtfully rendered
characters and their search for love and acceptance."

—*Booklist* on *A Rulebook for Restless Rogues*

**Also available from Jess Everlee
and Carina Press**

*The Gentleman's Book of Vices
A Rulebook for Restless Rogues*

A BLUESTOCKING'S GUIDE TO DECADENCE

JESS EVERLEE

carina press®

Recycling programs
for this product may
not exist in your area.

ISBN-13: 978-1-335-42856-1

A Bluestocking's Guide to Decadence

Carina Press
22 Adelaide St. West, 41st Floor
Toronto, Ontario M5H 4E3, Canada
www.CarinaPress.com

Printed in U.S.A.

For Nana

The emotional well-being of my readers is important to me. If you would like to see specific content warnings before you dive in, please visit www.jesseverlee.com/cw.

Chapter One

Emily

That there was a village hospital at all in such a funny little corner of Surrey was lucky enough; that it boasted eight beds, two nurses, a skilled surgeon within calling distance, and two-and-a-half physicians was a luxury.

The two physicians were the founders of the place, two gentlemen known in the village for their kind hearts and modern minds.

The half-a-physician was a young doctor (though *quite* an old maid at the ripe age of thirty) called Emily Clarke.

Emily wasn't half-a-physician because she was halfway-trained, but in spite of her full—and, she thought, rather impressive—qualifications, half-a-physician she remained in truth: half-paid, half-scheduled, half-respected, and only permitted to minister to the same half of the population that she herself was part of.

"I don't know how I would have survived without you, Dr.

Clarke. I'm grateful beyond words that the founders were so open-minded as to bring you on," sighed the woman Emily was thankfully releasing this afternoon, a patient she'd seen through a painful, highly personal problem that one of the founding doctors had forbidden her to speak the proper name of aloud in case a male relative should overhear it. "It's really *so* forward-thinking to have you here for this sort of thing. Could you imagine, having to go through this with a male doctor at the helm?"

"Forward-thinking indeed," Emily said as vaguely as possible as she helped the woman out of bed. It wasn't her job to help a patient put herself together after giving the go-ahead for release. The other doctors here, those *open-minded* founders of the place, didn't do that sort of thing. But the nurse always seemed to have an awful lot to do for those *real* doctors' patients whenever Emily needed her.

At least the patient was pleased. Though Emily's unusual occupation was not universally approved of, the tide was turning in that regard, as more people took the view her patient had expressed: that for propriety's sake, maybe women were best treated by other women. While Emily felt that was still a bit shy of the mark when it came to equality, she was glad the attitude had let her see this patient through until she was well at last and ready to return to her family, her dear cat, Daisy, and (Emily knew from seeing her around town) quite the collection of ostentatious hatpins.

"Do take care, Dr. Clarke," the patient said, offering a dainty hand in departure. "Should I or one of my daughters require your help again, can we bring you in for a house call? I know your father used to do quite a lot of those—"

"He did," Emily said as pleasantly as she could manage, which, frankly, wasn't very pleasant at all. "But I'm afraid I do not."

The patient's gaze drifted toward the door to the women's ward and the rest of the cottage hospital beyond it. She lowered her voice. "Do they not permit it?"

After her lauding of the founders, the patient's candid question was heartening. But it was also hard to answer. On the one hand, Emily hated to let someone mistakenly believe anyone had power over what she did outside this building. On the other, however, she had a reputation to uphold. The true answer to that question wouldn't help it in the slightest.

"Something like that," she said without a smile.

Trying as it was to half-work in a hospital where the patients called her *my dear* even as they complimented her skills, it was better than making house calls. As Emily knew better than anyone, houses had ghosts. Ghosts that could multiply should a physician fail in her duty. It was bad enough when a ghost was made in hospital, seeming to wail as she wiped their blood and her shame from her hands and then following on her heels for weeks. Ghosts made in homes didn't just follow the doctor; they stuck around for the family to deal with. Forever.

She would know.

While rational, educated Emily did not actually believe in ghosts, the fact of her disbelief had never spared her from their effects. Take her study, for instance. She had a lovely little study to retreat to after she sent Mrs. Hatpin on her way and walked home at the end of her shift. A woman like Emily needed a practical place for penning research papers, for keeping up with the thoughts of modern philosophers and religious critics, for the carving hobby that kept her hands and mind healthy. But it had once been her mother's sewing room, still haunted by the chests of fabric and the dressmaker's dummy that Father had not allowed her to relocate.

Still, the study was more her own than any other part of the similarly haunted cottage she shared with her father in the quirky village of Farncombe, Surrey. She sat in her rocker only partly shadowed by the dummy behind her, letting the day's shift melt from her fingertips as she put them to the task of carving a chess piece. When dragging a knife along the rough edges of a bishop-in-the-making had finally soothed her soul enough, she put her carving things away, shook out her apron, and got the broom in hand. Along with her books, her writing supplies, her whittling knives, and the assortment of pieces that came from the union of her hands and those beloved implements, Emily always kept a broom in her study to sweep up the wood shavings.

Tidiness couldn't eliminate the ghosts, but it did keep them quiet.

She swept carefully into every nook. It was incredible how dust could accumulate in the span of a day, so innocent and invisible at first, but eventually gathering into fluffy balls that bred like the guinea pigs they kept in the garden. Occasionally, she still encountered a button or needle that had rested in the groove of a floorboard since God-knew-when.

As she tidied up the edges of her small dust pile, a knock came. She knew whom it was and tried to ignore him, hoping he would go away. She'd have liked a few more minutes to prepare the place before the riskiest sort of ghost of all—a living one—could sneak in.

"Ems?" he called through the door.

She leaned on the broom handle. "What is it, Noah?"

"Can I come in?"

No, she whispered to herself. But her childish reluctance was uncharitable, and if there was anything Emily hated more than dust, it was thinking herself to be uncharitable. She opened the door, just wide enough to bring her face-to-face with her twin brother. Though one would never know it from the way Papa saved him a chair in the garden or had the cook continue to order a little extra as if Noah might surprise them any day now, it was his first visit back to Farncombe in over a year.

Noah didn't like ghosts, either, though he preferred to run from them, leaving the clean-up to Emily.

While far from identical, the twins did look like twins, both slim, both gentle-featured, crowned with unimpressive hair colored somewhere between that of a mouse and that of a straw heap. But the similarities ended where personality took its effect on their forms. Emily was visibly proper, modest, and correct, dressed with no frills or restrictive cuts, fulfilling her familial duties without complaint, while Noah had abandoned his natural place as Papa's protégé to study fashion and acquire a truly bizarre assortment of friends, taking on a sheen of city-dwelling cynicism and European decadence. As ever, his silky fabrics and the scandalous addition of pearls tangled in his cravat were of shocking contrast in the simple halls of their small family of studious, suburban Unitarians.

"What do you need?" Emily asked, still clutching the broom.

He shouldered at the door, like he wished she'd open it enough for him to get a good look around. "You disappeared so quickly after tea. I just wanted to see what you were up to, maybe ask after a game of cards or…chess. Goodness, you've been busy in that regard, haven't you?"

He nudged at the door until there was nothing Emily could do but either step out of his way or engage in a petulant battle that would be *so* satisfying, but too unjustifiable to indulge. She sighed and let him in.

"Don't step in that," she snapped as he came too close to her dust pile.

Thankfully, he avoided it, though he probably cared more about the state of his shoes than the state of her floor. He continued to the shelves that lined one of the study walls. Her many books were displayed there, along with rows of mismatched chess pieces, in all sizes, woods, and designs.

Her brother took down the most unusual of those orphaned pieces, an overlarge and curvaceous queen that still needed a final sanding and staining.

"Oh, I do like her." Noah brought the piece to the tidy desk and popped her atop the pages of a completed essay that was probably the more impressive product of Emily's efforts. He did not mention it. How very like Noah to fawn over her useless hobbies and ignore her true accomplishments, spinning the wooden queen around a few times like he'd taken her to a ball and the pages were simply a dais placed there for her majesty's display. "Where's the rest of the set?"

"There isn't one," said Emily. "She's decorative, too big to fit on a chessboard. I rarely finish the sets anyway. The pawns are a nightmare. There are only so many hours in the day, you know, between my hospital shifts and my other obligations."

She nodded demonstrably at the stack of essay pages. Noah flicked his eyes over the title page at last, pausing for a lengthy moment before giving the queen another twirl. "Well, I suppose she'll be alright on her own, won't she? She looks self-sufficient." He quirked a half-smile that was part affection, part scold. "Will you finish this one piece, at least?"

"Maybe," said Emily. "But I have finished that which actually needs to be done, so forgive me if I do not lose sleep over a chess piece's lack of completion."

She looked very pointedly at the essay again. Noah could not ignore it this time.

"Congratulations on that," he said. "Do you know who's to publish it?"

Emily's stomach knotted. It was her usual journal, of course. Who else? They were one of the only publications willing to take her work.

"Yes," she said simply, leaving the inevitability out of it. She didn't want his pity, or worse, his complete disinterest in a field that might prefer his decorative tailor's stitches to her fully-trained female ones. "I do."

"Well done, Ems. I hope it's a runaway success and you can afford to spend the rest of your days without ever having to set foot back inside the hospital."

"You think they're paying me for this?"

At last, Noah looked embarrassed. "Are they not?"

Her publications, she'd learned a long time ago, were not even worth the half-pay she got for her hospital work.

"Even if they were, it would never be enough to get me out of hospital work. Assuming I even wanted to get out of that in the first place, which I do not."

"Sounds like miserable work. Though you do love your misery, don't you? Have at it, sister. I'll continue to wish more pleasurable days upon you in your place. That way you can blame me if it works, and you won't have to take responsibility for your most unfortunate happiness." He smiled. It was annoyingly good-natured. "Anyway, will you come downstairs with me? When you're finished with…that." He nodded at the dust pile. "I'd like to spend some time with you while we're here. David would too. I know he's in a rough spot and it's a bit hard to witness, but I think your company would do him a lot of good."

Noah had not made this trip home alone, but with his loving companion, David Forester, a very ghost-prone man who was visiting the quiet cottage in hopes of shaking off an especially bad one. The better air and distance from his troubles in the city were having a positive effect on his nerves. While she felt sorry for his situation, she remained shrewdly aware that she would have to sweep his room out twice when he went back home.

"You two have hardly been without me for a week," Emily

sighed, returning to her task as she fitted the broom under the rocker, going after the final specks. She'd stayed with Noah over the summer, as reluctant to be in London *studying obstetrics like a proper female doctor* as Noah was to have her there. But she'd finally checked that box, getting the training that everyone said would be the very backbone of her private medical practice that she did not intend to ever start. While it was true that hospital work could be grueling and full of horrors, it was better than devoting every day to difficult labors like the one that had taken their mother and broken their father. "Aren't you sick of me yet?"

"Oh, I am," said Noah, light and teasing and certainly true. "But David's not. Would you make him one of those tonics you mix up sometimes, the one with the poppy flowers? And then join us for a bit. He values your friendship, you know."

Emily was tempted to snap that while he and David were essentially here on holiday, she was not, and had a very early shift tomorrow.

But that was selfish, and selfishness wouldn't do. Noah was right: Emily was well-suited to helping David through his nervous troubles this evening. She had the skills. The poppy flowers. The greater ability to sit with suffering than Noah did, because while he'd been traipsing around London and Italy studying beauty, Emily had been here, taking up his abandoned post to study hundreds of sources of pain, sickness, and death. She could help. And, as always, if she *could* help, she *would* help. She *had* to help. To do anything else would be uncharitable, and to be uncharitable would be…

Well, honestly, she supposed it would be very relaxing.

But that sort of relaxation was not in her reach. Because Emily was a *good person*, and *good people* did not let their talents go to waste when someone nearby was suffering.

"I'll meet you in the kitchen," she said. "Put the kettle on for me, and I'll handle the rest."

"*Grazie, sorella.*" Noah kissed the air dramatically in her direction. He stepped around her dust pile again, then turned back to give the study one more look as he took the door handle.

"You know," he said slowly, "I'm surprised but glad to see that Papa finally let you redo Mother's sewing room. It had gotten so bloody depressing I could hardly stand it."

"Still a bit depressing," Emily muttered before she could stop herself, eyes flicking to the unused dummy in the corner.

Noah snorted a dark little laugh. "True, but still far more than I would have expected possible for him. If he'd alter the rest of the house even this much…" He shook the absurd idea off. "Anyway, if you think a change to the curtains won't shock him into a swoon, I'll do up some better ones for you. These aren't quite fit for a, well, for a sturdy and independent queen like yourself."

He gave the chess piece another twirl upon the pages, and left.

Alone, she got the dust heap put into the bin under her desk. Then she gave the whole room a quick second sweep, to make sure she got out whatever bits and pieces Noah had tracked in on his excessively stylish shoes.

Chapter Two

Jo

London's West End
Two Months Later

That infuriating second button was loose again. The smooth horn jiggled ominously between Jo Smith's fingers as she closed her favorite waistcoat over a chest that had once challenged even corsets.

"Well, fuck me," she whispered, squinting into the glass and tugging on the checked wool here and there in hopes of taxing the bugger a bit less. To no avail. The button slid to the edge of the buttonhole, holding fast for now, but wriggling on its stitches like a fish on the line, threatening its inevitable escape. It might not be today. Or tomorrow. But a most impolite failure loomed over its future.

She should fix it before she dragged her arse from her home to her shop. She was a bookseller these days, by far her most respectable and public-facing position. If she was going to be so scandalous as to wear men's clothes in the first place, she had to do it right: tidy cravats and shined shoes, starched shirts and brushed tweed trousers. It had been a change of mindset, to look so tidy all the time. In other lives, she'd mucked stalls and milked cows, mended hems and mixed cosmetics, risked her fingers setting type and risked her arse arranging that type into obscene publications. It was only in the past year that something like a loose waistcoat button would register as a problem that needed prompt tending.

She dug around in her bedside drawer for the sewing things she was pretty sure were in there, sifting through cheaper buttons, beat-up business cards and burlesque handbills, a worse-for-wear rosary, scraggly pen tips, and a few inexplicable pieces of moveable type she must have wandered off with at some point (two *a*'s and a *Q*, sans-serif). She found the needle she was seeking when it stabbed her in the thumb, and the thread when she mistook the tangle for a spider and yelped. Loud.

Whoops. She cringed as she snatched up the innocent spool. Her husband—if you wanted to call him that; he was really more of a legally bound friend—didn't work their bookshop directly, and still kept the later hours of the less-tidy half of their business. Though they'd done well enough to keep separate sleeping quarters for years now, their apartment wasn't what you'd call spacious. She listened for a moment for a sign that she'd woken him up, preparing herself for a good and deserved teasing when she admitted why.

Fortunately, there was no stirring; she would escape that particular embarrassment for now.

Back to business. Squeaking heavily onto her mattress, she got the tangle off the wooden spool with her teeth and got the needle threaded on the fifth try. She removed her waistcoat and pointed at the troublesome button with the business end of the needle.

And there she stopped.

This bugger was constantly threatening to run off; it was

going to need a hardier stitch than the one she'd been using to resecure it. She knew one, didn't she? A better button stitch? She tipped her head back in thought, staring at the ceiling and feeling how the dark hair she kept knotted at the nape of her neck squished against her starched collar. Her grandmother had taught her a button stitch years and years ago, when Jo was known as nothing more than a particularly bothersome farmer's daughter back in Ireland. Gran had shown it to her in hopes that better button placement might settle her frustrations with the way her dresses fit. That had not quite been the issue with the dresses, but the memories of Gran's concern were sweet, and the stitch still came in handy.

Or, rather, the shortcut version Jo had taken to using came in handy. She'd gotten lazy with it over the years, too bored by the need to reinforce her pawned and off-the-rack gentleman's wear to do it properly. But she'd become friends with a fancy tailor, who'd helped her get her hands on her first properly fitted waistcoat. It fit tighter, and its horn button was heavier than the wood or bone she was used to. Clearly the combination of her bosom and the button's heft called for more skillful measures.

She tentatively poked at the fabric a few times, mind blank and fingers itching for their shortcut…

That blasted stitch was probably written down in Gran's book. Jo had nicked the little handwritten compilation of wisdom, remedies, and devotions before running away for good after that one dear relation passed on. It was rightfully hers, she figured, as Gran's favorite and the bane of everyone else's existence. The rest of the O'Donnell family back on the farm could still ask each other for reminders on things like this. Jo, on the other hand, knew she would have only paper and ink to guide her adult footsteps, so across the sea into England the book had come along with her.

Quiet as she was willing to be while still plagued by a *tiny* bit of resentment that her husband, Paul, didn't have to get up at dawn, she passed by the closed door to his room and through the parlor, headed for the study where they kept their books.

While every other area of the home was lavish and artful, those beloved shelves—those of a lifelong printer and his bookish wife—were packed, every gap filled in at whatever angle necessary to fit the books, so many of them that they were stacked on top of the shelves and the floor in front of them too. Little dime novels were smushed in between important literary tomes; the works of saints and homemakers untouched for years but never discarded; instruction on everything to do with getting words put down on paper, from printing to inkmaking to bloody handwriting analysis. And unfortunately, there was no reason as to the placement, no groupings by subject or author or alphabet. Jo and Paul very much enjoyed their odd way in the world, but that way had never been the most thoughtful or organized way.

Jo started scanning from the left, hands in her pockets and her eyes glued to the myriad spines that had been collected or printed-and-bound by her and Paul over the years of their marriage, searching out that ratty spine that was embedded deeply in her memory. Fuck. It could take an hour to hunt this thing down in such a disheveled, disorganized, neglected wall of treasure. All she managed to spot was some new scandalous stock from the erotic press they ran out of a Holywell print shop, the titles *The Ruin of Renatta Cunny* and *The Sailors' Tryst* sticking out obviously and obnoxiously in substantial stacks on the bottom shelf.

Blimey, they shouldn't keep that many copies at home. When had he brought these over? It wasn't good practice to keep these here. She made a mental note to bitch heartily at her dear husband until he took the lot back to the print house cellar where it belonged.

She glanced down the hallway. Did Paul know where Gran's book was? She considered waking him up, to ask him about it and scold him for bringing too much stock home...but no. Neither situation was urgent, and she needed to get the shop open. As she went back through the parlor, she spotted that a biscuit tin had been left out on the low table before the fireplace. Good biscuits. Ones she hadn't realized they had.

She smiled with affection in spite of herself. Just like that prat of a husband of hers, up snacking on the good stuff into all hours of the night without her. She popped the lid off and was just scooping a few up to eat on the way when she heard the sound of a creaking bedframe and footsteps from down the hall.

Jo looked up from the tin to see Paul in the doorway, the familiar, slim figure of him draped with a fur-trimmed dressing gown that hung from his shoulders as if from a clothesline. There was a brief look of panic on his features and a quick glance behind him to the bedroom. Then his blond pencil mustache twitched with amusement.

"Caught in the act," he said, clucking his tongue. "Here I thought you were industriously making your way to work, only to find you've become a biscuit thief instead."

"Don't mind me, I'll be out of your way in a second."

That guilty look came back over his face.

"What's the matter with you?" She laughed and reached for her hat. "Anyway, you don't happen to know where my gran's old—"

"Paul?" came a high-pitched voice from his bedroom.

Oh. So he had Vanessa here. As Jo's hand finally settled onto her hat, she noticed something else she hadn't: the mermaid-shaped coatrack by the door held not only Paul's things, but a woman's coat and hat. Paul sometimes dressed so ostentatiously that she hadn't thought much of it, but on second glance, that

hat with its faux birds and flowery branches was a bit much, even for him.

She caught his guilty eye. What was he acting so strange for? Vanessa had been coming round for a year, almost. Bit unusual that he hadn't asked Jo to clear out and snag a room at her sapphic society so the two of them could have a night together like he usually did, but in the end, Jo and Paul kept to their own affairs and liked it that way. Jo couldn't say she was friends with Paul's eccentric lover, but they were friendly enough that a chance overlap in their presence was nothing to be so awkward about.

But as she opened her mouth to ask about it, she was cut off by footfalls and a tired voice:

"Paul, I think my stomach will settle best with a few of those—"

Vanessa Garcia—the Spanish actress that Paul had fallen head-over-heels for after a particularly ferocious production of *Macbeth* at The Strand Theater—froze in the doorway, her eyes wide and cheeks flushed bright red when she spotted Jo by the door, like she expected Jo to fly into a jealous rage at any moment.

It was ridiculous. If Jo was jealous of anything, it was no more or less than Paul's ability to hang on to a pleasant re-lationship with a pretty woman, which was something she'd never managed herself.

"Morning, Vanessa." Jo averted her eyes, in case it was the woman's disheveled appearance that had her so shaken, rather than an expectation of jealousy. Vanessa had a pale complex-ion, raven hair, and lips rouged to give a Snow White–ish impression. But this morning, her opulent (though obviously secondhand) dresses had been swapped for some abandoned old silk of Jo's, the paint on her lips dull and leftover. Her age—likely into her forties, though it was always hard to tell with an actress—was not as well hidden as it normally was, making her look more like the wicked queen than the titular princess. Not in a bad way, though. Nothing wrong with a good old wicked queen.

So why did they both look like they were hiding a body back there in the bedroom?

It was unsettling, like stepping unexpectedly upon a loose cobble. Jo returned her biscuits to the table and backed away toward the door. "I was just on my way out—"

"Oh, Joey dear, don't go," said Vanessa, voice clear, brow angled, diction posher than her status in a married man's bed would indicate. "Please. I'm sorry you have to see me in such a state—"

"No one needs to be in any particular state on my account," said Jo.

"Join us, will you?" Vanessa went on. She'd been in London a long time. Like Jo, her accent was nearly tamed, so it was strange to hear it breaking free this morning. Jo had spent just enough time with her to recognize the stress as Vanessa scrambled for her usual misty, dramatic way in the world. She reached out and took one of Jo's hands in both of hers, smiling like she was peering into the great beyond instead of Jo's very regular set of eyeballs. "I'm sorry to surprise you like this. I came over after my rehearsal very late last night. There was so much to discuss. Is *still* so much to discuss—"

"Discuss?" Jo alarmedly tried to get her hand back without snatching it, but her subtle attempt at detangling went unnoticed.

"The miraculous connection we'll soon share, my dear," said Vanessa. "I simply insist that you—"

All at once, Vanessa stopped her characteristic yet ominous gushing and went dreadfully pale. She dropped Jo's hand and sprinted to the water closet, slamming the door shut behind her. Jo blinked her bewilderment, then turned to Paul.

"Is she—?"

The unpleasant sound of sickness tripped her up.

"Hold that thought." Paul put one glittering finger up, then darted off.

Stock-still and ears strained, Jo listened:

"It will pass, darling," said Paul, chipper as anything.

Then Vanessa's voice, no longer even trying to remain clear, clean and English, but decidedly rough and weak: "Oh, I'm sorry you're seeing this. It's so embarrassing—"

"Don't worry about me. You know I work on Bookseller's Row, darling. I step in worse every time I go down there, no question… Better?"

"Much."

There were sounds of movement, the rattle and swoosh of water flushing down the pipes, some mumbled words, then Vanessa came back. She still looked awkward, but quite a bit better than someone who was sick ought to look. She took up a pitcher painted with bacchanalia and poured from it into a glass that she drank from gratefully.

"Are you ill?" Jo asked, awkwardly glancing back as Paul joined them again, looking a little frazzled. "Damn, I really ought to get out of your way. I—"

Vanessa cut her off with a tired little laugh. She looked across the room at Paul, and that's when Jo caught the sparkle in both their eyes.

Unfortunately, Jo had spent plenty of time in the company of sickness. Little siblings with stomach bugs. Dying animals on her family's farm. Friends at her rowdier club, not the sapphic society but the other one, The Curious Fox, where blokes were known to go overboard with the gin.

There was only one sort of sickness, in her experience, that came with even the vaguest possibility of *eye sparkles*.

Jo could not process the news at all. It might have been easier if Paul and Vanessa were treating the situation like the disaster it was, but once the sickness passed, they both seemed happy.

"Given I've made it this long," Vanessa said with the shameless ease of a woman very outside of polite society, hand on her unwed belly in a manner that would cause the average Englishwoman to swoon, "I simply assumed it wasn't possible for me. In fact, I thought the missed courses were signaling the official end of such things, and that the dreadful sickness I've had was something I ate. But at this point, it's undeniable. After a conversation with one of my housemates yesterday and nearly fainting at rehearsal, I knew it was time to tell my dear Paul about the situation and express my hope that he would share this joy with me going forward."

Jo stared between the two of them, dread soaking up through her like muck through the seams of bad boots. "And what does that mean, exactly?"

Vanessa got yet another dreamy expression, like she was about to set a stage with all her wildest dreams for the sake of Jo's entertainment, but Paul leaned forward on his knees and looked seriously into Jo's eyes.

"I know what you're thinking," he said quietly, the dreaded word *divorce* seeming to pulsate in the very air between them. "You're thinking the worst. But I swear—"

"It will be an *irregular union*!" Vanessa proclaimed, as if these words were an incantation for joy immeasurable. "You know we have already been discussing celebrating our love among our own community. Now, we can celebrate the life of our child as well! We shall find a way forward together. And—" She broke off, looking a bit more softly in Jo's direction. "We shall do it without approval of church or crown, as those mean nothing to us anyway."

Jo stared at the pair of them, furious with Paul for getting himself into this situation and incredulous with Vanessa, who, while odd, had seemed to have a half-way decent head on her shoulders. Had she gone entirely mental? It was one thing to celebrate love and life and whatever-the-devil when it was just two people involved. It was entirely another when things became a matter of bigamy and bastards. She had to know that, didn't she?

"Vanessa—"

But she'd gone green once more, and was out of her seat and off to the water closet before Jo could try to prompt a more reasonable reaction out of her.

Paul grimaced as he watched her go. "It's definitely mine," he said with a sigh. "I too become sick when the church and the crown come up in a perfectly nice conversation."

"Perfectly nice?" Jo hissed, keeping her voice under the sound of retching. "You do realize this is a disaster, don't you?"

Paul Smith. Paul Shanahan when they'd married nearly twenty years ago. A man she did not love in the way of the poets, but cared for and laughed with and built businesses right alongside. Now that Vanessa was out of the room, he should be looking at her in a proper state of panic at the way his carefully curated life on the margins was about to be upended.

Instead, he sighed. "Is it, though?" He took one of the biscuits but did not bite into it, his hands obviously hungrier for distraction than the rest of him. "With raids being what they are right now, and only promising to get worse come the new year and the new laws, I've already had to tame things down at the press. Might have to put some of the tawdrier vases up high for a while, but all in all..." He looked at her with guilt that could not hide a glow of happiness in his eye. "Not a disaster. Such a circumstance has, in fact, never seemed like a disaster. To me."

His last two words were so incredibly loaded that Jo was struck speechless.

While he'd said before that divorce—a shameful legal proceeding that would leave Jo in a very bad situation indeed—was not on his mind, the fact that she'd never given him the children he was technically owed was his ticket to it, should he change his mind. Church and crown be damned, she'd done everything in her power to avoid a similar circumstance, back when their marriage was still a functioning one. And the way it functioned now was no better in the eyes of those nauseating institutions…

"We should talk," he said before she'd gathered her wits. "Just you and me. As soon as possible. I know that this is—"

But then Vanessa was back, looking gray and frail. Though she seemed to think she was a few months along, Jo noticed that she didn't really look it. She'd never have described Vanessa as hearty, but in spite of her smile and her over-the-top assurances, she now decidedly lacked the heft and vitality that Jo's own highly fertile family had insisted was necessary to bear healthy children.

She suddenly regretted not having made a better effort to be friends with Vanessa. Maybe Paul wasn't thinking divorce yet, but Jo had a hard time trusting that Vanessa was truly alright with the status that an irregular union would afford her and her child. This worrisome physical state didn't bode well for continued optimism, either. At every disadvantage imaginable, what if she tired of her unmarried status? The insecurity that came with it? Paul loved Vanessa. Would he really deny her for Jo's sake? Jo, the wife who had given him friendship and monetary success, but nothing that could ever compete with love and a child?

If this situation was left to go forward on its own, Jo would be out on her arse by Christmas.

But what could be done? Oh, there were plenty of nefarious games to play, but that wasn't her way. So what on earth...?

Jo stared at this woman she hardly knew, yet suddenly seemed the arbiter of Jo's entire future, thinking fast and latching onto the first thing that might save her from a trip to the divorce court. The bags under Vanessa's eyes. Her obvious exhaustion. The tentative way she nibbled at her biscuits. Latched onto the idea that there was a problem.

And perhaps, that problem was Jo's solution.

"You know, dear Vanessa, while I am very happy for you, I'm concerned for your health," Jo blurted, loving and grasping onto the reason with both hands as she did. Jo would not be nefarious, but she could be *concerned*. She could be knowledgeable. Could, if she played it right and called on old ideas and skills she'd purposely tried to leave to the Irish housewives, be *useful to keep around*. "I think you should know that my grandmother was an expert in these matters, and I saw... *helped*. I helped my own mum go through it nearly half a dozen times with my younger siblings. I'll tell you, she made a great show of plumping up good and early. Your illness is concerning. Based on my, um, extensive experience."

Paul rolled his eyes at the notion that Jo's experience was extensive, but much to her surprise, Vanessa nodded grimly. "I appreciate that," she said, sending a wave of relief along Jo's spine. She could be *appreciated*. "I admit, I know next to nothing of the condition. As I said, I never thought it would happen for me." She put a hand to her belly in a gesture so soft, so loving, so full of wonder at what seemed to her a miracle that Jo couldn't bear to look at her until she'd knocked all that off. "What do you think I should do? I hate to think my baby is going hungry in there already!"

Vanessa was looking at Jo just as Jo had hoped she would: like a little secondhand expertise made her a genuine authority on the subject, and a person whom Vanessa should certainly not beg Paul to get rid of.

Paul, on the other hand, looked wary. He put a bracing arm around Vanessa's shoulders and tucked the edge of the old silk more securely over her collarbones. "My darling, if you're concerned that the sickness is beyond the usual bounds, we should discuss it with an actual doctor, as opposed to…um." He blinked a few times, clearly cycling through a few options before settling on, "A… Jo."

Jo rubbed the back of her neck, faltering a little. Before she could hedge what she'd said about expertise, an unexpected fire lit up in Vanessa's eyes.

"And what doctor are we supposed to speak to?" she snapped, rounding on Paul. "I'm an unmarried actress, Paul. Toxic to any respectable professional. If all goes well, my friends at home will help me though the labor. If it doesn't go well, it's the women's hospital in Soho Square, and then only if I can talk someone into granting me a bed—they're limited, you know, and to get one you must inspire pity in a paying member." She sighed, smoothing the sleeves of Jo's old silk. "They won't see *an irregular wife* when they look at me there, no matter how many parties we have to celebrate the union. They'll see a fallen woman, carrying a burdensome bastard who will get up to no good. And you mind my words, they will treat us accordingly." She shined those lit-up eyes back in Jo's direction. "Jo, if you have any help to offer, I would be so grateful. You obviously know quite a lot more than I do, and goodness knows, I trust you entirely."

As a person who was consistently dressed wrong, sailor-mouthed, and often a bit creative with the truth, that wasn't a compliment Jo had ever received before.

"Oh, don't say that," she said before she could stop herself. She laughed a little awkwardly. "Why would you say that? We haven't spent enough time together for all that."

Vanessa snuggled in tighter to Paul on the sofa, looking much happier there than Jo herself ever was. "Because Paul's told me all about you. Once he assured me that he'd be seeing this through with as much officiality as can be had, he told me everything, to make certain that *I* wanted to see it through with him just as eagerly. Everything that came up about you was as glowing a review as if he'd been talking of a dearly loyal brother or sister. And of course, I can see that what he said was true."

"How? I haven't done anything."

"I have my own expertise," said Vanessa with a certain smugness, that queenliness returning at last to her posture. "In the human condition. I've known what sort of person you are from the moment we first met, dear Jo. You won't steer me wrong."

"No," said Paul, a little edge to his voice as he looked at Jo while speaking to Vanessa. "She certainly *won't*, will she?"

Jo stood up at last, pacing a bit until she caught Paul's eye. She had a silent yet detailed conversation with him across the room, because one did not live so many lives over so many years together without learning to speak silently. But then what did it mean, when the person who could say *I know what you're doing; knock it off and talk to me properly later* with nothing more than a twitch of his eyebrow suddenly launched himself into a new life without you?

"Well, uh, it's not me, really, who's the expert," Jo said, fumbling a little over the admission. "It was my gran. So. I've misplaced her recipe book, but it should be on the shelf over there somewhere. Go ahead and give it a look if you can find it..." She grabbed her own coat from the clutches of the mermaid rack, a chill shooting up her spine even as she set to the task of warming it back up under the swath of tweed. She stared at the door she itched to escape out of. They'd find the book. Look it over. Give it back to her, if she was lucky.

And then what?

And then her usefulness would end. Her place as a legal obstacle would burn bright as ever. In spite of Paul's naïve reassurances, keeping her around would become a silly flight of fancy compared to what his child would face in its illegitimacy.

"Until then, though, try a bit of ginger," Jo blurted, much to all of their surprises. She wasn't even sure how she remembered that. Some tucked-back part must have sprung a leak. She felt the burn of the candied ginger she used to swipe from her mum's medicine cabinet, and the sting of the switch when she was caught because *it was medicinal* and they *could hardly afford enough as it was*. "And if ginger don't do it," she went on, "see how you do with a very thin potato soup. Coats the stomach. Might help you eat a bit more, but if not, it's nutritious enough on its own to see you through."

"I knew it," said Vanessa with that smug smile. "You'll be a delightful help to me, won't you, dear Jo?"

"Yes," said Paul, pure warning in his eyes now. "Practically a midwife, that one."

"Oh, I wouldn't go *that* far," said Jo with a modest shrug that might very well imply she would go that far. "But I can be of help. Certainly. Most certainly, whatever else is going on, I can be of help."

She was not an inconvenience, something to be got rid of when Vanessa realized how much better off she'd be if she convinced Paul to get that divorce that he was entitled to ten times over. She wouldn't be that.

She would be *help*.

"Jo—" said Paul carefully.

"Must run." Jo popped her hat on in a hurry. "Keep an eye out for the book for me—you know, to jog my memory of some of the details—and I'll start gathering some of the herbs we'll want for that second, um, part. The second...oh, what's it called?"

"Trimester?" said Paul, so dry his throat might have been filled with sand.

Jo tipped her hat and looked just to the left of his eyes. "That's the one!"

When one's husband is suddenly expecting a rather ill-advised baby with some perfectly nice actress that he chivalrously did not abandon to the slums of London, and one is not quite convinced this won't have disastrous consequences for one's own daily existence, it is reasonable to expect one's friends to engage in commiseration, complaint, and excessive consumption of whiskey.

But if Jo had wanted that, she probably shouldn't have chosen Charlie Price as the friend to tell first.

They were in the bookshop after closing. Charlie had stopped by after his day at the bank so his lover—one of Paul's authors—could get some writing done at home. While Jo's hands were busy patching up the broken spine of a collectable volume she'd acquired, and the other shop hand, Alma Merriweather, was off sweeping and humming industriously in the store room, Charlie was doing his part by being perfectly decorative on the counter with a parcel of the shop's secret inventory open on his lap. While the vast majority of their books were good and proper, Charlie had a preference for the fun ones.

"This is dreadful." Charlie squinted at the page in confusion. "I don't think he could get to the other bloke's cock quite like that from the position he's standing in..." He turned the book at an angle like the action might tip all the characters into a more sensible configuration. "I'm not convinced the third chap could, either..."

"I didn't promise you fine literature," Jo snapped. "Now, quit bitching about the mechanics of fictional fornication so I can focus."

He went silent, but she could feel him watching her until she'd put the cap back on the glue pot and settled the book safely to the side to dry.

"You're awfully cheery today," he said when she returned. "Any particular reason?"

Jo put her elbows on the counter and rubbed her hands down her face. "The Beast and his lady friend are having a baby."

Charlie did not say anything for long enough that Jo glanced up. She'd expected commiseration, but probably shouldn't have. Seeing as Charlie had once convinced himself that he wanted seven of the little buggers, he wasn't properly distraught at all. In fact, he looked cautiously excited.

"That sounds delightful, Joey. But perhaps also…complicated?" he added, clearly reading and adjusting to the scowl she gave his enthusiasm. "The Beast is not, um, what I meant to say is, this doesn't mean he's going to…"

He broke off. Positive to a fault, giving voice to unfortunate possibilities seemed beyond Charlie's capability.

"As far as I know, he's not dragging me to court for a divorce on account of my being a deserter, a cross-dresser, and a seducer of innocent lasses, so I suppose it could be a lot worse." She put her head back in her hands, thinking about what a fool she'd made of herself during the initial conversation. She hadn't even congratulated them properly. Paul, her best friend, her companion for life, and she hadn't congratulated him. "Could be a lot better too, though."

"How so?"

"Well, aside from being a bit of an arse about the whole thing, it might also have been better if I hadn't insinuated to his lover that I have midwifery expertise to help her through the sodding pregnancy."

She couldn't bear to look at Charlie after admitting it, but she didn't have to. He hopped off the counter and came around to face her, his own elbows just outside of hers and his dark eyes so wide she could bloody *hear* them gawking at her even with her own squeezed shut.

"Joey!" he hissed. "You did what, exactly?"

"Well, I didn't want to be useless, did I?" Her voice came in a squeaky, desperate sort of whisper as she finally looked up to where Charlie had gone very conspiratorial, clearly on the verge of a spectacular burst of laughter. "He don't want to get rid of me yet, but *she* will eventually, once she shakes the baby dust out of her eyes and realizes it's nothing but me standing between her and a lot more stability for that child of hers. What if she convinces him to get the divorce?"

"Aren't you two Catholic? Can he even do that?"

"This is *England*. What's the court care whether the Catholic church approves the split? It's the courts that matter, and I won't do well in court, mate. I haven't managed anything approaching a marital duty in a decade, and while adultery's not cut-and-dried when it's two women, a good lawyer could convince the wrong judge that I've broken my vows in that capacity, among other things..." Things she'd done to avoid being in Vanessa's situation, church and crown be damned right along with her. "I'm not exactly a sympathetic creature if I wind up on the stand."

Charlie mulled that over. "It's not jailable, is it? Anything you've done?"

"Some is, some isn't," she admitted, "though what *is* probably can't be proven."

"And you get to keep what's yours in the event, don't you? They passed a law to that effect a few years ago, didn't they?"

"Technically, yes," said Jo. "Lot of good it would do me, though. I had nothing to my name when I married him save for two dresses and an old recipe book I've lost, and we never bothered keeping our money separated. If he turns on me, it will be with exactly as much of our assets as he wants. Or *she* wants. See why I had to get into her good graces?"

Charlie thumped his hand down on the smut he'd been reading. Paul's smut. "Let's say it came to that. You really think he'll do much better in court than you will? Given this?"

"I'd sooner die than simper and swoon and pretend it's him that dragged me into his filth to save my own skin," she snapped, shuddering at the very thought of the things she'd have to say and the fate he'd suffer for it. If such a degrading ploy even worked. "I'm not a bloody rat."

"Is he a bloody rat?"

She sighed, considering it honestly. "No."

"Then why are you so worried?"

It seemed a reasonable question, but the anxious gnawing in Jo's belly thought otherwise. She was worried because she had to be. Because she'd been out on her arse before, and avoiding it happening again was more important than she could articulate.

"All I'm saying is that she and the child are suffering for the lack of a proper marriage already," she said, settling for a response that sounded as rational as the question. "She's too scandalous to get a doctor equal to the sickness she's suffering, and I'm the one standing in the way. I need to make sure I look like a help to her, rather than an obstacle."

"Here's a wild idea: why not help by finding a doctor, instead of pretending to be a midwife?"

"Where exactly am I supposed to find a doctor?"

Even as she said it, it came to her, and she knew the answer to that. Charlie did too, smiling at her through the realization.

"Feel like coming along to The Curious Fox with me tonight?" he asked.

★ ★ ★

Unlike Jo, their friend Noah Clarke only donned a full set of the wrong sex's clothes when he did drag on the weekends. Still, he was not exactly inconspicuous even on a ho-hum workday such as this, in pearl earrings, hair too long to be even called rakish, and an intricate shawl draped over the shoulders of his jacket. Jo and Charlie found him sitting by himself at his usual table at The Curious Fox, playing solitaire and sipping such an ominous and absinthe-tinged drink that he looked more like an oracle reading the contents of his crystal glass than a slightly chilly tailor relaxing in his lover's gentleman's club after a long day.

"Here for a game?" Noah said as they joined him.

"Can't afford it," Jo said. "Last time I played you I went hungry."

Noah smiled wickedly at his cards as he went on placing them in the spread upon the table. He winked when Jo caught him slip a bad card to the bottom of the deck. Apparently, he settled the odds in his favor even when he played himself.

"Jo has a question for you," said Charlie, determinedly clapping her on the shoulder. Clearly, he wouldn't let Jo back out of correcting her little midwife misstep. "About your father."

Noah's eyes snapped up from his cards, wary. It was rare to discuss families at the club. "What about him?"

Jo glanced around before she went on. While the owner was careful about who he let in, extra caution never hurt before saying something that could trace a bloke back to his life outside a club like this. But while Jo only came here occasionally (and lacked the appetite for what went on in the backrooms and private parlors of the place) she *was* acquainted with every bloke here tonight, and none of them was paying their table the slightest mind.

Still, she leaned in and spoke quietly. "He's a doctor, isn't he? And a radical one at that?"

"Radical might be taking it a bit far, but it's true enough in the important ways," Noah said slowly. "Why do you ask?"

Jo started in, but Charlie spoke first:

"Because Jo needs a very open-minded obstetrician and was wondering—"

Noah clutched his shawl to his chest and shattered the mellow clinking and chattering of the parlor with a flat-out scream.

"Joey's pregnant? Can that even *happen?"*

One might think that such a dramatic declaration would get a reaction, but the Fox's regulars were used to outbursts from Noah; they went right on with their own business. The only person who looked interested was the club owner, David Forester, whose gossip-loving head whipped up from the glass he was wiping so fast he seemed in danger of spraining something.

"Not for me, you idiot!" Jo clarified desperately as Charlie chuckled not-so-innocently and Noah scrabbled for the comfort of David's arm, the latter having materialized at the tableside with his eyes wide and his ears open. "It's for The Beast's girlfriend."

"Your husband's girlfriend," Noah said, coming down from the shock.

"Yes."

"Not you," said David.

"Fuck no."

"We've got to keep the girlfriend happy, you see," said Charlie. "So that she doesn't try to talk him into the divorce that would let them be a perfect little family without a stray sapphist in the attic, making things complicated. And also so she will let me hold her baby when it arrives."

Jo shouldered him roughly. "What the devil do you know about holding babies?"

"I'm an uncle several times over, and a very good one at that. Do you really think my family would even be speaking to me if it weren't for the children? They rioted in the streets when I was disinvited from Christmas." He waved a hand around the club, as if indicating the myriad reasons the disinvitation might have happened. "In fact, forget being a good uncle. I'm willing to bet that by this point, even my *maternal* instincts are better than yours."

"Bet?" Noah ran a finger along his stack of cards, making them snap against each other as he eyed Charlie. "How much?"

"It's just an expression; I'm not betting against *you*."

"Hmm." Noah went on snapping his cards, moping a little in David's direction.

David planted a kiss on the top of Noah's head, then turned his attention back on Jo. "So your husband is expecting a baby with this woman. And she needs a doctor, am I understanding the situation correctly?"

"About right, yes."

"And you're the one to find a doctor because…?"

"Because she implied she's useful in matters of midwifery," said Charlie. "Which, as you can probably guess, was a *bit* of stretch."

They all looked at Jo in horror until she huffed, "I'm trying to be useful now, ain't I? Securing the doctor and all that?"

"While the social dynamics wouldn't scare him off, I doubt the actual work of it would suit my father's practice," said Noah, returning to his solitaire game. "He's a surgeon, mostly, and nearing retirement. He doesn't come into town very often these days. However…"

He glanced over his shoulder at David, the two of them having the same sort of silent conversation as Jo could with Paul.

"However what?" Jo snapped, unable to take the suspense.

"His father probably won't," said David. "But his sister might."

"Sister?"

"She's a doctor as well," David went on. "A very good one."

"She's also a real piece of work," Noah muttered to the next card he drew, one which was promptly stuck back into the middle of the deck. "But if you're looking for a physician and not a drinking buddy, she might be a good fit. I could arrange an introduction."

Jo mulled over that unexpected possibility. A female doctor? She'd never encountered one of those before. "She'll work with someone in such a scandalous situation? And can she be discreet?"

"I think she can."

"Is she some kind of social reformer? Given the press we run on Holywell Street, I've gotten a pretty wide variety of responses from those sorts."

"To be honest, I would strongly suggest that you leave Holywell out of it, if at all possible, but as for the rest, it shouldn't be a problem. It's what most female doctors *do*—charitable medicine for other women. That said, I cannot ever promise a particular response from Emily. While I theoretically understand her habits and values, the fact is, she's got—"

"A mind of her own," provided David.

"I was going to say a stick up her arse, but that works too." Noah seemed to catch Jo's skeptical look, because he patted her reassuringly on the shoulder. "But she is a *very* good doctor. There's no denying that."

"And who knows?" said David, his bearded face going a little dreamy and pleasant. "Maybe you'll surprise us. I've seen stranger sets of people get along swimmingly."

He winked, and Jo found herself intrigued in spite of herself. "Oh," she said. "Then is she…?"

"Well, she hasn't said anything, but you don't exactly have to be a genius to notice—"

Noah swatted gently but scoldingly at David's arm. "Keep your matchmaking to the club, *amore*."

"Jo's a member. I can set her up if she wants."

"Wants?" said Jo. "I never said I wanted—"

Noah went on as if she'd said nothing: "Not with my bloody sister, you can't."

David, who had dedicated his life to enabling lovers, looked perplexed. "They're both lonely, and it's not even illegal. I don't see the problem."

Jo jolted at the words. "I'm not *lonely*—"

No one seemed too troubled by her resistance, Noah barreling right over her to go on scolding David:

"It's untoward in the extreme," he said.

"I don't mean any harm by it. Emily's like a sister to me too. I'd like to see her happy."

"It's not untoward in regard to Emily," said Noah, rolling his eyes. "It's *Jo* I'm worried about."

David shrugged, looking Jo over with an appraising eye. "I don't know, beautiful. Something tells me they'll get along better than you think."

"*Dio mio*, are you drunk?"

"I am not drunk," said David, clearly offended.

Noah turned back to Jo. "Looks like he *needs* a drink, then. A strong one. And frankly, Davy, so does Mr. Brady." He gestured to the bar, where a chap was waiting on David to return to his duties. As David reluctantly gave his lover a kiss and returned to his post, Noah went on. "I'll write Emily in the morning and get your friend set with an appointment. Meanwhile, ignore Davy, will you? The stress of these laws is getting to him, I think."

Back in August, Parliament had snuck chilling new restrictions into what should have been a reasonable reform. As raids becoming easier loomed on the press's horizon, so too did the vague notion of "gross indecency" bring dread to the blokes at this club, with David set to take on more risk to himself than ever before.

"There hasn't been any legal trouble, has there?" Charlie asked.

Noah shook his head. "Everything's been alright in that regard, actually. But only because of the work he's put in. It's a lot of pressure, you know, and his nerves…" He broke off, transmuting his grimace for a grin. "Let's just say there's been a little less sleeping and lot more talk of matchmaking and pretty decorations. Don't worry yourself about it."

Jo shrugged and laughed, though there was still a grim turn to Noah's mouth that proved his levity was false. Stress levels were indeed high at the moment. For all of them.

"Look, mate," she said bracingly, "if dreaming up matches makes him feel better, let him have it. It's not like he's going to get to me. Last thing I need is an affair with a bloody *bluestocking*." She couldn't help but laugh. "God, can you even imagine?"

Noah lifted his greenish glass to that sentiment as he and Charlie laughed.

"Fair enough," he said. Then squinted for a moment, and with the sort of friendly, thoughtless indecency that characterized this place, he reached out and tapped the loose button on Jo's waistcoat. "Remind me later, I'll tighten this up before we leave."

Jo clamped her jaw shut to keep from groaning with irritation. With all the distraction, not only had she given up on finding Gran's book, but she'd never gotten around to tightening that damned button up at all.

Chapter Three

Emily

When the weather allowed, Emily and her father, Phillip, took breakfast out in the garden together. Fresh air was as vital to health as the food they filled their plates with. This morning was chilly, but the early autumn air didn't daunt Emily, who simply put on an extra pair of woolen underthings and wrapped herself in a heavy shawl before heading outside with this morning's *Farncombe Journal* and a hot mug of lemon water.

Three chairs were tucked around the latticed white table in the garden. One for Emily, one for Papa, and one for Noah. While more chairs were sometimes dragged out of the shed for guests, the set-up inevitably returned to this silent, continued assertion that there was always a place for both of Phillip Clarke's children, and that he'd meant it when he said he would never marry again after trading his beloved wife's life for theirs. Three chairs. Three Clarkes. For over three decades now. End of story.

Emily swept the first of the season's fallen leaves off her chair and Papa's (leaving Noah's as it was; a bit of foliage certainly wouldn't hurt him all the way in London), then settled in to wait, reading and sipping until she heard the garden door open behind her.

Betsy, their dear old housekeeper, beckoned her over.

"Everything alright?" Emily asked.

"Your father wants you to join him inside."

"Whatever for?" Emily glanced at the sunny-enough sky, seeking a hint of the rain that was the only reason they would take breakfast indoors.

"Bit cold, he says."

"No colder than this time last year," said Emily. She decided against argument, though, gathering her things back up and joining her father in the parlor. The fire was going merrily about its business, and the small table was covered in coffee cups, porridge bowls, egg pies, and jam-laden toasts.

"So sorry for the change in plans, my dear," Papa said, gesturing for Betsy to fill Emily's cup with fresh coffee. "But I took one step outside, and proceeded to shiver my way back inside very promptly."

"It didn't strike me as that cold once I was settled in the sun," she said before sitting, thanking Betsy, and beginning to fill her plate. "But no matter. We're here now. Did you sleep w—?"

She paused, having caught Betsy's movements out of the corner of her eye. The housekeeper had procured the post and was glancing at Emily with a letter in hand as if it were headed for her as soon as she stopped talking.

Emily didn't trust unexpected letters. In her experience, they tended to come from men with unsolicited opinions. Over her time as a practicing physician, she'd learned that there was a near-infinite number of men, with infinite opinions they clearly believed she had infinite interest in hearing. She'd received letters regarding the appropriateness of her occupation, the contents of her research papers, and even—worst of all—lists of reasons why she ought to give a particular fellow a chance to prove that marriage was preferable to her unladylike work.

These irritating pieces of mail had dwindled in the last few years. The novelty of her position had waned, most people having had the opportunity to get their tiresome opinions off their chests several times by now. Her publisher was more careful about attributing her writings to Dr. *E.* Clarke, rather than *Emily*. And having passed her thirtieth birthday, only the most determined nonconformists had any interest in her well-aged hand in marriage anymore, and those fellows mostly knew better than to ask.

"Don't worry yourself. It's from your brother," said Betsy, smiling like she knew exactly what was running through Emily's mind. "Anything else I can get the two of you?"

Papa waved her on. "No, Betsy, go enjoy your own breakfast if you haven't yet, and an extra cup of coffee if you have." He turned to Emily as she left. "From your brother? Addressed to you only?"

"How odd," she said, examining her name on the envelope. When Noah wrote (which was less often than it should have been), he wrote to them both, giving updates on his sartorial successes, interesting sketches he'd done, or newspaper clippings from London that he thought they'd like. She rarely got anything addressed just to her.

"Feel free to wait until later," Phillip said, trying unsuccessfully not to look too curious. "I suppose there's probably a reason he wrote it to you."

But Emily was too curious to wait. She carefully broke the seal and took out the letter.

Dearest Emily,
I am quite certain that, somewhere along the line, I've acquired the right to ask a favor of you. Well, today's the day I'm calling it in.

"A favor." She took a fortifying sip of coffee to see her through whatever the devil Noah thought *she* might owe *him*. "He wants a favor."

"What sort?" Papa asked.

Emily read on, aloud this time, because if Noah had wanted discretion, he would have mentioned it right off.

> *I've been made aware of an expectant mother, unmarried and in unusual living circumstances, who may be facing complications but cannot secure the care of a doctor given her situation. As she is the dear friend of my own dear friend, I offered to ask if you would take on such a patient. Since this might give you the opportunity to build your own client list away from the stress of the hospital, I thought it would be mutually beneficial for all involved. (Except me. I get nothing out of this save for the satisfaction of a fellow human being helped.)*
>
> *Please send word if you can meet with them. They are willing to take the train into Godalming, so as to save you the trouble of coming into London outside your regular visits.*
> *In peace,*
> *Noah*

She read it over again, and then handed it to Papa so he could take a look.

"Well, isn't that a fascinating opportunity."

"Opportunity?" Emily repeated. "Interesting *idea* perhaps, but not an opportunity. I can't take such a woman on as a patient."

Papa's face grew very grim. "I know that your own upstanding behavior is a matter of great pride to you, Emily, but I've taught you better than to cast judgement on the lives of other women like that. You don't know what circumstances may—"

"That's not what I mean!" she said quickly, heat rising to her face at such a harsh accusation of ungenerousness. "Of course I'm above such petty judgements. I mean to say, I work at the hospital only. I'm not like you; I don't keep a roster of patients of my own outside of its structures."

"Something I have advised you to remedy for years." Papa said it casually, but she caught the way his eyes left hers for just a moment too long, fingers twitching a little on the way to his coffee cup. "Perhaps this is a sign that you should consider a change."

"Why is that?" she asked suspiciously.

"I won't be around forever," he said. "And the hospital, noble as the work is, is showing no signs of paying you your worth."

She moodily took up a piece of toast, glaring at it like the jam had inked her pathetic stipend right onto its surface. "If I continue to do my duties, and pray diligently upon the subject, the founders will see my value and change their ways long before you're not around, Papa. Goodness, I should hope we have plenty of time before we have to start worrying about that."

"I hope so as well," he said in that same tight voice. "But you never know how timing might work out, do you?"

He busied himself with the coffee pot, using both hands to steady the thing as if he were feeling a little shaky. There were certainly days when the hospital sent one back heavy-laden with thoughts of how quickly a person's circumstances could change. She suspected that's what was troubling him. Poor thing. Probably best to change the subject to its more practical aspect.

"You could try putting in another word for me," she suggested.

"I share my opinion on the injustice of your meager pay to those men at least monthly. Each time, they promise to 'take a look at things.' But my dear, if your generous assumption that they will ever do more than *look* proves incorrect, then if a time comes when I'm no longer able to work—or, heaven forbid, no longer able to do anything but commune with our Creator at last—"

"Papa, stop that—"

"Then this family will be in a tight spot indeed," he concluded with an eyebrow raised in implication. "We would not be immediately destitute, but to avoid that eventuality…"

Emily felt her face twist unpleasantly. "We would be reliant on Noah."

"Reliant on Noah." Papa nodded. "Whose spiritual gifts lie a bit outside the sphere of domestic security."

Papa's generosity severely outstripped Emily's own. She would not use those words to describe Noah's complete abandonment of his familial responsibilities. Her most generous interpretation was that he had no tolerance for the ghosts this life came with. He could have been the best tailor in town, so it wasn't just the medicine. And Farncombe was home to a nice little pocket of nonconformists, so two men living as quietly as he and David had this summer would have attracted little trouble. What Noah had done was bolt. He'd run.

And he'd done it without once stopping to ask what impact that might have on his own sister.

"So," Papa went on, a bit lightly, like he knew she was thinking ungenerous things about the owner of the third garden chair and hoped to snap her out of it. "It would be a good time, I think, to consider building a patient list of your own."

"I see what you're saying, Papa. But…even if you're right, I don't think that home-based obstetrics is the specialty that I would choose for myself."

"Why not?" Papa said, cutting neatly across Emily's subtext. "Statistically, outcomes are still best in the home with a trained physician, an arrangement a poor woman like Noah's friend may only be able to manage through your generosity of spirit. What better choice is out there for you?"

Emily stared at him. From her seat, she could see the ratty old shawl of her mother's that Papa still kept draped over the back of his favorite armchair, not far off from one of her sewing kits, which lounged like an immortal wicker cat beneath an end table. The devastation of another physician's failure all around them, day in and day out, and all of a sudden, her father wanted to talk *statistics*?

She blinked a few times, but he simply ate his breakfast and waited patiently for her reply.

Well, she certainly wasn't going to be the one to bring it up. It was too heavy to speak.

"Pure obstetrics..." she began, finding another convenient annoyance to blame instead, "is the only field anyone ever wants to see me in!" Yes. That was reason enough on its own, really. "I'm trying to convince my peers that I am fit to minister to any patient, man or woman. If I lean so far into the idea that female doctors should only treat female patients by taking on someone like this, then what good am I to the cause of women at all?"

"While I understand the frustration of your limitations, I would still encourage you to spend a little extra time in contemplation to figure out why you suddenly care more for a nebulous cause than for a fellow human being in need. That's not like you, Emily."

Caught in her lackluster excuse-making, Emily took a moment to eat. The conversation had left her stomach churning and her appetite miles away, but without sustenance, she would never get through the day ahead of her. Once she'd choked a few bites down, she said to her plate, "It's also a lot of responsibility." Though she tried to keep her eyes on her porridge, they drifted out the window to the three garden chairs that should have been four all along. "A mistake in this specialty... it echoes."

Papa reached out, hesitating for an odd moment, stretching his fingers, before patting Emily on the hand. When she looked up, she found a softness in his eyes. He finally understood what she was trying to say.

"As does a success," he said quietly. "Same in any specialty in which life and death hang in the balance. The field has come a long way in thirty years. It could go further still, with the right people leading the charge. What's more helpful? Waiting around for ignorant men to take notice of your daily grind, or scraping together what you've got and being part of something that will outlive all their prejudices?"

"Papa—"

"If the reasons I've given aren't enough, I have one more for you."

"What's that?"

He picked the letter up again and smirked at it. "Your brother has gone out of his way for a stranger in need for once. I think that this rare moment of social consideration is something we ought to encourage in him, don't you? Particularly seeing as we both run the risk of relying on his generosity later?"

"I still don't think we need to worry about that yet," said Emily, not liking the way Papa wasn't meeting her eyes again. "There's plenty of time for the two of us to save and set ourselves up for the future. Correct?"

"I have always diligently saved, of course, as have you," he said a bit vaguely.

Emily narrowed her eyes, watching him go on about his breakfast.

"Papa—"

"I hope you do it, Emily," he said at last, straightforward and without further room for argument. "There are many reasons it would be beneficial for you." He paused, considering her. "And for this woman. Society at large, as well, if that's truly the motivation you need right now."

Emily nodded, knowing she was not going to be able to

find a way out of this. Defeated, she stared out the window at three chairs, briefly more jealous than resentful for that streak of selfishness that had allowed Noah to escape the specters that she had accepted.

As promised, the woman in question (an actress by the name of Vanessa Garcia), her consort (a fellow with very little information given and the suspiciously innocuous moniker of Smith), and the female companion they and Noah all had in common agreed to travel to Emily's own home in Farncombe for the initial meeting.

It was a nice show of respect for Miss Garcia to take on the task of travel herself. It put Emily in a good mood as she prepared the parlor to receive them. Sunshine came through the curtains, making all the houseplants gleam in a smooth and straightforward way. She had her medical bag stocked with far more than she would need today; unlike the physicians she'd trained under, she felt strongly that doctor and patient ought to speak a bit before anyone was overly prodded, but it did make patients feel comfortable to see that she had all the same instruments and medicines that any other physician would. Depending on whom she was meeting, she would sometimes deign to wear a health corset under her clothes so as not to appear sloppy or overly modern, but seeing as that shouldn't be a problem in this crowd, she was able to swathe herself simply in her favorite gray jacket and skirt set, so slim and structured that a corset was silly so long as a woman kept her posture in mind.

Which Emily, of course, always did.

At the appointed time, Emily was seated in the parlor equipped with ginger biscuits, watercress sandwiches, and boiled lemon water to refresh her guests, ready...

And waiting.

They were late.

She shouldn't be too irritated. She *really* shouldn't. In fact, she *wasn't*.

Her foot tap, tap, tapped on the rug and her eyes glued themselves to the old grandfather clock that kept watch over time in the parlor.

It was probably the train's fault.

She could *not* fault the visitors for the train's shortcomings.

(Her foot went on tapping.)

She *would not* fault them.

(Tap, tap, tap...)

She *very actively did not fault them* for nearly twenty-three minutes before the front door creaked open. Thank *heavens*. Emily ensured once more that there was no speck of sawdust or cavy fur on her skirt, then stood with her hands clasped carefully before her, spine like a steel rod and her face fixed into the serious physician look she and the others at the women's medical college had spent evenings perfecting with one another. *You can trust me*, the look said. *I am capable. I am skilled. I am a* doctor.

Betsy came first. She did not have a serious physician look on her face. In fact, she looked a little amused. Flushed, even.

"A Miss Vanessa Garcia," she said with a nod as a beautiful woman dressed in cheap silks glided into the parlor. Emily assessed her automatically, accustomed to emergency situations at the hospital where she had to understand a patient swiftly: the woman's condition was not visible yet, hopefully not because she was still corseting; while she'd shamelessly applied cosmetics to her face, the paint could not quite hide her advanced age for a first-time mother, nor her uncommon pallor. She did not look particularly strong, much less prepared for the trials of childbearing than Emily's own mother had been, if her father's report could be believed—

Emily's increasingly dread-filled assessment was cut short as Betsy ushered another person into the parlor.

"And…" Here, the housekeeper's amusement cracked into an incredulous smile. "And a Mrs. Jo Smith."

Emily blinked in the sauntering sight of the second guest. It did not take much assessment to ascertain that Mrs. Jo Smith was not the unwed father that Emily had been expecting, though she had not dressed the part of female companion very accurately, either. While Emily fretted about whether she could get away without a corset, Mrs. Smith had not even bothered with a frock. For a moment, Emily questioned whether the woman had taken a bicycle from Godalming station, but no: those trousers were decidedly *not* a set of the split-leg women's "rationals" that were popular among Emily's physically active peers. Mrs. Smith was in full-on gentleman's attire—reddish-brown trousers and matching jacket, with a darker waistcoat and a blue paisley neckcloth. The coloring of the clothing brought out the dusky tan of her face and made the black of her eyes, her hair, her obscenely long eyelashes, look like coal compared to the pale peaches and living greens of the parlor décor. Lovely and ostentatious as Miss Garcia was, it was Mrs. Smith who suddenly had all of Emily's attention, everything else in the room fading as if the woman had stepped under the greedy glow of a surgical lamp.

"Dr. Clarke." Mrs. Smith extended a hand. Emily stared at it, too shaken to shake. Mrs. Smith smiled warmly. "Our introduction having been on paper, I'm doing my best. I tried to make Noah come along to smooth it out, but I lost that bet. Cheating blighter. Though I'm sure you know *that* as well as anyone."

Emily found herself without any reasonable script for this introduction. Her brother (who was not so strictly male as most brothers) sending a written introduction to his friend (not so strictly female as her title indicated), who was accompanying an unwed mother-to-be to meet with Emily, a doctor who had learned to equate respect with masculine treatment. And where on earth was the baby's father? Wasn't he supposed to be here?

"It's a hand, Dr. Clarke," said Mrs. Smith with a little wiggle of her clean, well-kept fingers. "I know we're here to discuss other parts, but I do hope you're familiar with this aspect of human anatomy as well?"

Miss Garcia gave a chiding little click of the tongue and a smile. "Goodness, Jo."

Mrs. Smith shrugged it off, unconcerned, but the chide did rekindle the connection between Emily's brain and her body. She hurriedly clasped Mrs. Smith's hand, smooth and warm, with a shake firmer than she was used to getting from people in trousers, who seemed to think a proper greeting might crush her little fingers.

Emily took her hand back quickly, trying to squeeze out the tingle before extending it to Miss Garcia. She kept her gaze firmly on the patient, deciding all at once that the best thing to do with Mrs. Smith would be to ignore her.

"Thank you, Betsy," Emily said to the housekeeper, her voice sticking. She cleared her throat. "I'll take it from here."

Emily set determinedly about getting them all settled in for what she was *certain* would be a *perfectly typical appointment, thank-you-very-much.* She put Miss Garcia on the settee, Mrs. Smith in the striped chair, Emily herself on the—

No sooner was Emily smoothing her skirt when Mrs. Smith moved to sit beside Miss Garcia, like she really did intend to play husband. Considering these were Noah and David's friends, perhaps Mrs. Smith *was* something of a husband to Miss Garcia. But that didn't seem quite right. And what would such an arrangement mean about the baby's father? She had been under the impression that he was part of all this, to the degree of planning to join them today, though perhaps there was more to that than she understood...

And good heavens, if Mrs. Smith was going to take the role on, she could have done it all the way. One did not graduate from the women's medical college without coming to understand the myriad reasons that someone who'd started life in one sphere might switch to the other later on. Emily could have been happily discreet and polite had she encountered a *Mr. Smith* who might have at least *attempted* to tame a bosom that was stressing a wayward waistcoat button in a manner that was *currently quite distracting*.

She cleared her throat again, pouring a little lemon water for each of them and taking a warm, acidic sip before going on.

"So, Miss Garcia," she said, hitching her gaze to the likely-fake beauty mark on the side of the woman's face so as to avoid looking at Mrs. Smith. "I want to thank you again for your willingness to come all the way out here. I understand that you're facing significant discomforts."

"Indeed." Miss Garcia smiled her way through the admission, though the expression could not hide her exhaustion.

"I could have come to you, you know. I make the trip to London frequently; it's no trouble for me."

Mrs. Smith sighed and crossed her arms, taxing her loose button to a dangerous degree. "That's what I told her, but then she *never could have witnessed the living space of such a fascinating human being.*"

Miss Garcia laughed and nudged her companion, leaning in toward Emily to say, "We're getting to know each other so very well these days, she and I." She laced her arm through Mrs. Smith's in a casual, girlish way that seemed to remove the possibility that they were lovers. "And she's absolutely correct. It is my life's work to observe how people move through the world, Dr. Clarke. I couldn't resist the pull of novelty in coming into your space. A doctor. A bluestocking. A respectable dissenter." She waved her spare arm here and there like Emily's roles were balloons she was releasing into the air. "No woman like that ever lets me near her, much less into her home. The trip was uncomfortable to be sure, but I have already been well-rewarded for the effort."

Emily wasn't sure how to respond to that. In her bewilderment, she made the mistake of locking eyes with the mysterious Mrs. Smith.

Mrs. Smith shrugged, looking like she'd been subjected to a lot of this sort of talk all the way here. "Did Noah mention she's an actress?" said Mrs. Smith. "Because she's absolutely an actress."

"An actress. Of course. Well, that's…understandable," said Emily, the somewhat inappropriate word falling from her lips before she could catch it. "Actresses, I suppose, do…find themselves in this sort of situation from time to time. Or so I've heard."

"Have you?" said Miss Garcia, one of her darkly lined brows cresting upward with interest.

"Yes." Emily settled her notepad carefully in the center of her lap. "And I must admit—"

"Here it comes," Miss Garcia muttered to her companion.

"I find it very admirable that you are approaching the situation with gravity and responsibility," said Emily, catching the look of surprise that crossed their faces. "Your presence here shows that your health and the health of your child is of greater consequence than your reputation. Many a woman in your situation would not even show her face before a doctor until the wedding vows were completed. That you've come when it was necessary, rather than when it was proper, gives an impression of very good character on your part."

Miss Garcia and Mrs. Smith stared at each other for a moment longer than was natural.

"What—ah—what wedding vows are you referring to?" said Mrs. Smith at last.

"Has the father abandoned you?" said Emily, directing the question to Miss Garcia. "I was under the impression he had made the decision to step up."

"He has," said Miss Garcia defensively. "He will. In fact, one might say he's loyal to a fault."

Though Emily was trying very hard to keep her focus off Mrs. Smith and her wayward waistcoat buttons, she could not help but notice how the words made the odd woman stiffen unhappily.

"They're not marrying," Mrs. Smith said very carefully, hastily, like she wanted to get her answer out before Miss Garcia could, "because they do not believe in the institution. Isn't that right, Vanessa? They're free thinkers."

Free thinkers. Free thinkers, actresses, and women in trousers. Noah's friends indeed.

"I consider myself a free thinker as well," said Emily tightly. "But it is one thing to think freely, and another to act foolishly. Miss Garcia, you really ought to reconsider—"

"Look, Doctor. They're a bit…freer," Mrs. Smith went on, eyeing Emily's gray skirt and jacket set with distinct disdain, "than you'll ever understand. They're arranging their lives in accordance with their principles, though. That's admirable as well, innit? If they believe the institution is oppressive, and their lives aren't the sort to be upended by lack of conformity, then why should they marry?"

The argument had gone to surprising detail and depth more quickly than was appropriate. Emily was missing something. Something important.

"Not that I'm sure it's *your* business, Mrs. Smith," Emily said sternly. "But even free thinkers ought to consider marrying for the child's benefit. To be born out of wedlock is—"

"A technicality," said Mrs. Smith, very pointed, sharpened by something Emily still didn't understand as she reached for one of the ginger biscuits and passed it over to Miss Garcia. "Nothing more or less than that in our corner of London. Now, Vanessa, dear, do eat something, would you? It's been a long trip; you're looking pale."

"Thank you, Jo." Miss Garcia sighed and stretched like her back was giving her trouble. "A technicality indeed. We're just full to bursting with them, aren't we?"

"What do you mean by that?" Emily asked.

"Well, the reason he couldn't marry me even if we wanted to is a technical one." She nibbled carefully on the biscuit before going on, much to the obvious chagrin of Mrs. Smith. "You are a sharp woman, Dr. Clarke. I can feel the vibrations of your intelligence from all the way over here. You will figure us out in due time, so I am going to head it off at the pass: he cannot marry me, because he is already married."

Mrs. Smith tipped her head back in annoyance that bordered on horror. "We weren't going to mention that."

"Well, of course we weren't, for fear you would think it a scandal," she said to Emily. "But I can see now that we will never get away with fooling someone like you. I can assure you, however, that the scandal is no more or less than you originally understood. You see, he would marry me if he could, but the wife is, as we have just discussed, a technicality."

"How is an entire *wife* a technicality?" A righteous rage bubbled up within Emily, one she'd have preferred to release all at once with a shout, but settled for allowing it to gently hiss. "And if he sees his current wife as a technicality, what might that say about how he sees you?"

"Oh!" Miss Garcia said with a sly little nudge to her companion. "She doesn't mind being technical, don't worry."

"She…*what*?"

"Why should she mind?" muttered Mrs. Smith, looking a little defeated. "A technical wife is the best sort to be, ain't it?"

Mrs. Smith.

Mrs.

Smith.

All semblance of a serious doctor's expression was lost as Emily's jaw dropped nearly to the floor.

"I..." she stammered as everything clicked together. "I don't understand."

"Let me explain it real simple," said Mrs. Smith, leaning her elbows on her knees and flashing those devious dark eyes up at Emily. "I wasn't getting any use out of him, so I popped a bow on his head and gave him to Miss Garcia as a present one Christmas. Very thrifty, if I do say so myself. Especially now that he's proven to be the gift that keeps on giving." She looked pointedly at Miss Garcia's abdomen.

"And...and you didn't bring him because—"

"Other matters called him off last minute." Every angle of her heart-shaped face was set into an unmistakable challenge. "But in the meantime, *I* have been tending to Miss Garcia's discomforts to the best of my ability. *I* arranged this meeting, and *I* know more about what she needs to take care of herself in this condition than he does. So I came instead, as the person best equipped to judge your qualifications."

Emily bristled at the waspish tone. "And just what makes you so equipped?"

"Try asking again later," said Mrs. Smith. "Once you've shown us you can do something other than nose around into the non-medical details of our lives. Nosiness is bad for your humors, and so your devotion to it isn't inspiring a lot of confidence in me just yet."

A dreadful heat rose to Emily's face. "I'm not...and even if I *was*, when you say humors, you don't mean—?"

A dark brow drifted upward. "The regular bodily humors, Dr. Clarke. I should hope I don't have to list them for a physician."

Humors? Who in their right mind would march in here, dressed a scandal, refusing to answer basic questions, and then start talking to a real, qualified physician about *humors*? Did Mrs. Smith really have that low an opinion of a female doctor?

Or, even worse, did this strange, fascinating woman actually believe in the influence of *humors*?

She tried to go back to ignoring her, but it was difficult. Not only was the uncommon beauty of hers a terrible distraction, but the sight of Miss Garcia didn't help Emily's nerves much either, weak and tired as the actress was. Trying to imagine this wisp of an actress making it through a first labor set all manner of dark predictions swirling through Emily's mind.

Set so firmly between doom and desire, she took out her record book and tried her very best to convince herself that she was remotely the doctor they thought she was.

Chapter Four

Jo

Noah claimed that his sister had a stick up her arse, but meeting the chit in person, Jo believed she'd managed to get that thing all the way up her spine, twisting the pointy end into the skull-squeezing knot on the top of her head. Dr. Clarke held her back so straight and her stomach so tight that Jo hadn't even noticed she wasn't wearing a corset until they all sat down. Physically, she looked enough like her brother—long, slim lines; sandy coloring; big, stormy eyes—that Jo found herself wondering if Noah had created his prettiest but most insufferable drag persona yet, just to fuck with her.

But no such luck there. She was caricature-like indeed, but decidedly too short to be anything but genuine. David's anxiety really must have been addling his brain something dreadful if he'd thought for a moment this was a match that either of them would have any interest in whatsoever.

Jo watched Dr. Clarke as she determinedly shook off all the earlier conversation and got down to business with the air of a schoolmarm with a stick that was coming for your bum in a bad way. She clenched a stylus above a pad of paper, leaving off any further discussion of circumstance to finally start asking Vanessa about her health and her history.

Jo had never trusted doctors, getting on well enough on the country remedies she'd picked up from her family before they turned on her. The scribbling of medical notes made her particularly nervous. They seemed very official. Very final. The way the doctor's petite hand clenched the pen and moved so methodically over the paper started up some sort of whirlwind in Jo's belly. She poured and picked up a mug of what looked like lukewarm water in the others' cups, not exactly her choice beverage, but available as distraction.

She took a sip of the stuff and nearly spat it out. Not being quite so ill-bred as all that, she opted to choke on it instead.

The ladies both turned to stare at her.

"You alright, Jo?" said Vanessa, in tandem with Dr. Clarke's grim "A problem, Mrs. Smith?"

Jo coughed and loosened her neckcloth a little. "What have you done to it?" she asked the doctor. "Is that lemon?"

Dr. Clarke blinked those eyes at her incredulously. They weren't quite as much like her brother's as Jo had originally thought. A little rounder, a little bluer, with a quaint sort of frown line slightly off-center between them. It deepened substantially. "Yes," she said. "It is lemon."

"Enough to clean the kitchen with, isn't it?"

"To clean... Excuse me?"

"I mean, I'll be alright." Jo swallowed hard, trying to clear the sourness from her mouth. "Don't worry about me—"

"I assure you, I will not."

"—but should you be giving that to her?" Jo nudged Vanessa gently.

"Why wouldn't I?"

Vanessa laughed and took one of the biscuits from a porcelain bowl painted with rabbits, of all things. "True, it's not my first choice," she said cheerfully. "But it's hospitable enough."

Jo hated to do this in front of Dr. Clarke, but she was developing a suspicion that this doctor might not be all she was cracked up to be. She didn't seem to know about the bodily humors. She was asking odd questions about Vanessa's corset. And now lemon water? It was suspicious. Jo wasn't a midwife. She wasn't an expert. She wasn't even a mother herself. But she *was* a woman who'd been around other women and knew a thing or two in spite of herself. She lowered her voice and said to Vanessa, "You overdo that stuff, and your baby will wind up with a sour disposition."

"Oh!" Vanessa put a hand to her chest. "Well, I've never heard that."

"That's because it's poppycock," said Dr. Clarke, casting a look sharp enough to stab through Jo's entire ancestral line. "Old wives' tales. Lemon water will help your nausea and, combined with boiling, keeps the water free of contaminants."

Jo met the stare with one of her own. "I assume your mum drank it plenty."

"I wouldn't know."

The line of her mouth growing grimmer than ever, Dr. Clarke went back to her notes, her questioning, her lemon water. Her face was so serious that she might have been about to tell Vanessa that she going to die of some dreadful fever within the hour.

It was dull, irritating, and a bit embarrassing to boot. Since Jo was no more than a chaperone—a chaperone that the doctor had clearly decided to pretend wasn't even there—she stood. As expected, Dr. Clarke gave no indication that she'd noticed Jo strolling toward the window.

As the others droned on about menses and motherly maladies, Jo took in the sight of fading foliage and well-fed fowl in the garden. It was a curious place, this cottage. Filled with books, live plants, and by all account every modern amenity she could think of, yet surrounded by the sort of fresh country air that Jo had come to equate with far more suffocation than the soot-choked streets of the city. Jo herself was not familiar with English suburbs, having only experienced the extremes of impoverished farmland or the bustling, foggy squish of London. She didn't know much about this in-between space, but she sensed that it was the sort of place that inevitably gave birth to Dr. Clarke's type.

And Jo *did* know her type. Sitting so pretty in her drab rational dress, speaking the grim speech of a dedicated bluestocking. Paul shared a printing press with a group of idea-driven pamphleteers just like Dr. Clarke, who couldn't bear to rally for the rights of women or the poor without also making it about the evils of gin, or dirty novels, or any amount of joyful leisure whatsoever. Never mind that polite society hardly liked these teetotalling, nonconformist sorts any better than they liked whores and smut peddlers—since they didn't care for society's opinion anyway, their harsh judgement stood firm.

No sense dwelling on all that, though. While Vanessa's conversation seemed to be going well enough, this was probably the last Jo would see of Dr. Clarke. Once another appointment was secured, Jo could doff her hat to this whole mess, and then... and then hope there was still something for her do, someone useful for her to be to this family that might find itself growing happily away without her.

She cleared her throat, spurred to movement. She paced behind the doctor, hands in pockets. Needing something to do with her eyes, she peeked over the sofa at the contents of Dr. Clarke's medical notes. She was glad the information was as prim and professional as everything else about the doctor, though a particular aspect of the script made her chuckle before she could stop herself.

Gaze trained, as it was, on the movement of the pen, Jo saw the second it stopped in its inky tracks, standing straight and tall against the paper.

Slowly, moving no muscle save for the ones required, Dr. Clarke turned her head toward Jo. "Yes, Mrs. Smith?"

Jo stifled another smile. "Nothing."

"Is there something funny about childbed fever?"

"I might have missed that that was the topic at hand," said Jo with a grimace and an apologetic tug on her own bun. "My apologies."

"Then what, pray tell," said Dr. Clarke, "is so funny?"

"Nothing, Doctor."

"Forgive me if I don't believe you to be giggling to yourself in the corner over *nothing*."

"It really is nothing," Jo repeated. "It's just—"

"Oh, Joey!" Vanessa clucked scoldingly from the sofa. "You're not looking at her handwriting, are you?"

Dr. Clarke looked sharply between them, her spine straighter than ever. "What's the matter with my handwriting?"

"Nothing's the matter with it," said Jo quickly, trying to suppress her guilty smile. "That's not what I—"

"Forgive her, Doctor," said Vanessa with a chuckle. "She's gotten to know me better in the past few weeks, but it's been a mutual discovery. She's a printer, you see. A book person. An enthusiast of the written word in all its forms. Spent far too much time in the company of manuscripts. If I'm not mistaken, it set her down the path of learning handwriting analysis."

Disconcerted, Jo rounded on her. "How did you know that?"

"There's books about it on your shelf," she said. "I can tell Paul's never taken a look at them, so they must be yours. Fascinating subject—I read through one of them just last week."

Jo didn't have time to be horrified that Vanessa was out there *feeling her vibrations* and *peering into her soul* when Jo wasn't looking, because the words seemed to break some thin edge of Dr. Clarke's patience as well.

"Handwriting analysis?" she snapped, turning farther toward Jo so rapidly that a teeny, tiny wisp of hair escaped from the clutches of her knot. "Please don't tell me you are not only looking over my shoulder at my notes, glaring at the lemon water and fretting about humors, but you are analyzing my handwriting while you're at it?"

Jo shrugged. "It seemed a quiet and unobtrusive enough activity to me."

"And exactly what *humorous insights*," she said with an emphasis that quaked that spidery strand of blond on her forehead, "have you gleaned about my *sour disposition* through your unscientific means, Mrs. Smith?"

That stray hair looked terribly weak and undefended against the barely contained anger that simmered within the little doctor. Normally, Jo would bark out just what she'd *gleaned* without hesitation, but something about that vulnerable fluff made her think better of it—in fact, had her suppressing an urge to sweep the strand back to safety.

"Just that..." Jo paused, searching the ceiling for some way to put it. "The vertical, um...the *verticality* of some of the letters is thought to indicate a passionate nature. That's all. Should come as no surprise."

"Passionate," repeated Dr. Clarke, lashes fluttering impatiently. They were soft, fragile, and tipped in blond. "I am passionate about my work, Mrs. Smith. Though I like to think it shows more in my demeanor than in my *handwriting*."

"Of course, Doctor."

With a warning look, Dr. Clarke turned back around, pen moving a little more self-consciously.

Jo caught Vanessa's eye. She looked a little uncertain, which wouldn't do. They needed to be better friends, didn't they? If Vanessa had read one of her handwriting books, then perhaps Jo could use that common knowledge to make an in-joke. People didn't like to ruin the lives of folks they had in-jokes with. So Jo grinned behind the doctor's back, using her finger to draw a lower-case *g* in the air, one with the lusciously long lower loop that supposedly indicated a sort of passion that was more commonly associated with the oldest profession, rather than Dr. Clarke's illustrious one. Vanessa bit her lip as she caught Jo's meaning, covering her smile with another sip of sour stuff.

The pen stopped once more. The head turned. The stray hair swished, lifted, and left itself at an improbable angle at the side of Dr. Clarke's face.

"What?" she said, exasperated.

"Nothing," said Jo innocently, crossing her arms tight.

"Perhaps," Dr. Clarke started, but her eyes drifted and her throat stuck for a moment. Jo followed her gaze down to where that waistcoat button was straining worse than ever. She'd tightened it up as best she could, not having found Gran's book in the towering mass of literature on the shelves, but it was already trying to give up again. Great. Now the doctor could judge her tidiness on top of everything else...

Though when they locked eyes again, a strange flush dusted across Dr. Clarke's cheeks.

Something dawned on Jo. The blush. The nerves. The swoopy letters. Maybe judgement wasn't actually the right word for the situation.

"Perhaps, what, Dr. Clarke?" she said, crossing her arms a little tighter and letting just one side of her mouth drift up in a challenge.

Dr. Clarke cleared her throat again, the flush going pale.

"Perhaps you would be more comfortable waiting in the garden while I wrap things up with Miss Garcia."

It was too chilly to be comfortable, and the little animals and autumn-bright plants all over the place were so quaint as to be almost painfully saccharine, but Jo did as she was told, waiting in the garden until Vanessa came out.

Jo's stomach instantly sank at the slumping sight of her, makeup-tinged tears streaming down her face as she gave the terrible news:

Dr. Clarke had denied her another appointment.

Jo's stomach turned a guilty flip as she thought back on her own behavior in the parlor. Chickens clucked, rodents scurried, and Vanessa sniffed into her handkerchief until Jo found her voice.

"I'm sorry," Jo said. "Oh, fuck, Vanessa. I'm so sorry. I didn't mean to—"

Vanessa shook her head, dabbing her eyes. "Believe it or not, it wasn't you."

There was a bit of relief in that. "It wasn't?"

"It was my fault entirely."

"But the lemons—"

"It wasn't the lemons," she sighed. "It's exactly the problem we knew we'd have."

Jo grimaced. "You told her about Paul's books, didn't you?"

"I thought I'd read her vibrations correctly," said Vanessa, like she was begging the whole universe to understand her mistake. "That more honesty would see us through. But alas, her free thinking has just the limits you sensed it would." Vanessa gave a laugh that was not related in any way to mirth. "Funny, isn't it? Everyone so concerned with whether Paul's sticking around, but in this, I'd be better off without him."

"Better off without *him*?" Jo repeated, shocked that she wasn't getting the blame for this. Even if Dr. Clarke's rejection wasn't her fault, her presence was still the root of the problem. That Vanessa still hadn't found a single negative word to say about her was so far beyond her comprehension that she couldn't help but blurt, "God, Vanessa, has it really not occurred to you...?"

"That it's *you* I'd be better off without?" she said with a wry little smile.

Jo shoved her hands in her pockets and shrugged, afraid to speak.

"My dear Jo." Vanessa sighed and smoothed her silks. "I do not want to be married. I have never wanted to be married. And I never will. It isn't in my nature, and I would not sell my nature for all the security in the world. You're not an object in my way. You are a person who is trying to help me, in spite of the fact that this circumstance is nearly as big a danger to you as it is to me. It is my blessing or my curse to be unable to look away from that, no matter how I might benefit."

"You mean it," Jo said.

"I do."

"I could kill Paul off, then," Jo joked. "Get him out of the way of your proper doctor. If you'd like."

"Oh, but my dear, my dear, what you still don't understand is that I love him," said Vanessa, half-theater, half-exhaustion. "I want him with me on the other side of this, living our lives in the way that suits our spirits. That's the irony of it."

"I could kill him off for now," Jo suggested, "then bring him back later when he's needed. I've got a couple books in the back of my shop dealing with subjects like that. Considering the sorts of people who come looking for them, I can't imagine that a bit of light necromancy is really *that* difficult."

Vanessa laughed through her sniffling nose. "Why don't you go tell Dr. Clarke that?"

"Noah wasn't kidding." Jo leaned on the fencepost, cross-

ing her arms and glaring at the overly wholesome sight of little animals creeping over to investigate her boots. "She's a real
piece of work."

A real piece of work, and a good physician.

Jo glanced back at the garden door. She could take this as a
blessing. Vanessa and Paul would need whatever little knowledge Jo could bring more than ever in light of this rejection.
But while Jo wanted to remain suspicious of Vanessa's motives,
that wasn't working quite as well right now. She'd hate to leave
a kind person, who meant her no harm and meant the world
to her dearest companion, in a dangerous circumstance without trying to fix it.

There had to be something Jo could say to smooth this over.
Stark and sour as she seemed, the buttoned-up Dr. Clarke had
a button loose somewhere. It was less obvious than Jo's own
literal one, but such was the nature of women's garb.

Which Jo, for her part, knew perfectly well how to loosen.

Chapter Five

Emily

Uncharitable.

That's what Emily had been just now. Uncharitable in the extreme. It hurt to have done it, a piercing stone in her shoe that demanded she run after the woman and take back what she'd said.

But something within her rebelled against her sense of duty at last. Something that had sprung to life upon meeting these strange people. This mother so certain of what she wanted that she'd risk everything for it. Her alluring companion wandering the earth clothed in full honesty without regard for whether she came across as scandalous or ridiculous. The *something* in Emily coveted their ease so strongly that when Miss Garcia mentioned the nature of her lover's publishing business, it screamed in a voice she could not ignore: *here's your last chance, your best-possible excuse, your reason for shutting this down before it begins. You'll never have to admit that your mother's ghost has left you unsuited to the only branch of medicine that makes financial and logical sense. You'll just say the scandal was a step too far. Everyone has their limits, after all.*

She warred with herself as she arranged the stray cups on

the tray for Betsy, unsure whether she wanted duty or this new thing to win. Before she'd made up her mind, she heard footsteps in the doorway.

Emily took a walk in the garden every morning, rain or shine, and so she knew perfectly well that it was too chilly outside today for Mrs. Smith to be sauntering back into the parlor with her jacket over her shoulder and her sleeves rolled to the elbow. Goosebumps stood up on the woman's forearms, raising the little hairs there.

Which Emily certainly did not like.

Did not even notice, really.

"Can I help you find your way out, Mrs. Smith?" Emily said, trying to sound as cool as the air outside even as she felt a flush cross her cheeks. "The west garden gate will lead to where your coach is waiting."

"Not just yet," said Mrs. Smith. Her tone was warmer than she obviously was as she crossed the room and picked her mug back up. "Wanted one more sip for the road."

"Of course. All this suburban air must be scratching your London throat up something awful."

Mrs. Smith, far from looking offended, smiled like she was a companion who'd told a genuine joke. "Look, Dr. Clarke—"

"I've made my decision," Emily snapped, hearing how her voice belied her indecision. "While I am sympathetic to Miss Garcia's circumstance, an arrangement *between* her and me isn't in anyone's best interest."

"Not anyone's?" Mrs. Smith leaned her hip against the back of the couch, a little closer than was comfortable. Her fingers twitched before vanishing into her pockets. Emily had seen that sort of twitch before, the twitch of a tobacco addict. She was struck by a devastating mental image of this woman lighting up a cigarette right in the middle of the Clarke family parlor, a thought not helped by the faint and dangerous smell of smoke and ink that seemed to emanate from her jacket. "There's no need to feign altruism with me, Dr. Clarke. I'm not one of your pamphlet-wielding bluestocking friends. I'll not hate you for doing what's best for yourself first."

Emily startled at the…accusation? Was it an accusation? Mrs. Smith made such selfishness sound almost positive.

"She ought to have a London doctor," said Emily, disappointed in how hollow her voice sounded, how uncertain. "Or at the very least, someone whose specialty resides in this branch of medicine. I am an emergency room physician, leaning toward surgery like my father before me. It will be more suitable all around for her to find someone else."

"You're worried about your reputation," Mrs. Smith went on, as if she'd said nothing at all. "You think working with her will hurt your standing, which, I assume, is shaky enough as it is. I can't blame you. She understands her place. And I think I understand yours."

"I somehow doubt that," Emily blurted. Mrs. Smith smiled wickedly, like it was the exact response she'd expected; Emily could hardly believe she'd been lured into participation. She straightened the wrinkles from her jacket and her conduct. "But never mind. Good day, Mrs. Smith."

Mrs. Smith did not move to go. If anything, she settled in further, hip cocked out like she could stay right where she was forever.

Well. If she wasn't going to go, Emily would. She wasn't going to stand here all day. She collected the tray and started for the door.

Mrs. Smith blocked her path, reaching for the rattling cups. "Let me."

"No."

"Let me do *something*." A hint of begging crept into her tone.

"Miss Garcia won't do as well with the sort of help we can get in London. It's all there in your little notes—"

"My passionately written notes?" Emily snipped, brow up.

"Yes! That's the point," Mrs. Smith put her hands on the sides of the tray, dangerously close to Emily's, the two of them staring at each other over the fixings. She'd seemed taller before now, an enormous sort of presence, but she wasn't actually that much larger than Emily. Not vertically, anyway. Emily's eyes dipped to that strained button and back again to a pair of eyes just as black, just as shining, just as…

"Passion!" Mrs. Smith's hands tightened on the tray with an obvious and bursting abundance of the stuff. "Passion is the point, isn't it, Dr. Clarke? Doctoring. It's your passion. You think you'll be better off without us, but you won't be. The denial of your passion will stick in your mouth like this bloody—" She cleared her throat. "This blast—" Once more. "This *lemon* water. If you're going to spook at the circumstances of your most desperate patients, why are you even doing this? I can't imagine that becoming a physician was the easiest path for you. Why bother with all that if not for passion?"

Because someone had to do it.

The words flashed so brightly in Emily's mind that they quite nearly lit up her tongue, the room, the whole household. With her father having refused any expansion of his family and her only brother choosing to play dress-up for profession as well as for pleasure, what other options had there been?

Marriage or medicine, those had been the options. And she'd been incredibly lucky to have even that much say. Clearly Mrs. Smith didn't understand that not everyone was in a position to go traipsing about at pornographic print houses and questionable clubs in trousers.

Her options had always been limited and always would be. That passion for the work had come along in its own time was a great blessing and a balm to her resentment. But it was not enough to lead her into a frail woman's birthing room. If she could feel guilty for her own mother's death, something she'd taken no conscious part in, how would she ever keep her sanity if harm came to her own patient?

Yet, how might she feel to learn the poor Miss Garcia had died of sepsis in hospital, or of something preventable at home with her actress friends?

Emily's determination wavered. But she quickly came to her senses. If Emily took on this patient, in this specialty, under these circumstances, she would be pigeonholed into these same cases for the rest of her life, because it was exactly what the world believed she should be doing already. She would receive accolades for her goodness, her social concern, her sober charity.

And then she would be considered ruined for any other type of patient, with any other type of malady. The perfect "female doctor," doing the most generous, feminine, matronly "female doctor" things. Miss Garcia might end up alright, but eventually, someone wouldn't. And when the stress of seeing families torn apart, ghosts born in place of children, empty chairs and unchanged sewing rooms, runaway sons and left-behind daughters bickering with each other about what the bloody point of it all was, she would have no way out. No way back to some other specialty. Nowhere else to go.

As she stared at the figure before her, she was filled with an infuriating and burning sense of want. Not just for the woman herself, but for what she represented. Who she was. How she was.

How Emily never, ever could be.

She yanked at the tray, taking it back into her own hands with surprising ease. Mrs. Smith hadn't been clutching it as hard as she seemed. She wasn't that desperate, and frankly, neither was Miss Garcia. The woman's paramour—Mrs. Smith's husband—probably had enough money in his business to bribe someone closer to home. It would be better anyway; they wouldn't have to work out whether doctor or patient had to spend the last weeks of the confinement in a strange place. Everything would be simpler.

"I am not taking on Miss Garcia," she said. "I am not taking on any obstetrics patients for the foreseeable future. Not taking on any private patients, in fact. I am too busy at the hospital, and that's simply the reality of it." She hesitated, gripping the tray with the full force of her guilt. "But do tell her...tell her to loosen that corset immediately. It is not helping her sickness in the slightest, and might even be causing its severity." She tried to stop there, but a ghost appeared from her training in London, screaming at her with all the breath it never got to take: "And if she's going to continue wearing one, she must switch to a maternity model within the next two weeks. Remind her that those were created so she can *expand* the lacings as she progresses, never to hide the condition. That is a tragically common misunderstanding of their purpose, with devastating consequences."

"See?" said Mrs. Smith with an impressed sort of chuckle. "You can't help but—"

"I have helped all I can." Emily forced the words out through her teeth and the ghost back into the recesses of her mind, refusing to take even one more look at that beguiling grin before it shattered her into a million pieces. "Good day, Mrs. Smith."

Emily wasn't as relieved as she'd have liked after Mrs. Smith's departure. Fortunately, there was a full day's work ahead of her. Due to this strangely-timed appointment, she still had an afternoon at the hospital. Between the assessment of maladies, the fraught task of convincing male doctors of her diagnostic opinions, and the comfort work of pillow fluffing and blanket fetching that the troublesome nurse refused to handle for her yet again, there was very little time to think about her brother's bizarre friends.

She arrived home with her body pleasantly exhausted. After some time whittling at a new queen's curves in her study, a simple supper, and the swapping of hospital stories with Papa, her muscles ached for a bath, an herbal infusion, and the mattress. Since she and Papa had their home's plumbing brought up to the cutting edge of sanitation every few years, she had quite a lovely bath to look forward to, with a porcelain clawfoot and hot tap in a dedicated bathroom. A soak was always just the thing after a trying shift.

But the thoughts started up as soon as she'd gotten her hair unpinned, like they'd been twisted in the coils and were suddenly set free. She found herself wondering what it might be like to let one's hair down and see, not frizzy blond waves, but a lush, coal-black tumble that Mrs. Smith had certainly been hiding in her own voluminous, messy knot.

Madness. She shook the idea off, starting up the taps and letting them splash into the tub while she undressed.

And yet, the crashing sound of water could not chase out the next thought, which came when she started on the buttons of her blouse. With a slim figure and a tailor in the family, Emily's simple clothes fit modestly and impeccably, each button secure and every piece of her well-situated even by society's corseted standards. While everything about Mrs. Smith's attire had been decadent and incorrect, it was that loose button, that barely contained excess of her form, that suddenly had Emily slipping on her own fastenings, blinking her eyes like mental images could be cleared the same as soot.

She shouldn't let this woman bother her so much. She turned the cold tap down, letting the water go scorching. When she'd finally hung her outer-clothes and put the underthings in the washing basket, she gave herself a good, hot scrub with carbolic soap. That epitome of cleanliness would certainly take care of the day's troubles, in addition to its microbes.

The tactic failed. As did the calm application of her healthful woolen night clothes and the careful braiding of her damp hair. She boiled and infused some water with chamomile, rosebuds, and lemon peel, adding a few drops of the gentle tonic she'd been sending to David. Far from distracting her, the task was tainted with accusations of sour babies that had her smiling to herself as she recalled their ridiculousness. She had to remind herself that there was nothing cute about such myths. She added an extra lemon slice to her infusion and brought it to her room, where she tried to read but could not, because the text had her wondering: Might there be something to the idea of handwriting analysis after all?

She snapped the book shut on the nonsense coursing through her. Enough was enough. Perhaps it was misplaced guilt over turning Miss Garcia away. Or the disappointment her father had expressed over supper when she'd told him that the appointment hadn't gone well. Or annoyance at the audacity of Mrs. Smith to show up here, practically wink with those long lashes of hers, and act like any of them could just do as they pleased. Like she obviously did.

Whatever exactly had stirred up these torments, they were clearly becoming *hysterical* in nature and would need to be treated as such.

The conscious recognition made an impatient warmth blossom between Emily's legs. She used to try to talk herself out of this, but science was on her side. Far from causing blindness or other problems, the release of feminine frustrations was medically indicated.

With her heart picking up at the anticipation, she went into her bedside drawer and very quietly drew out the smooth, polished wooden instrument that was her favorite. Snug in bed as she was, she kept the bottom buttons of her union suit fastened. The frustrations of Mrs. Smith were certainly not worth the bother of crossing the cold floor to clean up. She opted instead to glide the tip of the instrument along the seam of her sex through the cloth, swirling around the clitoris and back down again, until her breathing became harsh, her limbs grew tense, and when she knew she needed *just a little bit more*, it was the image of a strained and swelling waistcoat that propelled her into the crisis that would let her put this from her mind forever.

Chapter Six

Jo

As much as Jo hated to see such an insufferable creature proven correct, Dr. Clarke's stingy suggestions around loose lacings and lemon water did improve Vanessa's appetite in the weeks that followed.

Even worse, Vanessa was nearly as enthusiastic about Jo's questionable contributions of ginger, potato soups, and the cutesy folksongs she kept pulling out of her arse on the unfortunate evenings that saw all three of them at home at the same time. She was doing her best to avoid being home with Paul entirely, since he used those opportunities to attempt serious conversations about the future of everyone's living arrangements, and she was still too mixed-up to deal with that. But while she'd mostly avoided being alone with him, and managed to be *very busy with something* whenever she couldn't, Vanessa kept asking for her company and support after rehearsals. The folksongs ensured these evenings were light and bright; even at his most annoyed, Paul wasn't the grim, practical kind of monster who would interrupt two women belting "Molly Malone" at somebody's blossoming belly. It was far too quaint.

Quite by accident, she'd found that being *impenetrably quaint* was even better armor against awkwardness and decision-making than being *demonstrably helpful*. Fortunately, because each of their employment and social habits came with very different hours, these occurrences were infrequent enough that Jo hadn't yet needed to go so far as to knit wee things too darling to disturb.

Which was good, because quaintness did not come easily to her, feeling as false as the paint on Vanessa's lips. She'd left quaintness back in Ireland. She certainly did not remember how to knit, for God's sake, and Gran's book still hadn't turned up. She'd found a few more dime novels that had gone missing from collections. An early Dickens volume that was probably worth a pretty penny to the right collector. Even a slew of embarrassing old photographs of herself from back when she'd thought she belonged in front of the pornographer's camera rather than setting his type out of sight. But no sign of Gran's book.

Incredible, really. A bit of a misstep, a span of neglect, and next thing you knew, someone—no, some*thing*—something you'd known all your life could simply vanish, never to be seen again.

It was becoming a problem. She could not quite let herself feel the gravity of what it might mean to have lost the only object she had from the one family member who'd never betrayed her; once she started feeling that sadness, she worried she'd never come out of it. But there were practical concerns as well. Aside from Jo's inability to get that button to stay put for more than a handful of wears, her feeble attempts at quaint and enjoyable evenings with Vanessa had led to a conversation that was not quite as horrible as the one Paul was plotting, but came close:

"Oh, and you'll be with me when the baby comes, won't you, dear Jo?" Vanessa declared, clutching Jo's arm and half-swooning as she so often did, even when she was feeling perfectly fine. "Judith back at the actresses' home has caught a few babies for friends, and she'll do it for me, but given…you know." She would never, ever say *my age*, even though Jo knew what it was by now. "And that we didn't find a doctor after all… I'd just feel so much better to have someone like you there with us."

"Vanessa," Jo said, half-pleading because all this bloody nesting had made her nearly as attached to this woman and her child as she was to the husband she was still pretty certain she was going to lose any day now. "I'm not a midwife. I don't really know what I'm doing. A farmgirl picks a few things up. That's all."

"But those few things are better than nothing," Vanessa insisted. "And while your hands are not skillful, I think we both know that they are very kind. Whatever happens to us in that childbed, kind hands will make all the difference to me."

Bloody hell! Kind hands? What was Jo supposed to do with *that*? Not to mention the obvious fear that lived behind the dramatic sparkle in Vanessa's eye. This shit was real, was really happening, and with Dr. Clarke having been nothing more than an annoyingly beautiful waste of time, it looked like Jo was going to have to figure out how to be quaint *and* helpful.

And as she had no experience, no friends who were of any help, and no idea whether she'd find her gran's advice in time, she had only one companion to turn to. The only one she'd had longer than Paul:

Books.

Fortunately, she had plenty of those in her bookshop, and much more organized than the ones at home. Paul had bought Morgan & Murray's off the worst bookseller in London as a cover operation for their press a few years back, and had turned most of its care over to Jo. While it had been a damned process getting the neglected shelves in order, the upfront work Jo had done on the place was certainly paying off now. Finding the medicine and motherhood books among her inventory should prove easy enough.

Though it was a Sunday—often a sleepy, lazy day for women who were not particularly welcome in their parishes—the shop employee, Alma Merriweather, came down from her flat above the place when she heard Jo thumping around. She stood behind the counter by habit, quietly watching Jo's stacks grow. Once it had become a rather formidable fortress, she peeked out from between the columns. "Joey?"

"Yes?" said Jo from the stepladder, wishing she was just a smidge taller as she reached for a volume at the very top.

"What are you doing, exactly?"

One more stretch, and she had the book in hand. She tucked it under her arm and brought it down, placing it directly in front of Alma. "Becoming an expert in midwifery."

Alma picked up the book, peering at the parental title printed across the cover. "Is this about Dr. Clarke rejecting Miss Garcia?"

"Bugger Dr. Clarke," Jo snapped, resenting the way that irritating woman's bright, severe eyes flashed through her mind. "Bugger all those high-minded doctors, in fact. Let them have their lances and their mercury and their lemony dispositions." She started taking books from the stacks she'd made, reorganizing them by urgency. "We don't need them."

"You seem very serious about this all of a sudden," Alma said. "I thought you were only playing the expert for your own benefit."

"You're absolutely right." Jo set aside one of the most promising of the volumes. "I am a terrific prat, and only acted like I could help so she wouldn't run me off with a pitchfork. Sadly for her, though, I might genuinely be the best she's got. I saw a new side of her in Surrey and... I can't leave her on her own. I've got to help. I'm still no expert, but I've got a lot of books, eh? And my grandmother must have delivered a hundred babies back in the day. As for hands-on...well... I watched my littlest brothers come into the world, not to mention all the calves and puppies, so it's not like I lack an understanding of the basic mechanics."

Alma looked skeptically at the stacks. "When you explain this to Miss Garcia, I strongly recommend you leave the puppies out of it."

"I'll need my gran's own book too, of course," Jo went on, patting one of the piles like it was the old friend that would see them through this. "No O'Donnell woman ever expected doctors or hospitals to be involved in their breeding. She practically wrote a bloody textbook of her own to see her granddaughters through. I never did pay much attention to the relevant pages, but I know they're in there."

A curious look crossed Alma's face. "Never?" She bit her lip, hesitated, but pressed on. "I mean to say... I know you and Paul began your marriage as a proper one. And you are...well..."

"Catholic?" Jo supplied with a wry look. She and Paul did try not to call attention to that socially indecent fact of themselves, hardly better than their occupations, depending on the audience. Downplaying it was usually simple enough, but Alma had been working for the Smiths long enough to have caught on. "Let's just say the page I liked best listed some teas that let me stop flipping and get back to work."

"Not very Catholic of you."

"You clearly haven't talked to enough of us after a couple strong drinks."

The turn of the conversation seemed to hit Alma hard. Jo suddenly regretted that she hadn't thought that possibility through before she started tossing motherhood books around. Having once found herself in Miss Garcia's situation, without Miss Garcia's sense of freedom or independence, Alma had her own troubles and tragedies related to the subject. This position at the bookshop, and her little home above it, was a very fortunate and very unlikely fate, one that Jo was proud to have been able to provide.

"Alright?" Jo asked.

"Well enough." Alma sighed and opened the nearest tome. "It's just so hard, isn't it? Sometimes it seems that none of us is unaffected, in one way or another."

Of all things, it was Dr. Clarke's tight jaw and rigid posture that flashed through Jo's mind, framed with that wispy, out-of-place little hair. Though the doctor's home had been filled with comfort, something must have been hard for her too, in this world that saw all of them as little more than property for someone else's propagation. A true life of ease did not create a woman so full of barely buttoned rage…but no. Jo wouldn't allow this little scratch of compassion to take hold. Something might have been hard for Dr. Clarke too, but that didn't give her any right to take it out on Vanessa.

It was almost worse that her advice on the corset had been spot-on. It brought into sharper relief just how much better off the poor woman would be with some proper care. That Dr. Clarke was refusing to give further help in potentially more dire circumstances was rankling.

"Anyway." Alma leaned across the counter. "I think that if you needed more support with Miss Garcia, I might be able to bring a perspective of my own. I've been through it myself, you know, start to finish. I even nursed my little one for a few days, before the nuns found better circumstances for her."

Found better circumstances. Alma's way of spinning gold through the disaster of her ruin bordered on heroic. "Are you certain it wouldn't be too taxing on your nerves?"

"Quite the contrary," Alma sighed. "It might give meaning to the situation, on the nights when I'm up wondering what the devil it was all for."

"That's very good of you. Thank you." She paused. "I'm getting hungry, are you?"

"Famished."

"Let's fortify ourselves before we carry on with all this, shall we? Doesn't seem like work for an empty stomach at all."

"Agreed!" said Alma, clapping her hands together girlishly. "Let's bring something back from Bradigan's across the way. It's my favorite."

Jo glanced out the window toward Bradigan & Son's Coffee House, an eclectic spot run by another former member of the English Martyrs mission church where Jo had landed when she got to London.

Now *that* was a life she'd packed up and left just as thoroughly as she'd left her first home. She'd met Paul at that church. Raised in London from birth, he'd been childhood friends with the Bradigans and others like them from his first days at the parish school until long after he'd grown into the eccentric bachelor who printed all the church's handbills, songbooks, and documents. When Jo married him, she'd thrown herself fully and sometimes even happily into the life they were building in the parish community, but those friendships were worse than awkward now. Even the odd family who owned the coffee house, a clan scolded for being uncommonly friendly with radical groups of Protestant dissenters, couldn't stay on good terms with Jo and Paul once they'd changed their last name from Shanahan to Smith and moved on to print scandals on Holywell Street.

Jo didn't relish going into that coffee house. While she couldn't regret her more authentic existence, it was bloody depressing to be reminded that every authentic move she'd made had required complete severance from everyone and everything she'd known. Popping into Bradigan & Son's was about as appealing as hopping on a boat back to her birthplace. But Alma was positively glowing at the mere mention of it. It wouldn't kill her, she supposed, to grab the girl what she wanted.

"What should I get? I've never been in."

"But it's so close by!"

"I've got my reasons."

"Get the cinnamon-raisin cake," Alma said. "It's divine!"

"Cake? For dinner?"

Alma waved a hand. "Oh, I'll eat a proper dinner too. But it's the cake that matters, so make sure not to forget it or we might as well have gone somewhere else entirely!"

The coffee house smelled of its namesake's elixir and something slightly too close to funeral incense to be entirely tasteful. The whole place struck Jo as ten times more decadent than the decadence she'd been accused of. No mermaids to hold your hat, but rather poorly done paintings of the Blessed Virgin amid a dull, earthy color palette. It was all a bit mismatched and confused, but seeing as the assortment of customers was similarly ragtag, she supposed the assault on beauty fit well enough.

No one she used to know seemed to be in, thankfully, some narrow bloke behind the counter instead. He talked so fast to the pair at the counter that he must have had a barrel of coffee already to be able to sustain that pace. As Jo took her place in the queue, she heard him conclude the monologue with "And will it be your usual, Mr. Clarke?"

"*Certo, gratzie,*" said the customer in a soft voice that Jo had never heard outside the pink-lit parlor of The Curious Fox.

Before Jo could figure out what she was supposed to do in this situation, Noah Clarke and David Forester turned around, freezing when they saw who'd taken up the place behind them in line. They all had a heartbeat's span to decide whether they knew each other outside the walls of the club. Since Noah and

David were known by name to the staff, she touched her hat, making her eyes say: *up to you*.

Noah smiled, then David did too.

"Miss Jo?" Noah said carefully, as if he wasn't sure he'd really recognized her. "Is that you?"

"Is indeed." She shook their hands in the solemn, proper greeting that would catch no notice. "I wouldn't have expected to see you in a place like this."

"My family and a few others from our chapel back home come out to hear talks put on by one of the London congregations every few months," Noah explained, glancing up the rickety staircase. "Afterward, we come here to socialize. Not my choice of an afternoon, but it's a chance to see my father and sister while they're in the city. Well, my sister this time. My father wasn't feeling up to dealing with the trains today."

Jo's head whipped around to the staircase too, so fast she nearly lost her hat. "She's here? Dr. Clarke?"

"Oh yes," said Noah. "She never misses these London talks, come hell or high-water."

"Hmm." Jo was tempted to storm up there and give Dr. Clarke all the hell and high-water she could manage. "Well, I'm just here to get some food to sustain me while I read up on how to help Miss Garcia do the same, whilst she and her baby waste away into nothing with naught but myself to care for them. Let your sister know that for me, will you?"

A chaotic mischief crossed Noah's face that was hardly less devious here than it was when covered in cosmetics at the club. "You could tell her yourself, if you'd like. Our meetings are open to all."

David gave them both a warning look. "Are you trying to cause a scene?"

"*No*," said Noah, putting an offended hand to the drooping bowtie on his chest. "But Emily would more than deserve it, if I were. I know she can be *prim*—" he said it like he very much meant a more colorful phrase "—but I also know her to be generally good and practical, and far as I can tell, there was no good or practical reason for her to turn Miss Garcia out. I was horrified when she told me. Our father was too. And, quite frankly, I know we wouldn't be the only ones, should someone *happen* to mention that my sister refused to care for an unwed mother before a room full of nosy social reformers."

"He is definitely trying to cause a scene." David took Noah by the arm. "Let's go. Take care, Miss Jo."

"No longer interested in getting the two of them talking, then?" said Noah, all false innocence.

"My interest was in them *talking*," David said, "not arguing in public. Let's go."

He dragged Noah off to the staircase, but as they started up, Noah turned and winked his formal invitation for Jo to come cause whatever sort of scene she liked.

"Help you, ah, Miss?" said the man behind the counter. He looked her over curiously, but was not as shocked as people usually were when they encountered her for the first time. She could appreciate that and returned his politeness as she ordered the cake and some more suitable foods to bring back to the bookshop.

Then she requested that he hold it for her for a few minutes while she went upstairs to visit with an acquaintance that she was very eager to have a chat with before she left.

"And do tell the Bradigans," she added, filled with deviously bright spirits, appreciating this place far more than she had at first, "that old Jenny Shanahan sends her compliments for the outstanding decorations."

Upstairs, she found a mixed group of somberly dressed men and rationally dressed women, done up in the muted woolen colors and old-fashioned cuts that marked their political position. Every last one of them stared at her. Clearly, strangers even more eccentric than they were did not often wander up into the private meetings.

Her gaze drifted to a few chairs under the breezy open window. Out the corner of her eye, she saw Noah rising to introduce her, but the full fixture of her attention locked without delay on the woman sitting beside him.

Dr. Clarke, strapped securely into gray skirts and a simple jacket, had gathered her hair into that same skull-squeezing bun. She was uncorsetted again, but so slim and erect it hardly mattered. No cosmetics. No jewelry. No nonsense. Jo would have recognized her anywhere. A clawing sensation sprang to life low in Jo's belly, a throbbing annoyance that was almost thrilling in its intensity.

When Dr. Clarke spotted Jo, she blushed spectacularly pink all across her porcelain face. She turned with barely contained rage to her brother, but he was already up and rapidly gliding out of her reach.

"Miss Jo!" He took her in for a delighted handshake. He smiled at their curious audience, their heads cocked for information about the oddity in their midst. "Just a friend of mine that I ran into downstairs. She runs the bookshop across the way, Morgan & Murray's."

Once she'd been explained so adequately, most of them went back to their own coffee cups and conversations, and Noah led her to his spot beneath the window.

As Jo's shadow fell over her, Dr. Clarke stared determinedly into the glossy black puddle of coffee in her cup. She glared at it so intensely that one might think she was attempting to telekinetically turn the bitter beverage into a dagger with which to stab her brother. Or maybe Jo. It was hard to tell, just now, which was the greater object of her ire.

Noah dragged another chair over and placed it between himself and his sister, with David across looking distinctly miserable about this turn of events. Once Noah sat her down, he settled into his own place, looking every bit the person who played the part of the meddling, gossipy Miss Penelope Primrose during the Fox's drag parties. "No need for introductions, are there? Seeing as you've known Mr. Forester for some time now, and have also had the pleasure of making my sister's acquaintance just last month."

He procured a cup from somewhere, almost magicianlike, pouring and passing it to Jo as he smiled and blinked innocently.

Jo took the cup, feeling waves of irritation coming off the doctor. But what should she be so miffed about? It was Dr. Clarke who'd sent Jo and Vanessa on their way. Jo was perfectly within her rights to be here. In fact, if not for preferring to avoid coffee house owners who remembered her by retired aliases, she might have visited with this group before now, given the proximity of her shop and her friendship with one of the regulars.

With that in mind, she met the doctor's lack of hospitality with an equal air of comfort, kicking an ankle up over her knee and sipping the rich coffee with relish.

"Thank you very much, Noah," she said casually, eyes slipping sideways to Dr. Clarke's stony face. "I can't stay long, but a bit of good brew like this will do me good."

"Oh!" said Noah with slightly exaggerated surprise. "And where you do need to rush off to?"

"I only stopped over to pick up a little dinner for myself and my coworker." She glanced at Dr. Clarke, who now looked like she was trying to turn the coffee not into a dagger, but into a broadsword. Jo smiled. There was something satisfying about getting under her skin. "We're reading up on women's medical matters so we can help our ailing companion Miss Garcia. You remember Miss Garcia, don't you, Dr. Clarke?"

Dr. Clarke finally met Jo's eye. "Of course I remember her," she said, moving her mouth as little as possible. Jo noticed that they were well-formed lips, plumped, perhaps, by their incessant pursing. "And how is she?"

Jo drank from her cup and stared the doctor down, even as she kept her voice pleasant. "Still having trouble eating much. But I'm doing my best to become a suitable childbed companion. All on my own. With no help, training, or even compassion from the world outside."

The coffee-scented air crackled between them. The doctor, obviously, wanted to snap, and Jo sat in as relaxed a fashion as possible, raising her eyebrows and just daring her to start.

David cleared his throat, far more uncomfortable with the tension than the smug-looking lover beside him. "It's good of you to be there for her," he said in a light, even voice.

"It *is* good of me, isn't it?" She lifted her cup toward Dr. Clarke, who did not opt to toast Jo's goodness. But that was alright. She was in *a room full of nosy social reformers*, after all. If she raised her voice a notch, someone else might lift a non-intoxicating glass to her upright actions.

"Regarding the plight of unwed mothers," she went on with a heavy sigh, peeking to ensure she had the attention of a nearby group, "I don't see how punishing the indiscretions of working-class women does any good for our society. Give the girl some help, I say, and you'll see how willing even our most reviled are to create lives of meaning and contribution."

Over Dr. Clarke's rigid shoulder, another drab and frowning sort of woman raised her own cup. "Hear, hear," she said, confirming that Jo's performance had successfully roused her social sentiments. "And perhaps, become more willing to instill the resulting virtues in her offspring, so that they might avoid her mistakes."

Jo may have read a few dissenter pamphlets in her day, but

never before had someone looked at her in all seriousness and used the word *offspring* in conversation about human beings. Fuck. Though it took every shred of self-control she possessed, Jo managed not to laugh, not to even smile. She just nodded right along, then nudged Dr. Clarke, a tiny touch that made the doctor jump and scoot to the other side of her chair.

"See," Jo said, smoldering with satisfaction. "Someone agrees with me."

The frowning woman turned her grimness onto Dr. Clarke, who waved her hands back and forth like she was erasing Jo's words from a slate. "I don't disagree with you, Mrs. Smith," she said hurriedly. Once the attention of Mrs. Frown was diverted elsewhere, she lowered her voice and muttered to her coffee, "Nothing about any of this bothers me in the slightest."

Oh, but it did. The palpable heat of her annoyance was more delicious than anything coming out of the coffee house kitchen. Jo was ready for her next helping before she'd even finished the first.

"Glad to hear it, Dr. Clarke," she said, still a little on the loud side. "I suppose I misunderstood your position. I was under the impression that you turned Miss Garcia away due to her scandalous circumstances."

"I didn't turn her away because she was unwed," Dr. Clarke hissed, eyes darting to the others nearby. "I would appreciate it if you did not imply—"

"No, I know you didn't turn her away for that," Jo interrupted, making to pat the doctor's hand where it was settled on the arm rest.

Dr. Clarke snatched her hand back as if from the jaws of a lion. "Good, because—"

"I thought it was your judgement against the father—a man you've never even met—that led you to make ungenerous assumptions about a woman who ought to have been respected as an individual soul." She sipped her coffee innocently. "Do you agree with that as well, Dr. Clarke?"

There were some mutters and nods from those listening, and a few suspicious looks in the doctor's direction. Noah looked poised on the edge of a cackle, while David stared at the floor with a grimace on his face.

"I understand," said the doctor, in a shaking voice that just barely carried beneath the building chatter of Jo's new admirers, "that you are trying to humiliate me."

"Indeed," Jo said pleasantly. "Is it working?"

"No," said Dr. Clarke. "The whole act strikes me as petulant, childish, and unkind."

The unexpected word sent harsh flare of temper through Jo's belly.

"Unkind?" she snapped, her feigned air of intellectual ease dropping as incredulity took over. "Me? You're the one who turned her out. How am I the unkind one?"

"Because you're only doing this to upset someone you know nothing about. You aren't here to change my mind. You're here to enrage me and cause me trouble with my own community." Somehow Dr. Clarke managed to straighten her spine even further as she said with a heated glare, "So yes. You are the unkind one, Mrs. Smith."

Jo got to her feet before she knew what she was doing. Enough of this shite. She turned to Noah. "You were right," she said. "Your sister really is a damned piece of work. You can bloody keep her."

This outburst garnered more attention than the glances and mutterings of before. Every eye in the room was on them now, seeming confused as to how Jo had gone so quickly from rational to tempestuous. Tongues clicked; whispers flew. Good. Let them see a few feathers get ruffled, a few buttons out of place, a little decadence. She'd lost the audience, but that was alright: Noah and David aside, she couldn't care less what these people thought of her.

In the spirit of that, she gulped down the rest of her coffee before setting her cup down hard enough to make the spoons rattle. She strode out of the parlor, slamming the door shut.

She wasn't even halfway down the stairs before she heard the door and more footsteps behind her. At the bottom, she turned to tell Noah she was fine and apologize if the scene was more than he'd bargained for.

But it wasn't Noah following her.

It was Dr. Clarke. And she'd brought enough fire along to rumple her jacket and send a few flyaways out of her bun, catching the light of the hallway sconces like the halo she clearly believed she possessed. She gripped the rail with one hand and her skirts with the other.

"Mrs. Smith, I have worked too hard to have you misrepresent me like that in front of my peers." She grasped her skirts tighter and pulled them out of her way, high enough to flash tight boot lacings and the soft cream of a practical woolen stocking. Her rigid heels clacked on the steps until she was two above Jo, pointing a finger inches from Jo's nose. "You will go back up there and apologize for the spectacle you have made of my family."

Jo blinked, overtaken half by a matching anger and half by something a bit more entertaining. The swirl of intensity and embarrassment had made the prim doctor appear almost wild. So *this* was what she was bottling up so carefully.

It might be appropriate to snap back at such fervor with a harsh quip of her own, but Jo suddenly lacked the motivation for it. It was actually a relief to see all that tension released at last. It suited Dr. Clarke to make demands from the fire in her belly instead of the list in her head.

Jo shook that off. Her business with the doctor was done.

"Don't worry," she said. "They're your friends. Not mine. In a few minutes, they'll remember all your most admirable qualities, and the only spectacle I'll have made is of myself. Good day to you."

Averting her eyes from the stormy vision on the staircase, she went to the counter for the bundled food that awaited her.

But once she'd gathered it up and turned for the door, she nearly dropped it all when she found Dr. Clarke standing so close that their skirts would have brushed, had Jo been wearing one.

"Mrs. Smith, I insist that you set things right."

How was this interaction not over yet? She tried to go around the doctor, but was blocked by a hasty side step. She snorted out an astounded laugh before she could help herself, then went the other direction. When Dr. Clarke blocked her yet again, she shifted the packages in her arms and shouldered the doctor out of her way. Given Dr. Clarke's stony demeanor, Jo expected her to feel like a cold statue, and was so shocked to feel a soft, yielding arm against her own that she nearly stopped in her tracks.

But there would be no stopping and no softness. She pulled her own arm tight to her side and whisked to the door, only to find her hands were too full to open it.

She tipped her head back. *Fuck.* Those severe heels clacked up behind her, and a small hand appeared on the door handle.

In the most reluctant act of chivalry Jo had ever seen in her life, Dr. Clarke held the door open. "After you."

Jo eyed the windows in hopes of spotting a more suitable escape, but they were overlaid with wrought iron and stained glass that looked unlikely to budge. Plagued by a prickling awareness of the doctor as she passed through the doorway, Jo went out onto the street without a glance or a thank-you.

When the door shut behind her, it was with Dr. Clarke on the wrong side of it.

Was this woman really going to follow Jo back to the book-shop? It was absurd. And yet, that's just what she did. The whole way, Jo was dogged by clicking heels and the furious swish of skirts. When they arrived beneath the Morgan & Murray's sign, Jo peeked through the window, hoping Alma would save her, but it seemed she'd gone upstairs.

Dr. Clarke drew breath to launch into something or other, but Jo cut her off.

"If you're going to do...whatever this is," she said, "then at least make yourself useful and get the door for me again, would you?"

Dr. Clarke pursed her lips, sealing up whatever she'd been about to say. Yes, it was certainly that pursing that plumped them. It would add up to quite a bit of exercise if she did it as often as Jo suspected. The habit was a trying one, but the effect, at least, was admirable.

Dr. Clarke tugged futilely on the door handle. "It's locked."

"Of course it is," said Jo. "This is London. Can't leave our doors unlocked like you probably do out in Farm-Brush—"

"*Farncombe.*" She shook back one of those wispy hairs that were always trying so desperately to escape her wrath. "Where's the key?"

A smirk crossed Jo's face. "The key is in my pocket, isn't it?"

Dr. Clarke's cheeks flushed an impressive pink that trailed down her smooth neck and vanished into the high, no-frills collar of her frock. Jo fleetingly wondered how far such the flush went, particularly with her blood flow unrestricted by a corset. Was she one of those porcelain sorts whose whole chests brightened under the influence of shame?

Or passion?

Jo realized that her gaze was drifting along with her musings. But it wasn't her fault that Emily Clarke was as pretty as she was insufferable. Seeing as this would be Jo's last look at the woman, she supposed it was as good a time as any to make it a thorough one. It wasn't as if she would actually fetch that key; she was probably about to storm off, never to be seen again and muttering about impropriety all the while.

Though what little of Dr. Clarke's visible skin remained bright red, her demeanor remained determinedly stoic. Far from running from Jo's challenge, she met it head-on, slipping her slim fingers straight into Jo's front pocket to feel around for the key.

Jo nearly dropped her burdens as shocking warmth shot from the clinically confident touch into all the most interesting spots nearby. It took until the doctor's eyes narrowed for her to unstick her throat enough to choke out, "It's the, er, other pocket."

Arms still full of boxes, she couldn't watch Dr. Clarke's hand slip from one pocket to invade the next one over, but she could sure as hell feel it. Her fingers were supposed to feel like steely, pinching forceps, but they did not. They were soft, ticklish, and far more pleasant than Jo liked to admit.

At last, the key was procured. Dr. Clarke seemed to have reached the maximum of redness a while back, so it was impossible to say whether she'd been as affected by the action as Jo was. She unlocked the bookshop door and held it open.

"Well?" said Dr. Clarke impatiently when Jo remained frozen at the threshold. "Go ahead."

Snapping out of it at last, Jo passed through the narrow doorway into her shop. Though Dr. Clarke's skirts were of a narrow sweep with little in the way of a bustle, the garment swelled just a bit too far to avoid a brush of gray wool against Jo's calves, the sensation making her heart stutter uncomfortably.

She unstacked the boxes on the counter, peering up the staircase. Jo was torn between calling Alma down as reinforcements, or sparing her the trouble of dealing with Dr. Clarke, who had come along into the shop's interior without an invitation.

Exasperated, Jo wanted to grab Dr. Clarke by the shoulders, using the excuse of shaking her or turning her out to feel that velvety humanness that only appeared when they were touching. Instead, she crossed her arms over her middle, tight enough to strain the waistcoat button she still hadn't gotten around to mending properly.

"Dr. Clarke." It was supposed to be a snap, but came out as a frustrated huff. "What are you *doing* here?"

Dr. Clarke twisted the key in her hands and then held it out. Jo kept her arms crossed as something petulant reared its head and refused to let her do even the smallest, most reasonable bit of Dr. Clarke's bidding.

"You embarrassed me," said Dr. Clarke. She firmly held the key out yet again, though her voice was gentler than it had been.

Jo considered snatching at the key, but she since couldn't bring herself to do it with the proper force, she opted to wait until her ire could peak again. "It ain't my fault that your motives for turning Miss Garcia away were unpalatable to your friends."

"What do you know about my motives?" Dr. Clarke looked her up and down for the sake of demonstration, but turned red again. The fury left her voice, replaced with something unexpectedly shaky. "I'm so *glad* you get to prance around in trousers, giving your husband away for Christmas, and living without any expectations hanging over your head. We aren't all so lucky, however, so I would appreciate if you could at the very least—"

"Lucky?" Jo had been called a lot of things over the years. Reckless. Scattered. Brilliant. Foolish. Pretty. Dapper. Confusing-as-all-get-out. But she could not recall anyone accusing her of being *lucky*. "You think I was born into the situation you found me in, Dr. Clarke? That my parents swaddled me up in a fine gentleman's cravat until I was big enough for them to say, '*Go on, Joey*'—as if they picked that name for me on day one—'*go live how you like. Do whatever you please.*'"

Dr. Clarke stared at Jo with her purse-plumped lips parted, but no words spilled from them this time, angry or otherwise. She looked lost, like she'd only just found herself in this shop by magic.

The air between them softened, but was still far from comfortable. Soft, sure, but also tight and impossible, like the first breath in a silken corset. For the first time since meeting this woman, she wasn't angry or frustrated. She felt pity. She'd assumed that a woman who put stock in luck couldn't become a physician, but based on the dazed look on Dr. Clarke's face, she felt as trapped as Jo had as a housewife. The rejection of Vanessa clearly had more to do with that unhappiness than it did with Paul's press.

Jo finally reached for the key between them, feeling the contrast of cold metal and smooth skin.

Dr. Clarke looked at their hands, still clasped around the key. Jo startled at the realization that neither of them had pulled back yet. That she didn't really want to pull back. In fact, she wanted to push into the contact, lacing their fingers and asking what she was so unhappy about. If she cared what she looked like to her nonconforming peers above all else, she'd have taken Vanessa on. So what was holding her back?

Slow, finger by finger almost, Dr. Clarke let go of the key, smoothing her hand distractedly down her skirt. Distracted and *distracting*: Jo was mesmerized by the movement until the hitch of breath, a precursor to speech, brought her gaze up to the doctor's mouth instead. Lips not pursed, but parted with words clearly waiting at the threshold, words Jo suspected might be unlike the others she'd heard fall from them…

A skittering clatter at their feet stole their attention, nearly deafening in the close, pulsing air. A button peered up from the floor like a nosy black eye. Jo tried to step back, feeling absurdly like she'd been caught at something, but her back was to the counter already.

And though Dr. Clarke had the whole world behind her, she didn't retreat. Instead, she stooped, flashing the very top of her tight bun, which gleamed golden in the sunlight. She picked the button up and straightened, squinting clinically at it. With an automatic air, she lifted it to its original place, as if testing whether she'd found the right spot for a puzzle piece.

The spot being, of course, the edge of Jo's waistcoat that fell over her breast. The faint whisper of pressure had Jo feeling how her heart thudded against the fabric like it wanted to reach out and grab the button back itself. That was the job of Jo's hand, but she didn't trust that part to do it, either. Her fingers itched, not to push Dr. Clarke away and snatch back her property, but to behave just as devil-may-care as Dr. Clarke thought she was, pulling her closer and breaking the threads of whatever flimsy button kept the doctor herself so put together.

But before she could do anything, proper or improper, there was a creak on the upstairs floorboards. Dr. Clarke stepped back in a panic, sweeping at her wayward flyaways. With one last, wide-eyed look, the doctor turned, skirts swishing, and all but ran out onto the street, back to her own world, where the shirts were starched, the coffee was strong, and the buttons were secure.

"Joey?"

Alma's voice from the staircase startled off the desire to chase Dr. Clarke down. And thank goodness, really; there was no way Jo cared enough about the woman to do something *that* ridiculous.

The key to the shop was still in Jo's hand, but her button was not. The trouble of sewing it back on was solved: Dr. Clarke had run off with it. Jo slipped the lonely key into her pocket, so recently breached by soft, steady fingers, then turned to the counter and started opening the parcels of food in a daze.

Alma joined her in the task, ignoring all the proper food she'd promised to eat as she sneaked a pinch off the raisin cake.

"I was starting to worry," she said. "What took you so long?"

Jo looked over her shoulder and out the window, as if she might still be able to spot a flash of gray wool and wispy hair.

"Honestly?" She broke a bite of crust off her pie. "I have no idea."

Chapter Seven

Emily

"You *grabbed Jo's bosom?*"

Emily threw a gambling chip at her brother across the table in his tiny but lushly decorated parlor. He happily added it to his own substantial stack of winnings. According to his complicated house rules, all chips thrown in rages became the property of the assaulted party.

"I didn't grab anyone's bosom!" She snatched the deck out of David's hands so she could take her turn to deal. "It just protruded farther than anticipated." She shuffled the cards furiously as Noah and David laughed. "Would you stop it! I only brought it up so you can give the button back and pass my apology along."

Her explanation didn't change their minds. David in particular was pursing his lips over a smile as Emily dealt.

"What's that look for?" she snapped.

"Well, it's just—" He shrugged and looked over his cards, arranging them into a new order. "*Apologizing.* It's not known to be your favorite activity."

Emily stared at her own cards, hardly seeing them. Even if

she'd been able to pay attention, she couldn't remember which cards were set as the wild braggarts this evening anyway, and would have lost the hand in any case.

When she'd been deservedly decimated and Noah pulled the chips to his side of the table, she glanced at David. While their friendship had been spotty, they'd known each other long enough that his observation about her character felt stickier than it might have, had it come from someone else.

"What did you mean by that?" she asked him. "I don't have anything against apologizing."

Noah snorted with laughter before David could answer, the lace on the cuffs of his shirt fluttering in a way Emily thought looked very uncomfortable as he arranged his chips.

"What?" She tugged at the edge of her own blessedly simple sleeve. "I apologize when I've done something wrong. Humility and amends-making are essential virtues."

"Sure. You *humbly make amends* when you believe you've done something wrong," Noah half-agreed with a matching one-sided smile. "But considering how rarely you admit your own fallibility, I'm suspicious of your sudden contrition regarding a…what shall we call it?"

"An accidental brush," said David without missing a beat.

"Nice, Davy. Very tasteful," said Noah. "*An accidental brush* with a woman who had publicly humiliated you not ten minutes earlier. I can think of at least a dozen worse things you've done without the slightest interest in apologizing."

"Is that so?" Emily huffed. "Go on, then. What dozen things come to mind?"

Noah drew breath to back up his claim, but David cleared his throat.

"Instead of ruining our evening with that," he said firmly, "why don't we brighten it by getting her to admit why she wants to apologize to Miss Jo."

"This again?" said Noah, scolding and a bit mysterious.

"What again?" Emily asked.

David shrugged shamelessly. "Nothing. I just think that under the right circumstances—that is to say, without a patient between you or a chapel's worth of busybodies looking on—the two of you might be able to have a nice conversation. That's all. I wonder if your desire to apologize for nothing is really just an excuse to explore that possibility."

They looked her over like the answer was scribbled somewhere in the red flush that swept across her cheeks. The last thing she wanted was for these two to think they had a point, but she feared there was no way out. They'd spot this flush if she stayed. They'd notice her retreat if she excused herself from the table with some trite excuse. It was hopeless. She waved the notion off as they played another hand she barely noticed, too aware of all the little looks moving around the table like card trade-ins.

"*So*," said David at last. It was a big, meaningful *so*, stretching out over the table as he stood up. "*Are* you interested in exploring a conversation with her?"

Emily wished she could clutch her feelings as close to her chest as she did her cards, but it was no good.

David nodded toward the nook of a kitchen. "Let's put the tea back on, shall we?"

Taking the hint, she followed him. At first, it seemed like a silly excuse. It didn't take two to light a stove and fix a pot. But as she noticed how he hesitated with the matches, she changed her mind about the assumption.

"Davy, are you doing alright?" She took the book from him and lit the burner herself, waving at him to handle the tea leaves instead. "You seem very on-edge lately."

"Much going on," he said, a bit over-bright. "Nothing to worry about. I have it handled."

"I'm still appalled at how Parliament handled the Criminal Act Amendment," she said carefully, knowing that it was the looming changes to Britain's laws that had exacerbated his nerves. "It was supposed to be such a reasonable thing, a move to protect women and girls. I still don't understand how this 'gross indecency between men' got to be part of it at all."

"No one does," David said, unconvincingly casual. "Because it became part of it at about three in the morning on the night it passed."

Horrible. Emily shook her head, trying not to let her frustration dig in too deep. "Do remember, Davy, that if you need a break from the stress of the city, there's always a place for you back home. I know it did your nerves a lot of good last time you came to visit. Perhaps it's time for another reprieve from your city concerns."

David shook his head and forced a chuckle. He dropped his voice low, still casual, but now with a hint of the conspiratorial. "Much as I'd love that, it's a tough sell for some. It's a balm to my nerves, maybe, but not as much to his."

"Noah won't?" Emily lowered her voice too. "I know things haven't always been easy, but I was under the impression we'd put a lot of that behind us. Did Papa or I do something to put him off during that last visit?"

"Don't think so. It's just…there's a lot of memories out there in the village, aren't there?"

She got the sense he was softening Noah's words again, as he tended to do. "David, would you be clear with me, please? What did he say?"

David ran a hand down his face and sighed. "I believe his exact words were *I swear to God, if I have to look at that sodding sewing kit under the end table for one more day of my precious life, I'm going to claw my own bloody eyes out.*" David winced. "I'm sorry. You asked."

Emily could only maintain a satisfying level of annoyance with her brother for so long before she grew too tired to do anything but agree with him. Not that she could admit it; it seemed cold for the two of them to bond over their exhaustion with Papa's peculiar method of grieving. But quietly, very quietly, she couldn't blame him for anything except how he'd abandoned her to it.

"You could come on your own, you know, Davy," she said. "If he won't, and you want to, you're still welcome—"

"I didn't drag you over here to talk about me, Emily." He leaned against the counter, fixing his face into a very meddlesome expression that meant the other line of conversation was over. "We're here to talk about you. Do you want to see her again? To apologize?"

"Well, what if I did?" she said, giving into his deflection, but tucking the other subject away for later. "What difference would that make? She despises me."

David's grin implied it made all the difference in the world. Made his whole day too, if she wasn't mistaken.

"Well," he said. "You could apologize for what she despises you over, to start. Rather than apologizing for, you know. An accidental brush."

"As I'm sure Noah has told you in more colorful terms than I can imagine, she despises me for turning her friend away." Emily took the strainer from the pot and shook the soggy leaves into the bin. "And while I could apologize, I don't know that she would care much. The deed has been done."

"So undo it." David took up the pot and started back to the table with it.

"I can't."

"Why not?"

"I encouraged speculation that it was because of their circumstances, but it wasn't," she admitted, lowering herself back into her seat. "Though I obviously can't remember our mother, I live surrounded by the repercussions of such a tragedy, and do not happen to have a nice little place in the city where I can escape them." She glanced at Noah, who opted to become very busy with his cards. "The training was bad enough, only taken on because the hospital wouldn't employ me if I didn't acquire it. I fear that my constitution is not suited to the work."

"You don't have time to be so picky about your specialty anymore, though," said Noah, his voice pitying and maybe—just maybe—a tiny bit guilty. "You need to build your own patient list with whoever will have you. And quickly, don't you? Before. You know."

He waved his lacey hand like he was being obvious, but Emily had no idea what he was talking about.

"Before what?" She was struck by a memory of Papa's recent caginess, all his implications that he felt the end might be nigh. A spark of panic lit in the bottom of her belly. "Noah? What are you talking about?"

Noah and David shared a shocked look.

"He hasn't told you?" Noah said carefully, like he couldn't believe it.

"Told me what?" Emily snapped, clutching her teacup.

Noah touched his fingertips to his thumbs a few times before squeezing his hands tight. It didn't look like any of his usual flourishes or Italian-inspired emphatics. It was a quiet and fearful movement that Emily didn't like one bit.

"That stiffness he's had in his fingers," Noah said quietly. "It's been worsening. He's fairly certain it's, you know, rheumatic gout. Which, for a surgeon, will mean his retirement. Not quite yet. But sooner than he'd have liked. He really didn't tell you?"

Emily sat back in her chair, thinking back. Sensitivity to the cold. New concerns over money and stability. Opting to stay in Farncombe for this latest London talk.

"He didn't tell me," she whispered. "But he told *you*?" She paused, hoping she'd jumped to the wrong conclusion. "No. No, you figured it out, didn't you? He wouldn't tell you without telling me."

Noah, usually oscillating from playful to fiery, had become dreadfully quiet. "He told me," he admitted, that previous note of guilt becoming a full and obvious chord. "He said since they don't know if it's hereditary, I needed to know about it now, so I could save money or take on some apprentices in case I also hit a point of needing to retire. A rheumatic tailor isn't much better off than a surgeon, and since I'll have no children to take care of me, he wanted to make sure I was preparing for the future."

The unfairness was incredible. Here she was, fielding criticisms for sending off Miss Garcia, when her own father—the one who'd always preached complete equality between the sexes—had so obviously valued the fate of her brother's career over Emily's.

"I'm sorry," Noah said, still in that terrible, solemn voice that meant this whole thing really was just as awful as it felt. "It didn't occur to me that he hadn't told you."

"How did it not come up between you and me before now?"

Noah smiled rather uncomfortably. "I can't say it's a topic I'm keen to bring up very often."

Once again, it was infuriatingly difficult to blame him; nearly every decision in both their lives had been made to further their professions. Hard work and a meaningful place in society were values they shared, even if they went about the particulars differently. It was what they had in common, aside from the gloomy sense that their father would happily have traded both of them back for another day with his wife.

"Well," she said quietly, clacking a couple of her gambling chips together. "Let's not…let's not panic about either of us inheriting it. The cause may be atmospheric or dietary or any number of things. We'll look to our health and the rest will be up to God."

Noah lifted his teacup with a half-smile. "You always conjure up the most thrilling toasts, *sorella*." She hadn't meant it as one, but she clinked his mug anyway as he went on. "And what of your work? Leaving that up to God as well?"

"Better him than Papa, apparently," she said, unable to keep the bitterness from her voice. "Why would he tell you to prepare for something that could be decades off, but not inform me that my entire life will be upended in the next few years? They might not let me continue at the hospital without him, you know. Sometimes I get the sense they are only tolerating me so that they can keep him on call for surgeries. In spite of my best efforts, I am nothing on my own."

Papa and Noah were right. Emily needed to be able to support herself, and at thirty, starting fresh in a new occupation or else trying to find some financially stable husband who would take an old maid like her was a waste of time she didn't have. She needed to build her own patient list, the sooner the better. And the soonest possible involved returning to the only people who had ever approached her as their first-choice.

Miss Garcia. Her scandal of a paramour.

And Mrs. Smith.

"David," she said. "I need to contact Miss Garcia. This is no accidental brush. I need to make this right, for all our sakes. Do you know where I can reach her directly?"

"No," he said. "All the correspondence has gone through Miss Jo."

"Miss…" Emily faltered. "You mean Mrs. Smith?"

"Mrs. Smith?" David chuckled. "I'd forgotten that was how you knew her."

"Can you put me in touch with her again, then? I have apologies to issue."

David grinned. "I think that would be lovely!" he exclaimed. "And I could certainly arrange a cordial meeting for the two of you before you leave town."

Cordial meeting. Something about those particular words out of the mouth of a notorious matchmaker was decidedly suspicious.

Still. As Emily thought back to those dark eyes and a refusal to conform that pushed even other nonconformists to their limits, she couldn't bear the thought of letting this one chance to see more of her slip by.

"An extra day in London would pose no problem for me," she mused. "Will you send off a note, if I write one up? If she agrees, we'll meet. But!" She put up one finger in warning. "For the love of all that is good, David Forester, you will plan nothing *too* cordial, do you understand me?"

"Oh," said David, grinning again. "I understand perfectly."

To the most esteemed Mrs. Jo Smith (should she be generous enough to open this parcel rather than tossing it straight into the fire as would be more than reasonable given the circumstances),

It has been brought to my attention by our mutual companion Mr. F— (as well as the stirrings of my own conscience) that I owe you and your friend Miss G— a considerable apology for my lack of reasonable human feeling and compassion. I regret the shameful behavior I have displayed, and would like to make things right with all of you.

I can stay in London for up to two extra days before my responsibilities call me elsewhere. If you would pass this message along to Miss G— I am more than willing to see her for a proper exam. In addition, I would like to apologize to you personally, for the events of this afternoon. I was the unkind one.

If either of these meetings is possible and desirable, please inform Mr. F— as soon as possible so that he might make appro-

priate arrangements. I offer the coffee house as a possible meeting place, but please suggest another if you have something in mind.

Most sincerely, and with the greatest regret and hope for reconciliation,

Dr. E. Clarke

Chapter Eight

Jo

"You've had a letter," said Alma, when Jo arrived at the shop the next morning.

Jo found it on the counter, noting the return address.

It was from Dr. Clarke.

She tore into the envelope to find a profuse apology. If Jo didn't know better, she'd assume it was their mutual companion Mr. F—Forester, that meddlesome matchmaker—who'd sent this in a conciliatory scheme worthy of a dime novel. But Forester had the open-topped O's of a gossipy people-pleaser, while this script was tidy and perfectly slanted, complete with those swooping, lusty descenders she'd noticed in Surrey. The hand was undoubtedly Dr. Clarke's.

And if the hand was hers, the sentiment must be as well. As Jo scanned the words once more, leaning over the bookstore counter, she caught herself smiling.

She shook that foolish happiness off, though, trying to settle into more fitting temptations. The part of her that never wanted to forgive Vanessa's poor treatment wanted to throw the letter on the fire as was suggested in the greeting. A petulant, tit-for-tat part wanted to respond with a devastatingly polite rejection. Yet another very insufferable part longed to dig out those dirty old photographs she'd found on her disorganized shelves, select an especially rude one, and scribble *bugger off* right across the image of her own plump backside.

If she did any of those things, this really would be the end. She'd never see the woman again. Never be blighted by her presence, her opinions, her stiff-spined judgements.

Never see that intriguing fire within her set loose.

And more importantly, she realized with a jolt of her own selfishness, she would ruin the possibility of poor Vanessa getting that appointment.

Jo resigned herself to the fact that she *must* respond to the letter.

She also *must not* write that response upon a photograph of her own bum.

But she did not have to agree to a cordial meeting of her own. She could put Miss Garcia and Dr. Clarke in touch with one another and step aside, for good this time, praying that her success in finding a physician would propel Vanessa's friendly feelings through the birth at least. She could wash her hands of this particular scheme, and redirect her energy toward figuring out the next one. One that did not involve any bluestockings, but might start to involve knitting after all.

She could do that.

If she wanted to.

She pulled out a piece of paper, unsure what she was going to put on it. It was of thinner weight and rougher texture than what Dr. Clarke had sent. She unfolded the letter beside her own blank page, contemplating the contrast before committing any words.

While it was nice to forgo the daily risk of typesetting injuries that came with running the printing press, she suspected

she'd never lose her fascination for the mechanics of the written word. Handwriting quirks, ink thickness and color, the
nuances of paper, the ins-and-outs of typographical anatomy.
Not to mention covers and bindings and tin picture plates. It
was the difference between a dime novel and a Dickens compilation, a poor man's filthy postcard and an aristocrat's pseudo-
intellectual erotica, a medical textbook and Gran's scrawled
recipes. The words within were the most vital aspect, but the
trappings made a difference, even if most didn't think about
them much.

She ran a hand down each of the sheets: Dr. Clarke's letter
and her own impending one. The difference between the papers was fitting. To further the satisfaction, she picked a nib for
her pen that was a little overused and an ink that fell nice and
thick. This letter would be undeniably hers, much as the unexpected apology could have come from no one but Dr. Clarke.

As she penned her response, she imagined her correspondent's
severe but pretty face so clearly that she could almost feel that
softness the doctor hid under all that starch and scratchy wool
fiber. Jo could imagine she was speaking, rather than writing;
that there was no distance between them at all.

Dear Dr. Clarke,
Your letter comes as a surprise. I'll let Miss G— know your
offer and put the two of you in contact to arrange an appoint-
ment yourselves.
As for a cordial meeting between the two of us…

Jo paused. While Dr. Clarke had certainly done wrong by
Vanessa, her crimes against Jo hardly warranted some formal
apology. Jo did not need Dr. Clarke's services. Did not expect
her cordiality or companionship. Didn't really even need that

button back, seeing as the waistcoat was doing better with a lighter-weight one anyway.

If Dr. Clarke should apologize for anything, it was that feeling of her fingers in Jo's pockets, the flash of her stocking on the stairs, the wrath and passion that had stuck to the matter of Jo's brain like pretty little burrs that seemed innocent enough until you tried to unstick them. After a childhood spent muddying herself up in wild country, she knew returning to the thicket to put those sticky blighters back never worked. You'd just come out with more trouble than ever.

As for a cordial meeting between the two of us, I don't think...

The bell above the door chimed. An inky-fingered young man was trying to fit a cart through the narrow doorway.

Abandoning her half-finished rejection, she sprang up to help the lad.

"Thank you, ma'am," he huffed as they got the wheels over the threshold.

"Why the devil didn't you bring this to the back door?" She resisted the urge to smack him upside the head only due to the cart between them. "It ain't going to fit."

The lad glanced over his shoulder. Jo followed his gaze to find that Paul was holding the door open with one hand, ushering the lad faster with the other. All the while, he stared over his shoulder, face pinched with paranoia.

That sort of look on a man in his sort of business got superhuman feats accomplished. Jo managed to slip the rest of the cart inside without half the trouble it should have been, clearing the way so that the delivery fellow and Paul could step inside.

Jo did not need telling that she ought to bolt the door.

"What are you doing?" she snapped. Paul was smoothing his mustache and clothes like he was perfectly comfortable now, but was still looking out the window instead of at her. "Why aren't you taking these through the proper door?"

"Well," Paul said brightly. "Because I didn't fancy that bloke following us into an alley just now."

He pointed to a man walking briskly away from the shop.

She left the lad alone, but did grab Paul's hat so she could smack *him* upside the head.

"You fancy showing him to the front door so he can nose around my business later?"

"Your business is the respectable branch of the operation," he said. "If I come in this respectable door, it means I'm probably carting respectable inventory."

She crossed her arms. "Are you?"

"Bit of both, believe it or not. These are from home. I went through the shelves for your grandmother's book."

Jo's mood threatened to brighten in spite of herself. "Did you find it?"

"Alas, not yet," he said. "But I'm optimistic it will turn up in the next go-round, and in the meantime, I did find quite a lot of other things that—as you said—ought to be stashed at the print house."

"Then why come here?"

He reached in and grabbed a hand-sized stack of the paper-bound adventure novels that Jo snacked on like cakes in her spare time. "I'll bring those troublesome ones down to the Row when I get the chance, but figured I'd bring your things along first."

Jo stared at the books. *Her* books. *Her* books being moved out of *her* house.

"Th-those are mine," she said shakily. "Why are you bringing them here?"

"To save you the trouble of coming after them, of course," he said, his voice very light but his eyes belying a darker edge.

"You're going to such obvious pains to avoid being home with me. Looks like a lot of effort. As your oldest and dearest companion, I thought I'd make your endeavor to never speak to me again a bit easier. So here you go; all your favorite books are here now. One less reason for you to head home in the evenings."

She wasn't sure whether to be relieved that he wasn't actually moving her things out or annoyed to death that he'd done something so characteristically obnoxious to force the conversation she'd avoided.

"Bloody hell, Paul." Jo snatched the books out of his hand. "Did you seriously drag my shit all the way here for a stunt?"

"You know I love a good stunt." With a flashy, unconvincing show of good humor, Paul paid the lad for his part in the ridiculous show and sent him off. Once he was gone—and another glance at the street had been spared to be sure there were no further followers—he looked back at her with decidedly less humor. "You can't avoid this forever."

"Oh yeah?" Jo challenged. "Seems to be going pretty well so far."

Paul ran a frustrated hand down his face. "All I want is to have a bloody discussion, Jo. Like the friends we are. The friends we have been for years. Please."

"There's nothing to say," she said, so firmly it almost sounded true. "Our—" He'd said friendship. She should too. That's what they were. But there was distance between them now, a sense that their futures were no longer as entwined as they'd been. The word felt like nails in her throat, far too painful to make it out. Something else made it, though. Something that, when it appeared, proved decidedly cold:

"Our *arrangement* is what it is."

"Joey—"

"Look, Paul. Vanessa is a lovely woman who you've cared

about for a long time. If you'd done this with some young thing who meant nothing to you, we'd have something to talk about. But this is just one possible result of a situation we all agreed to. Plain and simple."

"Ah yes. So plain. So simple." Paul rolled his eyes. "I know this isn't what any of us planned for, but do you really wish I'd left her to it? Is that what this is about? Because that doesn't sound like you, Jo."

"That's not like me, obviously."

"Then please, for the love of all the unholiness we have dedicated ourselves to, will you let me ask what we're doing about the living situation?"

Jo wanted to start unloading the books, to do something useful and comforting with her hands, but seeing as half of them belonged in the secret cellar under the printing press and the other half belonged back home, it wasn't a great option.

"Look, Paul. You've done it. You've cornered me. Say what you want to say, will you? You want me out?"

Jo hadn't quite realized how badly she'd been fearing it until she heard herself say the words. She feared confirmation of what she knew in her bones: that another reinvention was on the horizon, another life abandoned, a new start forced upon her.

Paul was a theatrical sort of chap, but the way his jaw dropped and his brows went up had no artistry or charm involved. He looked a decade younger. A decade less sure of himself. A decade less happy. At last, he looked how Jo felt.

"Is that why you haven't talked to me?" he said quietly. "You think the second I get you alone, it will be to kick you out?"

He looked so crestfallen that Jo wanted to backtrack. But what good would that do? They'd started this inevitable conversation; to stop now would just prolong it.

"I know you want them with you," she said instead, rationally as possible. Because it was rational. Being rid of the mistake you married when she started getting in the way was more than rational. "I know you, Paul. I married you, didn't I? I know how you are when you're in love. You want them with you."

"Of course I do. And that's exactly why we need to talk, Jo," he pleaded. "It's just something to discuss. Frankly, I haven't even gotten *her* to agree to it yet; she values her independence so highly, and—seeing as you've gone so terribly out of your way to make her love you nearly as much as she loves me these days—she values your say in the matter. She won't even consider it until she has your full blessing. There are practicalities, Jo, but that doesn't mean anyone's being kicked out of their home. Give me a little more credit than that."

"Why should I?"

Paul raised an eyebrow. There was a moment, a fragile little moment, in which they could choose to laugh at her melodramatic reply. There was a list a mile long as to why she should believe him. They'd been lovers, and spouses, now business partners and dear old friends. Never had either of them betrayed the other like that.

And yet, Jo couldn't shake the feeling that this would soon change. After all, her parents hadn't betrayed her, either. Nor her parish here in London. No one she'd relied upon had given a hint that she'd soon be out on her arse. Not until the day they crossed the lines that forced her to scrape up whatever she could carry and run.

She opted not to laugh.

"You're right, Paul," she muttered. "I'll just have to trust you, won't I? At the end of the day, it's all yours anyway. I'm sure you'll make the very best decisions possible, given the circumstances. I only ask that if you decide there isn't room for everyone, that you allow me to continue working at the bookshop until I've gotten on my feet."

Paul stopped even pretending to seem casual and confident, allowing himself to look baldly hurt. She felt like a bit of an arse, but why should she? It was true. Though the laws on wives' property rights had changed in her favor since their wedding day, habit and trust had led her not to keep their items and assets as separate as she should have, especially given the tricky nature of his enterprise. There was very little she could prove belonged to her. Not in the house, not in the publishing business, and not even in the shop that had become her lifeblood.

"Since when," Paul said, "is that how we've seen things?"

"It's the way things are, Paul. The truth of the situation is that I will have to tolerate whatever you decide," she hissed, daring him to agree with her, to lord this fact over her. This uneditable shift in her greatest friendship would be easier if he proved he'd been a wanker all along.

"The truth? It's not the truth of anything," he all but sneered. "It's the bloody law, maybe, but I'd like to think that by now, we are not in the habit of confusing the two."

"Easy for you to say."

Before he could gather up another highly-reasonable-sounding rebuttal, she whipped around toward to the counter without any idea what she was going to do when she got there. Fortunately, Dr. Clarke's letter peered up at her. A perfect distraction. A perfect way out of this conversation.

"Dr. Clarke has had a change of heart regarding Vanessa's case," Jo said, waving the letter around before jotting the doctor's address on a bit of scratch paper. "You ought to contact her and set something up. In the meantime, I agree to nothing. I don't want anyone else moving into my home, not even someone I admire as deeply as Miss Garcia. She values her independence, and so do I. If you want to shake that up, Paul, you're welcome to do so at any time. Say what you want about *truth*, but the *law* says it's in your hands, and that's something you're just going to have to face."

She passed the address to him with a final-enough glare that he rolled his eyes and tipped his hat.

"I wish you wouldn't do this," he said. He put up a single finger between them, glaring irritably around it. "Don't mistake me; we've been together long enough that I'm not surprised you're doing it. But I wish you wouldn't."

He left, peering with the barest trace of caution up and down the street for pursuers as he did.

Jo returned to Dr. Clarke's letter. All of a sudden, the rejection she'd planned was less appealing. She felt sickened by what was happening between her and Paul. Perhaps a bit of time with a doctor—a pretty, intelligent, and sharp-tongued doctor at that—was just what she needed.

As for a cordial meeting between the two of us, ~~I don't think~~ *I find myself surprisingly open to the idea. As for a place to meet...*

Her sapphic club, Miss Withers's Orchid and Pearl Society House, was the obvious place. She had a standing invitation to bring friends along to its prettily decorated parlors anytime. As different as Jo and Dr. Clarke were from each other, the doctor was actually not so different from Miss Withers and some of the other women in the society. It was part of her...well, not *appeal* of course; she was far too prim to be *appealing* to anyone, but it was part of what made Jo more convinced that friendliness between them might be worth exploring. She'd probably fit right in.

But Jo wasn't sure she *wanted* Dr. Clarke to fit in. She'd enjoyed seeing her tightly bound edges fraying on the staircase. In fact, the more she thought on it, the more she felt that the whole point of seeing Dr. Clarke again was to inspire that unraveling once more. To see her off-balance, warm, human, and uncomfortable.

That's how Jo felt all the time now, after all. With everything so unstable around her, she liked the notion of going where she would have feet firmly on the ground, while her company wobbled a bit.

As for a location, I humbly suggest The Curious Fox. Mr. F——
is very capable of arranging a cordial meeting and I trust him to
handle the details admirably.
Most sincerely,
Miss Jo

She could see it now. Prim and perfect Dr. Clarke muddying her shoes up in the alleyways, wrinkling her pretty nose at the smell of cigar smoke and incense, shielding her innocent eyes from the Grecian-style artwork. If anything would shake her balance up while letting Jo sit comfortably in her own, it was The Curious Fox. They'd have to go off-hours, of course— the political situation was too dire to let outsiders see faces they could not unsee—but David Forester trusted the doctor well enough that he'd set up a little daytime chat for them. And the more she emphasized the "setting up" of it all, the more enthusiastic he'd be.

And the more embarrassed Dr. Clarke would find herself. More flustered. More interesting.

It was only as she was folding the letter up with a little grin at the mischief she was making, that Jo realized she'd signed the thing without a full name: just *Miss Jo*. She considered adding the surname by which the doctor knew her, the one she used for the convenience of it when first names wouldn't do. *Jo Smith* was technically the name she went by. She'd at least had a bit of say when choosing that surname, but it meant little to her, and who knew how much longer she'd be using it anyway? Was it really any better than Paul's original Shanahan or her father's O'Donnell? Surnames were certainly a matter of luck. Not to be trusted.

So she left well enough alone, improper though it was. It was satisfyingly different from Dr. Clarke's complicated sign-off, and undoubtedly more polite than the photo of her bum would have been, anyway.

Chapter Nine

Emily

There was a certain look given to Emily, when she told friends she was spending time in the city. The London Look. Since most of them rebuked things like fashion and society, it was typically social or political matters that brought them into town, and their outlook on the place reflected that in spades. The London Look was one that said, *be careful*. It said, *how good of you to do this thing in such a place as that*. It said, *hold your nose, dear, and be sure to wear dark colors so you don't spoil your dresses*. While that look was overblown for Piccadilly Circus, Mayfair, or Fleet Street, where she spent most of her time, it was a little more fitting for Soho.

She had a sneaking suspicion that Mrs. Smith—or, rather, Miss Jo, as she'd signed her letter—suggested The Curious Fox to shock Emily out of the meeting, but Emily wasn't as uncomfortable with the neighborhood as Miss Jo probably assumed. The Women's Hospital was right in the main square, for one thing, a place she'd trained at just this past summer. And of course, Noah had turned himself into the very stuff that Soho was made of, living close to the area and apprised of anything interesting happening within it. The Berwick Street market was good fun, a chance to meet interesting people and eat interesting foods that came to the bustling street from all over the world. Artistic eccentrics and the sight of poverty outside the context of charity work might bother her suburban acquaintances, but it did not bother Emily save for making her wish that the poor and the eccentric had a cleaner and more spacious place in which to exist.

She refused to yield to Miss Jo's assumption that she couldn't handle it. However, she did find that coming to Soho with David and Noah was a different experience.

Once they'd passed the familiar façade of the hospital and found vegetarian lunch fare from a Greek chap who'd parted with his cart's offerings for half the price when David smiled at him just right, Emily's escorts turned her down a little side street behind the market that would have had Emily giving the London Look to her own reflection—if, that is, any window or puddle had been clean enough to catch sight of it.

"There's no need to worry," said David happily, nearly tripping over a mangy little dog that growled like something twice its size until appeased by a scrap of their lunch that David had apparently tucked into his pocket for just this purpose. "I know it looks rough, but I promise you, the neighborhood is perfectly safe. Well, before sundown, anyway." He chuckled like these filthy back alleys were his own pack of ill-behaved but charming toddlers. "The club by day will be a lovely meeting place. Very private. Very comfortable."

"Perhaps," said Emily, her arms tucked tight to her sides for fear of what might end up on them if they touched one of the buildings on either side of their path. "I simply hope we won't be a disturbance to your usual patrons. It's all fellows, isn't it?"

"That depends on who you ask," David muttered with a

funny little sparkle in his eye. "But either way, I don't have any patrons coming in at noon."

"Davy's hardly even awake at noon, most days," said Noah.

"I brought a server in, though, don't worry," David went on. "To bring in your drinks or tend to other comforts. The fire. The lamps. Whatever comes up. I didn't figure you'd want *me* popping in and out while you're trying to get to know one another."

"Davy," said Noah. "I know you pride yourself on your hospitality, but do remember that this is an amends-making. Not a matchmaking."

"Sure, sure." David waved a hand, partially at Noah, partially in response to the flies gathering around a bin as they turned deeper into the maze of alleys. "But still. Just in case, wouldn't want her own brothers popping in to do the service work, would she? That would cut off any possibility, however remote—"

Noah groaned. "David Forester, you are incorrigible—"

"Incorrigible? If you're trying to insult me, love, you're going to have to dig a bit deeper. I *know* I'm incorrigible…"

They went on in this way, but Emily lost track of the banter as David's words pulsed softly through her mind. *Her own brothers*, he'd said. The two of them. The spirit of that was true enough, wasn't it? Though decidedly an outlaw, David had become like an in-law to Emily over the past few months. There was some other version of this afternoon, wherein a sister-in-law might say to a spinster like Emily, "*Still unmarried? We'll see about that! Come to my house, and do meet my cousin…*"

While the nature of their connection meant David could not bring her to a proper home to meet a proper match, Miss Jo's mocking suggestion had let him bring her to the place he had. Not just the fragrant food carts, glittering theater façades, and sturdy hospital doors of Soho Square, but into the alleyways that were largely quiet now, but soon would be the ones where actors went to smoke and take an undignified squat between scenes. The troughs and grates where the cart pushers dumped chicken bones and used grease at the end of the day. The shadowy corners where the painted women came down with the troubles that would bring them to the hospital in the end.

They finally arrived at a dingy doorway, which David proudly led them through to reveal his nightclub. His pride and joy boasted a draped ceiling, ostentatious decorations, and a truly shocking number of liquors lined up behind the bar (including, she noticed, heavier spirits like Irish whiskey and absinthe that she'd never seen in person).

As she'd suspected, the place was as decadent and morally dubious as the woman she was meeting here.

But she'd done this to herself. She was in a place so unsuited to her temperament because of her own ungenerous actions. So she swallowed her discomfort (and what felt like quite a lot of lingering incense and tobacco smoke in the air) and stood firm on a swirling, flowery carpet that probably looked a lot nicer under cover of evening and the red-shaded lamps that David ignored in favor of a few gas sconces.

"What do you think?" he asked.

"I think," she said slowly, "that there are more strong spirits and fewer articles of clothing on the painting subjects than I'm used to, but I appreciate your unique hospitality." A question popped into her mind so suddenly, so unbidden that she was blurting it before she'd decided to: "Miss Jo really comes here in the evenings? A place like this?"

"She's an anomaly in the crowd," David said. "But fits right in, in her own way."

Emily had never been the sort who thought curiosity was dangerous, but for once, she could see how others may have gotten that notion. Treading the same paths that Miss Jo did made Emily's curiosity about the woman hot enough to boil.

"How on earth did she find herself here?"

"Same as anyone." Noah crossed to the bar to help himself to the beer tap. "Friends with a member."

"Tagged along as a bit of a joke, I think," David went on with a little smile, as if remembering something so amusing that Emily's curiosity threatened to bubble over entirely. "The friend who vouched for her enjoys bringing a little novelty wherever he goes. Wanted to see what I'd do with someone like her."

Someone like her.

"What did you do?" Emily asked. "With someone like her?"

Noah chuckled. "What do you think? Played the gracious host and the perfect gentleman, tried to set her up twice, and then overcharged her for cheap liquor like he would for anyone."

"Equal treatment under my roof," David said.

"Let me rephrase," said Emily. "What am *I* to do with someone like her?"

"Well, that's much trickier," David went on.

Noah lifted his glass. "Indeed. You see, she's a bit—"

A sudden knock startled him silent, even as Emily was desperately hanging on for the answer that might see her through this ill-advised meeting with this ill-tempered woman in such an ill-chosen location.

The knocks went on longer and with more deliberate rhythm than was natural. Emily watched David pass through the layers of jingling curtains that obscured the doorway without blinking once until he'd returned with Miss Jo by his side.

The woman was resplendent, fresh, and perfectly at ease as she walked into this odd place. She looked less bookish than she had before, not quite dandified, but leaning in that direction, with checked trousers and a black feather tucked into her hat band. A thick, black braid dripped from the nape of her neck to the middle of her back like some wickedly tempting escape rope from reality itself.

Comfortable as she was here, her eyes did not scan and dart around the room at all. Instead, they locked right on Emily's, the entire scene so surreal that Emily began to wonder if she was in a dream.

"Afternoon, Doctor," Miss Jo said.

"G-good afternoon," Emily replied. "Thank you for coming. It was incredibly generous of you."

"Maybe." She smirked. "Or maybe I couldn't resist the idea of these two dragging someone like you into their den of sin for the day." Miss Jo reached into her coat pocket for a pack of cigarettes. "I'm sort of surprised you stuck it out. Especially once you saw the paintings."

Emily pulled herself up straighter. She was intimidated, but that didn't mean she had to show it. "I am a physician, Mrs. Smith. Would that every nude form I saw could be as healthy and strong as these fellows before us."

Miss Jo snorted out a laugh, clearly against her own will and quickly stifled. She straightened the humor out of her countenance and turned to David. "So. I've actually never been to the back. Do we get the private parlor upstairs, then?"

David's brows shot up. "The private parlor?" His gaze shifted uneasily to Emily, and he lowered his voice. "Look, Joey. I don't know what you think we're doing here, but Emily told me not to arrange anything *too* cordial."

Miss Jo laughed again, though this one was more forced. She pulled David away a few paces, under the guise of getting a light for her cigarette, but Emily heard her whisper under her breath, "I confess that I wanted to shake her up a bit, but wasn't trying to go so far as to put her in a bawdy house bedroom. I thought a private meeting would be in the private parlor."

"What exactly have you been led to believe is the point of the private parlor?" David hissed back, eyeing the doorway in question meaningfully. "The biggest bedroom is the most proper room I have. Trust me."

"Seriously?"

"What kind of place do you think I'm running here, Joey?" David rolled his eyes as he passed her a matchbook from his pocket. "You're welcome to sit out front—"

"And have you listen to our every word?"

"I wouldn't." He tried, but completely failed not to laugh at the idea he'd ever mind his own business.

Miss Jo looked a little frozen by this turn of events.

David took Miss Jo's hat and coat, heading toward the same nook he'd stashed Emily's in. "Just...don't overthink it. Go get comfortable. Last room on the right—it's the one with proper chairs and everything, so you won't even have to sit on the bed. There's champagne on the table of course—"

"Champagne?" Emily blurted.

"—but I'll send someone round with specific drinks in a moment. Your usual?"

"I guess," said Miss Jo.

"And Emily?"

"I don't suppose lemonade is a possibility?" she asked, trying not to glare too obviously at the liquor as she wondered which of those sparking poisons was Miss Jo's "usual."

"Certainly it is!" David gently guided them through a door propped open along the back wall. "And lemonade would mix just splendidly with that champagne."

"I don't often take spirits, actually, and I think that given the circumstances—"

"Oh, I know that," said David, opening a second door and

shooing them inside. "Goodness, do you think I don't pay any attention? That's why I just put out *champagne*, rather than *brandy*. And since I knew you wouldn't want me barging in on you, I'll have Bonnie come round with the other things in just a moment."

Jo turned a skeptical eye on him. "Who's Bon—?"

But with that, Emily's dear brother-outlaw just smiled, patted them both on their shoulders, and closed the door behind him on his way out.

Chapter Ten

Jo

Jo and Dr. Clarke stood shoulder-to-shoulder as they took in the reddish lighting, the pillowed chairs and chaise, a fourposter whose pretty trappings couldn't hide how it sagged with the weight of all it had seen. There were more cosmetic pots lined up on the vanity than Jo had seen outside a pharmacy, and a scrap of dressmaker's lace stuck out at the bottom of a wardrobe she knew was filled with more extravagant drag than she ever went to the effort of indulging in herself.

A creeping sheepishness started at the bottom of her belly, crawling upward until she felt her face bloom with a blush that hopefully wouldn't be spotted in the moody lighting that belied the actual hour.

"I know we're here so that you can apologize to me," Jo said. "But now, I owe you one as well."

"You really let David orchestrate this to get under my skin?" said Dr. Clarke. "I suspected it, but thought I was being paranoid."

"I did," Jo admitted, wondering if the scent of some cheap rose spray was always present, or if it had been used to cover the deeper smell of cigar smoke, mismatched musk colognes, and carbolic soap. "Though for some reason, I didn't think he'd take it quite this far."

Dr. Clarke, whom she'd expected to be having palpitations by now, simply stared at her with a lifted brow. "That was awfully foolish of you, wasn't it?"

Jo paced over to the fourposter, almost running her fingers along the embroidered counterpane before some preposterous story of Charlie's skittered across her mind and made her think better of it. She peeked in one of the bedside drawers and quickly thought better of that as well, slamming an impressive assortment of creams and oils back up where they belonged.

She turned to Dr. Clarke, whose face was warmed and undeniably beautified by the unnecessarily romantic lighting. "Is it possible the man doesn't know the difference between a chat and a honeymoon?" asked Jo.

That was when Dr. Clarke did the most surprising thing Jo had seen yet.

She threw her head back and laughed.

It was the first time Jo had heard her laugh. It was quiet and high and a bit raspy, like it didn't get oiled up very often, but was also intensely pleasant. It ended soon, leaving Jo wishing she was a bit funnier, so she could extend it.

"I've known Mr. Forester for half my life," Dr. Clarke admitted on the end of her final giggle. "And yes. It's more than possible; it is absolutely inevitable. The fact that you thought otherwise is more charmingly naïve than I ever would have expected from someone like you."

Jo loosened her tie, that sheepishness coursing through her along with another sort of tingle that was a little softer and a lot more troubling.

"Are you saying you came here knowing exactly what we

were getting into?" she asked. "I assumed I was dragging you into a dreadful surprise."

"Well," said Dr. Clarke, eyeing another anatomically impressive painting above the fireplace. "A few things are surprising, but only due to lack of imagination on my part."

"Yet you still came?"

"I hold humility and amends-making as high virtues," Dr. Clarke said. "Higher even than avoiding...well...whatever precisely those are for."

She pointed to an umbrella stand that did not hold umbrellas, but slim rods wrapped in satin whose purposes, Jo thought, were pretty obvious in context. And it was hard to say in this light, but was that a little gleam in Dr. Clarke's eye? One that indicated perfect knowledge, even as she feigned proper ignorance?

"It's odd," Jo said suspiciously. "I wouldn't expect you to tolerate such behavior in your acquaintances."

"In my acquaintances? Certainly not," Dr. Clarke said with harsh finality. "And for a very long time, I did not tolerate it in David, either. But he's far more family than acquaintance at this point, and a family that does not allow for idiosyncrasies is a very fragile thing, isn't it?"

Jo startled at the words, eerily similar to something her grandmother had once said to her parents when none of them realized Jo was listening in at the keyhole. They'd been talking about her: her brash ways, her disinterest in courting, her wild insistence that she'd "live different someday or die trying." Gran had told her parents in no uncertain terms that if they kept trying to quash her spirit, they'd break the family apart. And so, they stopped trying to quash it until Gran died and her prediction came true.

"Well," Jo said, trying to regain what little footing she'd had. "I am sorry, in any case. Now that our roles are reversed, and I'm the one scandalized by David's complete disconnect from normalcy, I can appreciate the dastardliness of my own intentions."

"Why are you so shocked?" Dr. Clarke chuckled, her joy apparent in this laugh, even though it came quiet. "Don't you come here all the time?"

"Yeah, to play cards and drink out front with my mates," she laughed. "I've never been back here before. The other patrons aren't the sort I like to hunt down a bedroom with, if you catch my meaning." She paused, uncertain. "Do you catch my meaning?"

"Yes, of course I do." Dr. Clarke swatted at the air and settled herself on one of the armchairs. "Goodness, you're under the impression that I'm a complete know-nothing, aren't you?"

Cautiously, Jo joined her, selecting the center of the sofa so as to have just enough distance. Any farther, and it would seem like avoidance. Any closer, and she might have to start wondering if that vague lavender scent that kept cutting through the rose and debauchery belonged to the doctor.

"Are you ever going to smoke that?" Dr. Clarke asked.

Jo looked down at her hand, which still clutched a cigarette and matches. She'd taken them out from nerves, and had since forgotten about them.

"Maybe I am," Jo said, trying for stability. She'd come here for the sake of stability, after all. It was well past time she found it. Stability came quicker when she neglected to meet Dr. Clarke's eyes, but that was easier said than done. The garish club lighting did interesting things to the stormy blue of them.

"Well, don't let me stop you," said Dr. Clarke.

"It won't bother you?" Jo asked.

"Of course it will," said Dr. Clarke. "It's a disgusting habit. But you came here in hopes of horrifying me, so I'd hate to deny you this opportunity to do so. I'm used to it anyway."

Jo smiled in spite of herself. "Your brother's a right chimney, isn't he?" She opened the pack of matches, but didn't do anything with them, too distracted by the slightest hint of humor at the corner of the doctor's lips. "It's hard to believe that the two of you are related. Quite a bit different from each other, that's for sure."

"It's not that unexpected," Dr. Clarke said with a shrug. "We weren't raised in a way that actively squashed the particulars out of us, so it's only reasonable that there would be differences." She paused, head cocked such that Jo worried she'd let envy slip across her countenance. "That said," Dr. Clarke went on carefully, "even harsh childrearing allows for some variety within families. I assume your siblings aren't all quite like you. Or at least, I hope not, for your parents' sake."

A joke? Jo was too surprised by the fact that Dr. Clarke had a sense of humor at all to be offended by the contents. Still, the topic of siblings was a difficult one. Her idiosyncrasies soundly forbidden, Jo's place in her family had proven fragile indeed, though that rejection had never been her wee siblings' fault. She smiled anyway, because that's what one did. At last, she struck the match and lit the vogue, finding the way Dr. Clarke wrinkled her nose more soothing than the smoke itself.

"I wouldn't know," Jo said.

"You don't have any siblings?"

There it was. All of a sudden, Jo found a little footing. She was good at this kind of question. The sort that would let her make a mystery of herself.

"I had five," she said on a smoky, dramatic breath. "Last I checked, anyway."

Dr. Clarke looked satisfyingly startled. "You have at least five siblings," she repeated. "But you don't know what they're like, nor do you have a final headcount?"

"That's what I said."

"Shall I ask you what you mean by that, or would you prefer to leave it there for now? You seem quite pleased to have made an enigma of yourself, and I should hate to spoil the moment for you."

Jo's satisfaction wiggled a bit around the edges as the question threw her off-balance once again. When she said purposely mysterious things, people either pressed on or gave up; she could not recall ever having been asked which she would prefer.

"Oh," she said before she could stop herself. "Um. Well, it's just I haven't seen them in a long time. The eldest after me was only fourteen when I came to En—when I left home."

Fuck. Those piercing eyes, filled with a curiosity that was simultaneously shrewd and innocent, were slicing right through something that Jo considered to be impenetrable.

That might have been charming if the situation was actually what David had arranged it to look like. When Jo brought a pretty woman into a bedroom outfitted with rose spray and champagne for a quick and scandalous seduction, she wasn't quite so cagey with the details of herself. Those ladies loved to coax a grim or dramatic admission out of the dapper women they took up with, but it was only for the sake of heightening the intensity of their coupling. They certainly forgot every detail by the time their skirts settled.

But Dr. Clarke's skirts weren't showing any sign of budging, and Jo suspected that any detail she gave would be filed away in an exceptionally organized mind, where it would remain until the end of bloody time.

"So you are Irish, then," Dr. Clarke said. "I thought I heard it in your voice. Why do you hide it?"

"Why hide anything?" Jo snapped, a little harsher than she would have liked. Dr. Clarke didn't flinch, though. "What people know about you affects how they treat you, and depending on your company, Londoners don't always treat you very well when they find out you're from anywhere other than London."

Dr. Clarke smiled. "Fair enough. I suppose I've engaged in similar deception."

"Really?"

"Well, I'd prefer not to hide anything, of course," she said, slipping into that prim cadence again. "Truth is paramount. But...admittedly, I've had to stop putting my given name on research papers, opting for the first letter only. As you may imagine, Emilys aren't treated as well in the medical field as presumed Earnests or Edwards." She let out a sigh, her small frame shuddering with it. It was so lovely a sight that Jo found herself scrambling to put out her cigarette in the ash tray near the champagne bucket. She suddenly hated to think she was filling those lungs with something unsavory.

"Look, Miss Jo, can we call the situation between us even?" Dr. Clarke asked. She reached into her pocket and pulled out the button she'd stolen during their last meeting. "You regret your trickery today, that much is clear. Meanwhile, back at the coffee house, I admit I was a bit of an—"

"Arse?" Jo supplied.

"That's harsh."

"Prat?"

Dr. Clarke pursed her lips.

"...I dunno. Nitwit?"

They both laughed at how silly that sounded.

"Sure," Dr. Clarke said. "I was a bit of a nitwit, and you were a bit of a nitwit. But we possess obvious similarities. Maybe more than we think. Perhaps our wits might be put to better use with each other in the future? As...friends?"

Similarities? Jo still wasn't so sure about that, but she found herself hoping it was true. She stared at the button in Dr. Clarke's outstretched hand, then held out her own. Jo expected Dr. Clarke to drop the button in her palm, but instead, she placed it just gently enough that the very outer atoms of the skin brushed like static. Jo's fingers retracted instantly, clutching the button in a fist.

"I'm not sure," she said, feeling her mouth trying to twist into a smile. "Your particular nitwittery in the coffee house was pretty extreme. I'm not convinced that this matchmaking debacle, awkward as it is, is *quite* bad enough to call things eve—"

The door opened once more.

A heavily frilled and painted young woman bustled in with a clear voice, laden tray, and naughty eyes. David, always one to help a fellow friend in the shadows, had clearly paid her quite well to provide beautiful hospitality for the afternoon. Most likely, this woman was accustomed to providing *any* sort of hospitality requested, and seemed very cheerful about having been brought in to simply look pretty and pour drinks.

Or so Jo sincerely hoped.

As she went back out, Dr. Clarke peered curiously at the half-filled glass of lemonade she'd been given.

"I, er, think that's so you can top it off," said Jo, tugging at her tie and nodding toward the champagne bottle.

"Ah," said Dr. Clarke, nodding demonstrably. "Right. Very thoughtful." While her face remained passive, mirth danced in her eyes, more than could be written off as odd lighting. "So, tell me, as a regular in this place: Is dear Miss Bonnie usually the one bringing drinks round? Or has Mr. Forester arranged her specifically for our benefit?"

"You know what, Dr. Clarke?" Jo sighed heavily and raised her own glass, filled quite oppositely from the other with at least four damn fingers of whiskey. "I think you and I might be even after all."

"Glad to hear it." Dr. Clarke raised her skimpy glass and clinked it with Jo's. Just before she brought it to her lips, she paused. "In that case, do call me Emily."

"Really?" asked Jo, surprised.

"Might as well," the doctor—Emily—said. "You've already established a rather horrifying lack of decorum with your own 'Miss Jo' business. And to be quite honest, I'd rather not hear myself referred to as 'Doctor' over and over again. It's taxing." There was something heavy behind that sentiment, but Jo didn't ask, and Emily didn't offer. "And *Miss* Clarke is what people call me when they want to dismiss me. So Emily it must be, if you'll humor me."

"Of course," Jo said automatically. "I'll call you anything you like. Doesn't matter to me."

"*Anything?*" Emily said with a touch of a challenge.

"Anything at all," Jo declared. "Why not? I'll call you the queen if you like."

Emily snorted a bit of laughter. "I appreciate that, though it's probably a bit much."

"Princess, then?"

That one got a chuckle. There was something very addicting about that, wasn't there? Jo had come here wanting to get more rage and passion out of this woman, but getting a laugh out of her was even more satisfying.

As their conversation went on, mostly casual things like the weather or the friends they had in common, Jo found herself slipping more jokes in than she usually did. Each one that landed felt like she'd won a hand of cards. Though, when time continued to pass, and it became clear that this meeting, this apology, this whatever-the-devil-David-thought-it-was, was coming to a close, Jo found her mind shifting from punchlines to excuses for it not to end.

But end it must, of course; Emily had a train to catch.

"Though I shall be back," she said as she went for the door that would return them to the real world. "I'll need to check in with Miss Garcia monthly for a while, and then more frequently until we're closer to her confinement; at that point, I'll stay in the city, if I can arrange it."

"Would you care for another cordial meeting next time you're in town?" Jo asked.

"No. I've had quite enough of cordial meetings, I think," said Emily, glaring toward the champagne. Just as disappointment was starting to settle in the pit of Jo's stomach, she went on, "But I would be delighted to take tea or perhaps a walk through the park, if you're amenable."

Jo grinned. "Certainly, Princess."

"Oh, stop that," Emily scolded. "I shall be in touch, then, a bit closer to the time, to ensure it's not just the sconces and whiskey making you think you're interested in any further friendship with such a dreadful bore as I am."

"I'm immune to the effects of sconces and whiskey," said Jo. "I doubt my opinion will change much."

Though her words landed lightly, they left a bad taste in Jo's mouth as she followed Emily back out into the Fox's front parlor. Jo wanted to see Emily Clarke again, perhaps under circumstances more suited to themselves. But would a month apart change Emily's mind?

"Emily," she said, just before either of them could catch the eye of those waiting on them in the parlor. "Write to me in the meantime."

"Write to you?" Emily repeated. "About what?"

About anything, Jo wanted to say. But that might sound mad, so she reached for the first excuse that came to mind.

"I promised Miss Garcia I'd give her some of my grandmother's old remedies for discomforts," she said. "But I've misplaced the book. Maybe you could write a few down for me? If you have some? Like...like the lemon water recipe. I'd love to have that on hand, I think."

"It's simply lemon juice and hot water—"

"Yeah, but…how much lemon? And how much…how much water? I'd hate to put too much of either, you know. Might cause…problems."

"Problems?"

"Yes. All sorts of problems. Will you send the recipe to me?"

Emily blinked a few times; what Jo had just said sounded madder than the original sentiment would have. Miss Garcia did not need a recipe for bloody lemon water. And even if she did, they would be in touch on their own terms now, as doctor and patient. They wouldn't need to route such things through Jo.

"Alright," Emily said tentatively. "I…I suppose if you insist—"

"I do."

"Then I shall write to you in the interim," she said. "And pass along the…recipe."

Jo held out a hand so they could shake. "I'll be looking forward to it."

Chapter Eleven

Emily

Emily tried to read on the train, but the book might have been written in Noah's questionably accurate Italian for all she could make of it, mind whirring as it was with the weekend's happenings. While she'd planned a very basic visit—an interesting lecture, an afternoon at the coffee house, and a day with her brother, same as ever—instead, she'd gotten the news that her father's career was coming to an end, an appointment with her first private patient, and a surprisingly pleasant chat with a most unexpected person in a place she'd hoped never to find herself.

While Emily still did not approve of David's work, he was clearly talented at it. She was haunted by a sense that Miss Jo had seen their encounter as a romantic one, and it was troublingly difficult for Emily to avoid the association as well.

Obviously, though, the effect had been created with false lighting, cheap perfumes, and the sight—if not the taste—of chilled champagne lounging about on the table like a bubbly temptress. In fact, was there even such a thing as romance outside of those artificial trappings? Sure, she'd had her share of youthful infatuations at church and school, pointless and distracting though such feelings were. She'd even had what one might call a very close companion at the medical college. But unlike her brother's uncommon attractions, which were associated with bohemian artistry, European exploration, and forbidden passion, there was nothing more ordinary and dull than a couple of overeducated women who couldn't be bothered with the suffocating interest of men. Emily and her friend got their passions out of the way without any nonsense, same as they approached their work, their dress, their social considerations. They no more needed to cast red shawls over their lamps than they needed to don sparkling jewelry.

But Miss Jo didn't seem to see it that way. Her surprising discomfort, as far as Emily could tell, had stemmed from an assumption that all those trappings could have been for them, if only they'd taken the bait. She'd dressed herself like the most wicked of lovers in those checked trousers and that glossy black braid; she'd taken them to a spot that was explicitly, unapologetically debauched. While she'd wound up in over her head, she'd still had the thought, which was more than Emily could say for herself.

Why was it that she'd never had the thought? After all, her father had been so blinded by love that he was still stumbling in the dark of its absence decades later. Noah and David risked their freedom and possibly their lives every day. And yet a little champagne was outside of Emily's very imagination? A notion too impossible to even dream? How had that happened? It struck her suddenly as incredibly unjust.

It was a lot to think about, and the station wasn't far enough along the Southampton line to give her sufficient time to process it. By the time she arrived, she'd gotten nowhere. She still had no idea what she was going to say to her father. Not the foggiest how she was going to keep her wits in the face of Miss

Garcia's pregnancy and upcoming confinement. And hardly a blasted paragraph read in the book that had sat on her lap all the way home, more like a kitten than a source of knowledge.

It was nippy out, but not dark quite yet. She had her valise sent on ahead of her so she could get her blood back to flowing, her clothing aired out, and a little more time to sort out her thoughts as she walked the half-hour home. Home. To her father. Her arthritic father. Her lying father. Her father, who was not nearly as pleasant a thing to think about as Miss Jo's dark, smiling eyes.

She arrived to find her valise left on the porch by the delivery boy and her mind no closer to working out what to say to her father. She let herself into the house, where she heard his voice immediately, coming from the parlor.

Perhaps that was for the best. She'd face him now, and it would go however it was meant to go. She steeled herself and asked the Creator to fill her empty mind with the right words, before facing the doorway and drawing breath to say whatever she would—

But she stopped short, embarrassment creeping through her veins as she realized that it was not the housekeeper Papa was talking to, but someone else—Rochelle Baptiste, a Frenchwoman who'd found her way into their parish community some years ago and struck up a close friendship with the Clarkes. While it was not unusual to see her here, even to see the two of them alone in a situation that would be compromising for a woman of some other age, nationality, or political position, it was still shocking to stumble upon such a tender scene without warning. They were not indecent, but were not entirely *decent*, either, sitting together before the opened windows, their chairs pulled close as Rochelle dipped her fingers in a jar of ointment Emily herself had compounded, massaging it into one of Papa's hands—his arthritic, failing hands—as they laughed at some joke one of them had made. It was sweet. It was quaint. It made the charming sound of Miss Jo quipping "princess" echo through her mind.

She shouldn't wait, though. She should confront her father about his secret now. Her feelings about it aside, it was a practical task that had to be handled. She certainly would have, had she come straight from Noah's without today's decadent little detour. But she was apparently not as immune to all that nonsense as she had assumed. Why should she always be the one to ruin a lovely evening with practicalities and arguments? Didn't she deserve a break, just once, from being the cold killjoy they'd turned her into? Ruining their evening would ruin her own just as surely. Since she wasn't convinced she would ever feel quite this way again, she did not relish the idea of ending it so soon.

If it was Noah Papa wanted to talk to about the situation, let it be Noah who took up the duty of being the household scold for once. He knew what Papa had done, now. If he cared at all, he would confront Papa on the injustice of it. The men would right their wrongs without her having to interrupt her own good mood to harp, yet again, on why they ought to.

Instead, she went upstairs to her study, letting the uncanny dreaminess of her afternoon drift back into her limbs. It would be correct to change out of her travel clothes first, but if Jo could wear checked trousers, then Emily could bear a slightly sooty frock a few moments longer.

She grabbed up her whittling supplies, but it became clear that her distraction was not conducive to this hobby. If she went on like this, she'd spoil the piece—or her finger—in short order. She put the lot down. As she was going for her dustpan to clean up the mess she'd made, her eyes caught on an ink bottle, partly shadowed by the oversized queen that had been living on her desk since Noah put it there, during his and David's last visit over the summer.

She hadn't put it back because she liked its presence. There was something soothing about it, something comforting.

Something a little...devious.

I'll call you anything. I'll call you the queen, if you like.

Emily sat down at her desk. Though the chess figure had no eyes, no face at all, just a smooth expanse of cedar, it seemed she was looking at the ink bottle. Saying to Emily, *there's a whole life of drudgery ahead. Why bother with it now? You know what sounds nice now, don't you?*

Writing out that lemon water recipe.

Emily took out a sheet of clean, crisp paper, dipped her pen, and began to write. First the necessary pleasantries. Then the recipe, if one could call it that, done up with as many measurements and specifications as she could think of for something that was little more than a boil and a squeeze. But as she finished that up and was preparing to sign it, she realized there was no reason for Miss Jo to write her back. No dangling questions. Nothing.

She thought back on what awaited her in the future—the secrets, the uncertainty, the sense of unpleasantness closing in on all sides at last—and decided she wanted something to look forward to in her postbox. It wasn't perfume or champagne. But it might at least be a bit...fun.

She hastily added:

Awkward though the circumstances were, I want to thank you again for letting me redeem myself in your eyes. In the interest of more neutral ground when I'm next in London, I wonder where you might have suggested if you weren't actively trying (and failing) to horrify me...?

Emily typically tracked her time through the ebb and flow of her responsibilities. Her hours passed in chores and follow-up appointments, her weeks in hospital rotations and chapel meetings. Months were in trips to London and household management, and years stretched toward the vague notions of *stable*, *secure*, and *good enough* like plants toward the sun.

But in the weeks that followed, the keeping of time ceased to follow those rigid rhythms. Even the movements of sun and stars became little more than background lighting.

For the first time in her life, time became the servant of something unpredictable: Miss Jo's letters.

They started simple enough.

> *Dear Emily,*
> *Thanks for the recipe. It's absolutely disgusting, which I assume means it's very healthful. I'm pleased to report that a spoonful of sugar and a splash of whiskey does it wonders.*
>
> *As for a meeting place, I'd probably pick my ladies' club, rather than the gents'. I'm a member of Miss Withers's Orchid and Pearl Society. Have you heard of it? If not, do you need me to explain the name to you, or have you got the gist well enough?*
> *Miss Jo*

Nearly as pleasing as the fact that Jo too had ended her note with a question that demanded a response was the change in tone that came along with it. No longer assuming that Emily knew nothing about anything, prodding at the fault lines of difference between the two of them, now her words came laced with an assumption of shared understanding.

"*I've got the gist,*" she scribbled out in response. She saved her reading and responding for late at night, so that candles rather than autumn sun lit her enterprise. All her carvings, her diary writing, her evening meditation were forgotten in favor of this far more engaging activity. In the quiet of a house where both family and staff had long-since taken to their beds, there was something furtive about it. A trembly thrill shot all along her arm as she continued, "*I'm not familiar with The Orchid and Pearl in particular, but as a nonconformist and a bluestocking, I'm no stranger to such societies.*" She paused her pen, then added the all-important concluding question, "*Does that surprise you?—E. C.*"

She nearly ripped the whole thing up and started over. Goodness, was there any way for someone to read that question without imagining Emily batting her rather unimpressive lashes while she asked it? Yet, Miss Jo had been the one to initiate that flirtatious dynamic, all but nudging with one of her patched-tweed elbows: *Have you got the gist?*

The letter was sent on as it was penned from the first.

Some sleeps, some shifts, some appointments. A complete and unsurprising silence from Noah and her father. A quagmire of duty and anxious waiting, until the response arrived and time chugged pleasantly forward like a train on its way somewhere exciting at last. The next letter was longer, pleasanter, more familiar still, and Emily responded eagerly and in kind.

The post between London and Surrey was very efficient these days, particularly in a town so close to a train stop, and so their correspondence became quite regular, responses coming only a few days apart.

On the evenings there were no letters, Emily took supper with her father, sometimes joined by his companion Mme. Baptiste, sometimes not. Each time, she watched his hands and considered bringing up what she knew. And each time she decided against it in favor of retreating to her study to reread Jo's latest letter, work on her carvings, and fool herself into thinking Noah was sure to get around to the problem eventually. A smaller, more practical version of the curvy chess queen that might possibly fit into a whole set someday had become her obsession. Why argue over something she couldn't control, when she could finally sand the piece properly during one of those long evenings, making her fit to sit on the desk, an exact but smaller replica of the giant prototype beside her, impatiently awaiting the rest of the pieces, who started coming along slowly but surely.

The queens were the only ones to witness the private moments Emily spent in the company of Jo's letters, peering at Emily's dreamy smiles and blushing gasps with their blank, rounded faces, presumably wondering why this kept cutting into their maker's ability to stain them suitably and produce more subjects for them.

Emily did not mind such witnesses. A king might have been a little off-putting, but the queens, she figured, would understand.

The exchanges were such a refuge that it was easy to forget about the trouble with Papa entirely if she felt like it, because she and Miss Jo did not talk about any of that. They didn't talk about their work, or their churches, or the men in their lives. And while Emily had also been sending a few messages with Miss Garcia, answering questions and arranging their next appointment, they didn't talk about that, either. They talked of themselves, mostly, in banter and plans and the occasional innuendo:

"So how far down the path of nonconformity has Dr. Emily wandered?"

"All the way down to the women's medical college. I cannot say the nonconformity was especially prolific, but it was, as you might imagine at an institution of learning, quite educational. And you?"

"Six months at the nunnery. Very prolific."

It drove Emily mad. The personal details had her reeling with friendly sentiment, while the undercurrent of impropriety sometimes had her hitching her skirt up before she'd even left her study. There was nothing in the letters that most would find objectionable, and yet she kept them hidden like they were the stuff of the nearly-forgotten Mr. Smith's press.

And on that count, how ridiculous it seemed, all of a sudden, to have even pretended to hold *that* against these people, when these days, the mere glimpse of Miss Jo's thick scrawl was enough to light a fire between her legs?

Miss Jo's next letter came a few days later than expected, and on a different paper. Emily herself might not have noticed the difference, but she'd learned by now that Jo—who'd worked as a printer and a bookseller—put a lot of stock in the material matters of correspondence. She wasted no time apologizing for what she considered a very cheap and unpleasant writing surface:

"I didn't realize just how frequent our letters had become. I ran out of my usual supply, and this was all they had at the shop," she said. *"I might usually have waited until they had what I wanted—"* Emily took a grateful moment to clutch the letter to her chest, relieved to have not had to wait even longer than she already had for time to progress *"—but Miss Garcia mentioned that your next visit to London is growing closer. I didn't want to delay telling you that I hope we can still meet. A waste of money, maybe, but the only other writing surface I had at my disposal was a stack of my old postcards. Not that you wouldn't appreciate the view of me that the postcards offer (you would; it sounds like you learned to appreciate such anatomical models at the women's medical college), but because the postman might have stolen it if the sunlight hit the envelope just right and revealed the contents within, causing the very delay I was hoping to avoid…"*

View of me? Anatomical models? The postman? Emily was missing something, some joke she was too tired to catch. It had been a very long, trying day at the hospital. The sort of day where she could understand the impulse to swathe lifeless dummies in pretty fabrics rather than dressing wounds doomed to fester, witnessing final rattling breaths, and trying to figure out the mystery of why half her leeches had died overnight, all while handling the lion's share of her patients' nursing tasks.

She reread the perplexing comments about paper weight and postcards until it clicked. One of her old postcards. *Postcards.* An innocent enough term for Emily's polite society, but Miss Jo was decidedly outside of all that. When she said postcards, Emily had a feeling it wasn't Buckingham Palace on display.

For a moment, she just smiled at it like she did all of Jo's scandalous humor. But slowly, she realized that there was a further scandal. View of *me*, she'd said. Not a view of some arbitrary beauty. *A view of me.*

Had Miss Jo had found herself in front of a camera? The rest of her was bad enough, but that…that was so blatantly wicked that Emily's breath caught in her chest, her mind positively whirring…

And not, as it should have been, with disapproval.

Oh, goodness no. She turned the paper over and put it in her lap, frightened, all of a sudden, to even look at it. She'd let this flirtation go on, spurred and heated as it was by the odd setting of their last meeting. But this? This was too far.

Wasn't it?

Hot curiosity made the letter's position upon her skirts seem even more devilish than looking at it, like it was Jo's own head rather than the contents of her mind nestled facedown where warmth was gathering rapidly. She couldn't resist reading the letter again, and again, trying to ignore how thrilling her body found all this and find where she'd left all her sense. It was one thing to accept idiosyncrasies, or to reject the expectation of perfect chastity that caused more harm than good in the world. But it was quite another to approve of something so unnecessary, materialistic, and crass as dirty postcards.

She absolutely *had* to muster up something negative about this, even if it was only concern that Jo might have been taken advantage of. But try as she might, she couldn't convince herself of that. Jo had never given the slightest whiff of being some tragically fallen woman, small and scared and needing the kindly hand of a reformer like Emily and her friends. Unlike Emily, Jo had built her destiny bit by bit. If she'd wound up on the business end of a camera, it was because she'd wanted to be there.

With even concern out of reach, all Emily could imagine was that Jo *had* indeed written her message on the back of some indecent photograph. If Emily was this flustered over the *idea*, what might the reality have done to her? Surely *that* would have been too far? Yet still, the only negativity she could gather up was disappointment that she hadn't gotten to see it after all. And since she'd never been so crude as to behold such postcards herself, she wondered…

What did they look like?

"Emily?"

Nearly leaping out of her skin, she scrunched the scandal up and shoved it in her apron pocket, scrambling to her feet and calling, "Yes?" with high, false innocence that her father would see through instantly.

He tapped gently on the door before nudging it open. "Betsy called you for dinner. Is everything alright?"

No. Everything was not alright. Day after day passed without a word from him about his retirement. Noah had left her to deal with everything herself yet again. And somehow, brief and tiny as her protest against being the household nag had been, it had still left a crack in her constitution through which she could see a new perspective. She was not alright. All *wrong*, in fact, made more wrong still by how little it bothered her right now.

"I'm fine," she insisted. "Just distracted. I apologize, and shall be down shortly. I have to finish a bit of correspondence."

Papa gave her an odd look, as falsely casual as her own demeanor. "Your letters from London?"

Emily held her stomach in tight, calling on the professional skill of hiding emotion that was so vital to her continued presence in a field of men.

"Yes," she said simply.

"Do you want to tell me anything about those letters?" Papa asked. "There have been quite of few of them these past few weeks. Is there something important about them?"

She had convinced herself he wouldn't notice, but that was foolish. Jo's latest letter seemed to burn and glow like she'd stuffed live embers in her pocket. All of them smoldered like that. Was it really any wonder her father had smelled the smoke?

She wanted to tell him. Shocking though this last one had been, Jo's letters in general were exciting, new, something important indeed. They'd changed her. Impacted her. She was not used to keeping such things from her father, who would probably be pleased that she'd made a friend who expanded her consciousness and got her thinking from such new perspectives.

But that was back when she thought the exchange of personal joys and tragedies was reciprocal. If Papa still couldn't bring himself to tell her what was vital, why should she give him the satisfaction of hearing her good news?

"Just my new patient," she said calmly.

"Ah." Papa relaxed as he believed the lie. "Is she well?"

According to Miss Garcia's last letter, she was. But Emily wasn't thinking about Miss Garcia's letter. She was thinking about Jo's. And because of that, she found herself shaking her head as the wickedness of it proved suddenly contagious.

"No," she said. "Still quite ill. In fact, because of that, I was considering moving our next appointment up a bit, to see what I can do to improve her condition. I meant to ask if you could cover for me at the hospital this weekend, so I can get to London…with a little more time to spare."

Dearest Jo,
I am still very interested in seeing you again when I return to London. So interested that I have arranged to come earlier than anticipated, to ensure I can dedicate a full evening to socializing. I look forward to seeing you along with whatever "views" you may allow me to appreciate…

Jo's response came a few days later. It was very brief. On one side of it were the words *Let's meet at our own place this time*, followed by the address of The Orchid and Pearl Society House.

On the other was quite a view indeed.

It was Miss Jo herself, at least ten years younger. Had Emily not known who it was already, she might have been impossible to recognize, covered in cosmetics and curls from the neck up, and covered in nothing but a black corset and knickers from the neck down. She was blowing a kiss and smirking at the camera, her eyes full of a devious light.

But that wasn't where the delight and decadence ended.

Because the Miss Jo of today had made sure that she was represented in the artwork as well. She'd doodled a few details atop the original; a bowler hat, a mustache, a bowtie, and a cigar streaming inky curlicues toward the border had been added with care.

The feeling Emily got when she looked at it, joy and laughter and an instant flare of heat between her legs…it wasn't like anything she'd encountered in a schoolgirl infatuation or practical arrangement at the college, that was certain. It was just as garish and unnecessary as she'd assumed. But rather than filling her with disgust, the combination of beauty and comedy ran her straight through with happiness she'd been sure was out of her reach until this one utterly irresponsible moment.

She ignored the nagging of her conscience, her morals, her intellect as she packed the more flattering of her simple skirts up for the weekend. So what if she'd stretched the truth of her trip to London a bit? What did it matter that she was still foolishly waiting on the respect from her father and brother that seemed unlikely to ever come? Who cared if she'd happily partaken of a vice that would appall nearly everyone she knew? Everything was changing anyway. In fact, if she could not figure out how to convince the hospital to keep giving her shifts once they no longer needed Papa's services, or to get more than one desperate actress to actually pay her to practice medicine in *any* specialty, everything might very well be ruined.

If Miss Jo's companionship was proving to ruin her a bit further, well...

Maybe she could explain, while she was at the task of ruination, exactly how one went about starting over from scratch to build up something just a touch more decadent.

Chapter Twelve

Jo

It was a risk, sending the photograph.

She shouldn't have done it. For so many bloody reasons. First and foremost, Paul had heard evidence of further snooping around the press on Holywell Street last week. The political pamphleteers they worked alongside without much fond feeling had found it in their hearts to let him know someone had been by, asking suspicious questions.

"I swear I'm not here to force you to discuss the baby," Paul assured her when he came to let her know, the rings on his fingers flashing in the sunlight as he waved them reassuringly. "You seem quite content to save all practical discussions until you can have them with the child itself. While I question whether the two of you will be able to hammer out a living arrangement on your own, I respect your decision to give the wee one a voice in the matter."

"God, you are ridiculous—"

"I am simply here," he went on, "to let you know that while we are not fucked, you need to keep your head down, be on the lookout, and if you see anything suspicious, please do not opt to save it for the birthing room like you are doing with the rest of our problems."

It was hard to tell how worried to be. This sort of thing happened now and again, and had never proven too difficult to get out of. They were very careful with their enterprises. Paul's distress was more palpable than usual this time, but based upon his delivery of the news, she suspected it was fear for his domestic future that had him so on edge. After all, he was still waiting on Jo to start behaving like a reasonable person, and in the meantime, Vanessa had taken ill again in the last few days. Jo couldn't bring herself to fix her part in his distress yet, but she still cared enough for the blasted idiot that she pitied his position and promised to be on her best behavior.

Sending a naughty photograph to her prim penpal was not exactly her best behavior, coming not only with a chance of discovery through the post, but the risk of taking things a step too far with Emily and scaring her off.

But that's why she'd had to do it.

These past few weeks, Emily's letters had been a balm more powerful than anything out of a medicine bag. She was witty. She was smart. She was good and kind in a way that Jo hadn't really even believed a person could be, and there was a certain sensuality underlying all her buttoned-up trappings that seemed to slide under the layers of Jo's dapper dress to curl up in the center of her chest and purr for hours. Her upcoming visit had become a bright spot upon a future that was murky and uncertain.

She needed to make sure, though, that Emily did not forget who she was dealing with. Because if she forgot, and Jo got more attached than she already had, then the eventual remembering would be more painful than Jo could stand. Best to send a reminder now, so that neither of them got a nasty shock later.

While she'd hoped for a quick response to ease her worries

about disastrous discovery or tragic rejection, the weekend came too quickly. If Emily was either offended by Jo's photograph, or had sent on information about which train she was taking in, her response did not arrive in time for it to do Jo any good. Once she'd closed up the shop for the day, she was left with nothing to do but go straight to The Orchid and Pearl Society House and hope for the best.

Jo had sent word to Winifred Withers that she and possibly a guest would be at her place for supper. When she'd first started coming to the society house, it had felt presumptuous to invite herself over for meals whenever she felt like it, but it was Miss Withers's way. She wasn't old, only around forty, but there was something intrinsically matronly about the wealthy spinster; she liked to house, to clothe, to feed. And while she was always willing to do those things on-the-fly for a stranger, she preferred that those already under her wing give notice if extra plates needed to be set.

When Jo arrived as the sun was setting, she found Miss Withers in the lovingly decorated drawing room, sitting at the piano in a simple, tidy gown as she made notes in a music book. When she heard Jo's footsteps behind her, she turned to peer with a look half sweet and half scolding.

"You friend isn't joining us, then?" Miss Withers said. If one looked just right, they could imagine they saw the evening's guest list in her sharp eyes, names being scratched out and numbers updated in real time.

"Hello to you too." Jo took off her hat in greeting before popping it onto the rack. "And as for that, I'm not sure. She's not here yet, then, I take it?"

Miss Withers looked scandalized. "Why aren't you meeting her at the station?"

"She never told me when to be there." Jo shrugged and headed to the bar near the piano, where her favorite whiskey was ready and waiting just for her. "It was a bit of a hasty situation. I wasn't expecting her for another week."

A snort of laughter by the fireplace caught Jo's attention. Margot Levin was over there behind her easel, her black curls pinned back clumsily, paint stains on her hands and trousers. Jo hadn't noticed her before, but ought to have assumed she was here; for years, Margot followed Miss Withers around like a puppy. Margot was *always* here.

"What's so funny?" Jo asked, forgoing the whiskey bottle to shove her hands in her pockets and move to see what she was working on—she'd met Margot through the illustration work she did for some of Paul's authors, so there was always a chance she was working on something fun. "We don't all sit around pining half our lives, you know. Some of us move decisively."

Margot twirled her brush through a few colors on her palette until they'd blended as she wished. "I'm simply amused that you've found someone as decisive as yourself. More decisive, perhaps, what with her *hasty* arrival. She's got you a bit unbalanced, doesn't she?"

Jo peered at the start of a painting composed of Margot's signature satyrs and nymphs, ignoring her friend's playful eyes on her.

"I'm not unbalanced," Jo snapped, wishing her face wouldn't burn. "And anyway, I hope you've told Miss Withers that you're over here painting her in such scandalous poses, and nude to boot."

Miss Withers looked up from the piano, but Margot's eye-roll told her that it was just Jo causing trouble again. "Well, Jo," Miss Withers said, returning to her notes. "I counted your friend in when planning dinner. If she comes, do know there is plenty of roast for everyone."

"Oh, shit," said Jo. "I think she might be a vegetarian. I'm not sure, though; it didn't come up specifically, it's just a few things she said makes me wonder— Fuck, do you think…?"

She trailed off as Miss Withers shrugged. "She's not the only one. Plenty of bread and vegetables too."

"She's not unbalanced," Margot snickered, dipping her brush. "Not unbalanced at all."

Jo shoved Margot with her shoulder, but only when she knew the jostle wouldn't ruin the painting. Margot returned the attack by trying to dot Jo's nose in green paint, which she dodged at the last second, retreating to the table of hors-d'oeuvres and spiked punch. The Orchid and Pearl wasn't a large society, usually somewhere between five and fifteen of them in at a time, but it was certainly a well-catered one. Jo ladled punch into a goblet and wondered if Emily was as strict a teetotaler as she seemed, or it if was just that she'd wanted her wits at The Curious Fox—

The bell rang. Jo whipped her head toward the front hallway so fast she nearly sloshed punch straight onto the blue-and-cream carpet.

Miss Withers closed her music book and stood, smoothing her skirts and taking the goblet carefully from Jo, so as to avoid any further close-calls. "That's either Quinn and Tansy, or your most decisive and bothersome Miss Clarke."

"Dr. Clarke," Jo corrected automatically. "She's, you know, a full doctor."

Miss Withers and Margot shared a look over Jo's shoulder before Miss Withers went for the hallway.

"Someone's got it bad," Margot muttered, eyes fixed on the half-formed satyrs on her canvas.

"I have not," Jo insisted. "I don't even care for her, really. But she seemed like she could use, you know, the influence of a few people like—"

"Save your breath, Joey," said Margot, all sly smiles and patronizing love. "You hide your accent better than you're hiding your interest in this woman."

"I hide everything I wish to hide just fine. I am an impeccable enigma," she said petulantly, peering after Miss Withers and worrying at her waistcoat button as she strained to hear who had arrived.

"Good evening," came a distant greeting from the stoop. "My name is Dr. Emily Clarke. I've brought along my invitation from Miss Jo, though I would prefer to leave it in my suitcase if possible, for reasons that are particular to our common acquaintance."

How wonderful to hear her voice again after all their letters! It was just as tight and proper as she remembered, with that same failing attempt at a low pitch. It had been difficult to imagine that voice sounding out the instances of dry wit she often penned, but as she described the reason she didn't want to flash Jo's invitation, it made sense. Unlike Jo, who sometimes felt like she was a dozen different people stuffed into one suit, Emily spoke just the same, no matter what was said.

But there was no time to be fascinated by that. Jo needed to look like she was doing anything but lurking around, straining for snippets of a voice. Not that she *was* doing that. She wasn't. She *wouldn't*. But it sure looked like it right now, and if she wasn't careful, Emily would be smirking at her just the same as the others were. She got her punch back up and took it to the powder-blue chaise behind Margot's easel, where she could not so easily fall victim to knowing glances. She crossed her legs. Uncrossed them. Fluffed the bolster. Flipped it over. Drew the untouched goblet to her mouth, then changed her mind…

Miss Withers led Emily into the drawing room, and what struck Jo first was how perfect she looked in this place.

Emily marched in on those practical heeled boots, swathed in a traveling dress the same color as the inevitable station soot, clutching a valise in a simply gloved hand. She looked very much a woman who'd never, not once in her life, given a fuck what the world saw when they looked at her. Zero fucks about whether gents found her attractive. Same number given regarding whether she came across ladylike or butch in this crowd, a concern Jo herself remembered with sickening clarity. Jo had spent *two hours* getting dressed the first night she came here. But Emily, clearly, had not. Because Emily was Emily. She was comfortable and put together, and it showed in each assured step.

In the blue-and-cream drawing room, her eyes looked more like the sea than a storm. As soon as they fell on her, Jo leapt up, nearly spilling her punch again as she reached to remove a hat that she'd already taken off and left on the rack.

"You made it," Jo said.

"Seems I did," said Emily, shoulders square but face flushing. "It was easy enough to find. Your instructions were suitably revealing."

Her lips didn't even twitch with the joke; it was so straight-faced that a few weeks ago, Jo would have assumed the innuendo was accidental.

"May I put this down?" Emily asked once introductions were done, lifting her suitcase. Jo instantly reached out a chivalrous hand to take it, but Emily jerked it just out of reach. "I can carry it; I should just like to put it somewhere appropriate."

"Joey, why don't you show her upstairs?" said Margot, eyes flashing mischievously from behind her canvas. "Miss Withers figured the two of you would want to catch up before supper, so the parlor is ready for you. And of course, the usual bedrooms are all made up for anyone who needs them."

"My brother lives in town," Emily said. "And while there is room in his study, it has become crowded over there of late. The society house is accustomed to providing lodgings, then? I should hate to put anyone out, but it would be appreciated."

"Oh, visiting friends and wandering strays are always coming and going," said Margot brightly. "No trouble at all, so long as Miss Withers knows the breakfast numbers by midnight."

"Well, put me down for breakfast then," she said with a polite but confident nod.

"Speaking of, are you a vegetarian?" Jo blurted in her haze of wondering.

Emily turned back to her, all wave-colored eyes and frothy wisps of hair that could not be adequately contained during a day's travel, like it was the sea she'd risen from, rather than the suburbs. "Near to it, but not strict. Gratitude for hospitality is of greater importance than perfect adherence to a diet, so I am more than happy to share in whatever is offered. The only thing I strictly avoid is strong spirits."

"That should work, then," said Margot with a naughty little grin. "Seeing as Joey didn't pick the menu, we should have a few offerings aside from Irish whiskey available to you."

Emily not-so-subtly flicked her gaze to Jo's goblet.

"It's punch," said Jo defensively. "Bit of port wine in it, but nothing I'd count as 'strong.' Would you, ah…would you like some, Emily? I know you weren't keen on Mr. Forester's champagne, but…"

Jo trailed off as Emily looked suspicious and straight-spined again all of a sudden. But then she softened by a smidge. "Bring one along to the parlor for me. I find myself more willing to lose the edge of my wit in this location than the last. But first, my luggage?"

Jo filled another goblet, then led Emily toward the stairs. As she gestured with the glasses for her to go up first, nearly spilling again as she did, she felt a gentle hand on her upper back. She turned to find Miss Withers looking somewhere between scolding and amused.

"We'll have some refreshments brought up." She carefully

slid both glasses from Jo's hands. "You allow your attention to focus firmly on...what it's going to focus on anyway."

Emily selected an open bedroom and settled her valise on the stand while Jo watched awkwardly from the doorway.

"The water closet is right across the hall," Jo said, strangely pulled to be helpful somehow. "Just. You know. If you'd like to freshen up. It's got a tap."

The words fell a little stupidly between them, but Emily nodded with obvious appreciation. "Glad to hear it," she said. "I very much look forward to the day when they all have taps, hot and cold both. Far more sanitary."

Jo nodded, trying to push thoughts of every filthy pump she'd ever sipped from far enough away that Emily couldn't peer into her soul and spot the memories like specks of dirt.

"Is there, ah, anything else you need?" Jo asked. "I could have Miss Withers's maid come up to help with...like...your buttons or—"

"Believe it or not, the point of rational dress is not to look drab." More dry wit laced her words, though this time, a lingering smile curved their tones pleasantly. In spite of all the simple gray, the laughter made her look anything but drab. "All my clothing was consciously designed to be a one-woman affair. While I appreciate your hospitality, I require nothing more. I shall meet you in the parlor shortly."

"Do you know where—?"

"You pointed it out on the way up."

Jo started off, but before she'd shut the door all the way, she stuck her head back in.

"This is awkward, isn't it?" she asked.

"Yes," Emily admitted with another of those small smiles. "One of the more awkward things I've ever done, actually.

And as a physician, you can probably imagine that that's saying something."

Simultaneously reluctant to leave and practically running for the exit, Jo left the smiling and severe sea of Emily and escaped down the hall to what she affectionately referred to as the gents' parlor (much to Miss Withers's chagrin). It had been set up to look like one, though…or so Jo was told, having never visited houses rich and proper enough to have separate parlors for the sexes to retire to after dinner. In fact, she'd never been in a proper house at all, and had only seen rich ones after she found company that didn't even bother separating, since the women all smoked and half of them worked the streets on the weekends at least. Still, Jo knew that the décor—dark woods, sturdy upholstery, smoking implements and liquor carts and stately chess boards—were standard-issue for spaces dedicated to the constitutional restoration of upper-class Englishmen.

Though Miss Withers hated the nickname, Jo thought it was fun. She could light a cigarette and pour some whiskey by the stony fireplace, taking on the handful of gentlemanly traits she found enjoyable while leaving the bothersome parts behind.

Surrounded by the familiar scents of old tobacco and wood polish, Jo squished down onto one of the sofas to take up the punch and plate of fruits, nuts, and toast points that Miss Withers had seen safely set up on the coffee table, trying not to eat them all in her anxiety. As a woman of letters, Jo knew perfectly well that she sparkled better with a pen than in a conversation. What if Emily discovered that the real Jo—the one beneath the clothing and the puns and the postcards—wasn't as interesting as she seemed? That she was, in reality, just an Irish runaway and bookish wife who happened to have good taste in cravats?

Surprisingly quickly considering how long it usually took people to get out of the women's garb they'd arrived in, Emily joined her. The traveling attire had been swapped for a simple navy skirt, creamy cotton shirtwaist, and practical knitted cardigan. Her face was pink from a presumed scrub at the oh-so-sanitary tap, and she'd repinned the froth of her hair so the lines of her face were once again simple and severe. She looked like someone who would never accept Jo's invitation to anywhere in the entire cosmos.

And yet, here she was, staring between the two sofas that faced each other, clearly unsure where she ought to sit. Across?

Or beside?

The fact that it was even a question had Jo's stomach flipping worse than it had when hearing what women got up to at the medical college. She found herself scooting over on her own sofa, making space.

Jo half-expected the doctor to spook, but she actually looked relieved. She sat down with a soft, huffing sigh before seeming to remember herself and folding her hands on her lap. She remained very still, as if she had not a single need in the world, but Jo didn't miss how her eyes flicked to the tray of food before her.

"I assume you've had a very long day of work and travel," said Jo. "Help yourself."

Emily took up a point of toast with a gentle nod. "You were right to pick this place," she said, sounding a bit prim again. "Truly incredible hospitality. A bed, a meal, and a running tap are far from what I expected when all I really wanted was... I don't know what, exactly. To get away, I suppose. To indulge a bit."

"Get away from what?" Jo asked. "And indulge in what?"

"Get away from everything," Emily sighed. "And indulge in anything."

"Except strong spirits."

She nodded. "Precisely."

"That's not very specific," Jo accused.

"Well, you deserve it for the mysterious comments you're apt to make, don't you?" Emily took a nibble off a toast. "Don't deny it, Jo. You purposely pique my curiosity, only to leave me unsatisfied over and over again. It's only fair you let me partake of the fun."

Jo stared at her as those words soaked in, genuinely unsure whether the innuendo was intended. "The fun of being mysterious, you mean?"

Emily picked up her glass and peered over the rim of it, eyes flashing with a new sort of wickedness. "Sure. That's one aspect. But you know how to have all sorts of fun, don't you? Your recent correspondence shows that well enough."

Jo had long since lost the decency to even pretend to blush. "That was fun, at the time. Not something I'd do again in a hurry, but the person I fancied I was then enjoyed the excuse to get done up."

"The photographer, he…" Emily faltered. "He treated you well?"

"Oh yeah," she said, thinking back to that day with the detached feeling that was so often packed up with her memories like a sachet of mothballs, acrid and annoying, but necessary for safe storage. "Yeah, he wasted a shit-ton of coal keeping a good enough fire going for me. Blankets and tea between the sets. Very kind chap. Haven't seen him since we moved to print, but I wouldn't be sad to run into him again." In fact, if not for that useful sense that her left-behind lives belonged to someone else, she might have been sad to have fallen out of touch with him. "Why do you ask?"

"I should just…" Emily faltered. She brought her punch to her nose, like the vapors might hit her strong enough on their own to see her through whatever was making her blush so bright. She went on in a rush with her eyes squeezed shut: "I should hate to think I had enjoyed something that was terribly unpleasant or degrading for you."

Jo couldn't help but laugh at the reaction. Goddamn, how long had it been since she'd talked to someone with a mind-set quite like that? Normally, she'd find it annoying. Maybe quaint, at best. But she'd already gotten the sense that Emily's strict attitudes came from care, not judgement, and so it was actually sort of…well…sweet. In a way.

"It would be disingenuous to pretend every postcard you pick up will have such a happy story behind it," Jo said carefully. "But enjoy my pictures all you like, Princess. I'm just glad to hear it was well-received. I was thinking it might scare you off."

"Were you trying to scare me off?"

"I was trying to make sure that if you were scare-offable, it happened sooner rather than later."

Emily nodded, satisfied with that answer. She did the same little song-and-dance with her goblet, smelling, almost tasting, thinking better and going for a bite of food instead.

"May I ask another question, Miss Jo?"

"So long as you aren't too attached to getting an answer."

"How did you go from that…" She reddened spectacularly, making a gesture with her hand that was quite vague, but that Jo liked to think was supposed to indicate knickers. "To…this?"

"That's a big question," Jo said. The way she'd shed old lives like a snake leaving its skin behind didn't make for terribly charming conversation, and seeing as Emily had traveled all the way here to see her, she wanted to seem charming at least through the appetizer course. "Can I ask a better one?"

"Oh? And what would that be?"

Jo leaned in, elbows on knees. "Which version do you prefer?"

"As much as I can appreciate both views," Emily said with a pragmatism belied by her continued flush. "Your creative additions to the former makes me think that it's the latter that is genuine. And therefore, the latter is the one I prefer and the one I came here to see." Though her face stayed soft for a moment, imbuing the words with a pleasant and flattering warmth, she eventually caught herself relaxing, and startled upright again. "Came here to seek," she corrected. "To seek assistance from. In my…my quest."

"Your quest for enjoyment?"

"Yes." Emily sighed. "I'm sure it's tiring to have gone through all the things you did to get here, Jo. The move, the nunnery, the husband, the postcards. But there are also downsides to knowing who you are and your place in the world from the day you're born."

"No fun?"

"No fun at all!"

Jo laughed. She wasn't sure if she herself was as interesting in person as she was in her letters, but Emily certainly was. In fact, she was much better for the proximity.

"And that's bothering you all of a sudden?" Jo coaxed. She herself was having a bit of an existential crisis. While she didn't wish such a thing on Emily, it was intriguing that she seemed to be going through something similar. "The unfunness of your position?"

"It would be worth it if it was getting me anywhere," she said. "I have lived every day assuming it was. But it's not. It was an illusion. Everything I've done, every sacrifice I've made, every good time I've turned down…it's still led me down a path where my future is entirely dependent on my father and brother, neither of whom, if I'm being honest, is…" She paused, reaching for the words she wanted. "Is especially… They have their own concerns, you see. And the fact that they see me as equal tends to blind them to the reality of… Not that they're *trying* to make things difficult for me, it's just that—"

"Are you trying to say that they have their heads too far up their arses to be of use to you?"

"Miss Jo!" Emily's eyes went wide and shocked. It seemed like it might be the end of their conversation until she grasped Jo's forearm. "That is *exactly* what I'm trying to say!"

"Well, that's good," Jo muttered, relieved.

"You understand, I'm sure," Emily went on. "Your husband is a radical, isn't he? I find that well-meaning as they may be, these sorts of men simply do not understand that their own enlightened views aren't actually protecting the women in their lives from the reality of our circumstances. It takes a bit more than that when there is literally no hospital in Surrey that will pay me my worth for the work that I do. No field that wants me save for the one I'm probably least suited to."

Jo's first thought was that she didn't actually relate to that. As a pair, she and Paul had put "reality" as far behind them as possible a long time ago, refusing its false promises in favor of a more unscripted life.

But she didn't want to correct Emily, and even more than that, she didn't want to linger on what a good friend Paul had been to her up until this point. Because at this point, he was a wanker, and that was all there was to it.

"Least suited to?" Jo said, latching on to that subject, rather than the more complicated one. "What are you talking about?"

Emily looked a little sheepish. "Now, I don't want you thinking I'm unequal to the task of delivering a baby. I am more than capable of the work. What I struggle with is the pressure of it. I know what it is to grow up in a home torn by the particular grief that can enter through the childbed. All my troubles, my father's troubles, my brother's...they trace back directly."

It took Jo a moment to wrap her mind around the nervous look Emily was fixing her with.

"Your own mother," Jo said when it clicked. "She..."

"I suppose in some sense, this makes me even better suited," Emily said, clearly not believing the words. "I am very driven to attain a better outcome for Miss Garcia, and, I suppose, will continue to be driven as I take on other patients. But I fear that if ever some tragedy happens that is beyond my control, or heaven forbid a result of my own mistake, I will be driven as mad as my father was when he lost my mother."

"That's why you wouldn't take Vanessa on initially," Jo said. "It wasn't Paul's press. You were protecting yourself."

"That's right."

"I wouldn't blame you, if you had to step back from it."

"That's very kind of you, but I don't have a choice," Emily explained. "As I said, I am not being paid a livable wage at the hospital, but my father is going to be forced into early retirement. I need an income. Private practice is the only way forward, without moving to London—"

"Why not move to London?"

"Because my father is on my very last nerve, but he has not been so dreadful that I wish to leave him alone in his old age." She sighed. "He's not infirm, and we do have such a supportive community back home, many friends and neighbors. But it's not the same as the company of one's family. If my brother would take on at least some of the responsibility, we might be able to make it work between the two of us. But that's not looking very likely."

"It's funny to hear both your sides of this," Jo said. "He makes you out to be some moralizing harpy."

"If he wants me to be less of a moralizing harpy, he is more than welcome to lighten my load a bit. As it is, I am harsh with him. Yes. It's hard not to be when someone leaves you in an impossible situation only to turn around and berate you for not being any fun. Lack of fun was not my choice. And seeing as my choices are narrowing even further, I bring us back to my goal for this weekend: to have a bit of fun for once, while I can. Accompanied, I hope, by someone knowledgeable in the subject."

Good God, had Emily been intriguing like this during their first odd meeting in that greenery-filled, lemon-scented parlor? Had Jo simply been so put off by a dull dress and a notepad that she'd failed to notice the wit, the sharpness, the—there was no other word for it—the *heat* that simmered just under the surface of this woman?

"Well," Jo said, scooping up her own punch. "If it's a little indulgence you're looking for, I'm knowledgeable enough to get the job done. And seeing as I too have troubles I'd rather forget for a few days, I can think of no better way to spend my weekend than being your guide in the ways of the decadents."

"Lovely." She peered into the goblet she'd been flirting with since she picked it up. "We'll start with this."

"Spirits," said Jo in a misty voice, as if she meant the other sort.

"Spirits indeed."

She moved as if to take a sip, but Jo put a halting finger on her wrist.

"Ah, ah!" Jo said. "Indulgence isn't meant to be taken quick like medicine. It has trappings." She lifted her own glass. "We have to toast."

"To what?" said Emily, lifting her glass as well, but not touching. Not yet.

Jo looked into the lovely face beside her. "To cordial meetings?"

"In all honesty, I'm not known for my thrilling toasts." She brought her glass just the tiniest bit higher. "So, I certainly can't think of anything more fitting. To cordial meetings."

And it was still very awkward as they locked eyes and clinked glasses, but wonderful as well. A decadent and a dissenter seated so close on the same sofa that one's skirts covered the toes of the other's boot, so different that they were nearly natural en-emies, with no real reason to have found themselves here, sip-ping punch that Jo found a little weak but made Emily's eyes bug and her cheeks go pink within moments.

"Very indulgent indeed," said Emily with that hand back on her chest, peering into the glass as if she expected to find wild little nymphs swimming around in there.

Jo laughed, grateful to be able to break the tension with the comfort of mirth. "Well, do you like it?"

"I don't know," she said, that line between her brows deep-ening in thought. She brought the goblet up toward her face, smelling and looking at it for a moment before pulling it to her lips. It was like she was running an experiment on it, sipping so slowly that Jo could only assume she was hunting down data with her tongue.

By the time Jo watched the final delicate swallow, she real-ized she'd been holding her breath in anticipation of the final conclusion.

"Quite good, actually," Emily declared. "Undoubtedly in-toxicating in certain quantities, and far too much sugar to ad-vise regular consumption. But there's something very bracing about it. I do think I like it." She picked up another of the toast points and allowed it to line her sensitive stomach before going on. "What do you think?"

"I very much prefer whiskey," Jo said.

A hint of a smile tugged at the corner of Emily's mouth. "Somehow, I'm not surprised."

Was that a jab? Who could say? And what did it matter? She set her own goblet down on the table, and when she leaned back, she was an inch closer to Emily than she had been before, turned toward her with an elbow up on the curving, wooden top of the sofa.

"So, Emily," Jo said, crossing her legs inward as she did.

"Seeing as we're being exceptionally candid here, I have to ask. When you say you're looking for lessons in indulgence, exactly what kinds of things—"

There was a knock on the parlor door, and before Jo could shout at whoever it was to bugger the fuck off, they'd already opened it. Jo tipped her head back to see Tansy Wickersham bubbling on the threshold. Though married and lacking anything resembling a grim or academic edge, she had a habit of dressing almost as plainly as Emily.

Shame, just now, that her disposition was not as polite and timid as her clothing.

"It's true!" Tansy said, coming around to the other side of the sofa to stare at the pair of them. As she did, Emily gasped and clutched her cardigan tight.

"Mrs. Wickersham?" Emily exclaimed.

Jo looked between Emily's shock and Tansy's delighted nods. Bewildered, Emily stood for a proper greeting.

"You know each other?" Jo stood as well, nervously trying to get on a level with whatever was happening.

"We go to some of the same talks," Emily explained, still looking a little shaken. "I… Goodness, Mrs. Wickersham, I can't say I ever would have expected to run into you *here*."

Tansy laughed. "Well, you're not very observant then, are you? As for you, well, I can't say I'm overly surprised by anything but your proximity to Joey in particular." She gave a little wink. "In any case, I simply had to come up and see if you'd noticed how *very* unsurprising it is that you eventually made your way here! Quinn's downstairs saying I conjured you myself. She's into all those pagan notions right now, though honestly, with a coincidence like this, I can't blame her this time."

Emily turned to Jo, blinking in confusion and distress as if the rhythm of it were some sort of code for help.

"What are you talking about, Tansy?" Jo asked.

"The chess set!"

When they both fixed her with more confused stares than ever, Tansy took Emily's glass and set it down. Bit brash and forward, but not so much as when she took Emily by the hand and led her to the chessboard near the window, always so neatly set with two armies of curving, feminine pieces that Tansy had found more fitting for this parlor than her own. "Oh, Emily, we all love it! You're practically a celebrity here already, though of course I didn't mention your name when I brought the set in. Didn't seem relevant."

Jo followed them with something uncomfortable flaring behind her ribs the second Tansy touched Emily's hand. She positioned herself between them, making them break that contact.

"What of it?" Jo asked.

Emily had gone quiet. Clearly, this was not some bizarre flight of fancy of Tansy's (who, as a Quaker from a family that made Emily look like an excessive socialite, used the excuse of this place to fly every imaginable fancy). Emily picked up the white queen, her fingers pinching the unmistakable curve of her majesty's lovely waist.

"She made it," Tansy stage-whispered. "I told you it was purchased from a friend who was quite adept with a whittling knife? Well, Dr. Clarke was the friend."

Jo was torn between admiration for the skill required for such a beautiful, intricate piece of work and something that felt unpleasantly like jealousy that Tansy had known about it first.

"Anyway," said Tansy, putting her hands on both the others' backs. "I'll leave you to finish up in here. Supper's nearly ready. I just couldn't wait to share this one. It's simply too much!"

With that she was, thankfully, gone.

"Goodness." Emily put the queen back where she'd found it. "That was all a bit of a shock."

"You know Tansy, then," Jo said a bit stiffly. "You're… friends?"

"I wouldn't go that far." Emily peered toward the nearly closed door like she'd seen some unlikely imp pass through it. "Particularly since even the friendship I've shared with her has been…with sort of a different Tansy Wickersham. Goodness, I don't think I've heard her say that many words at one time before. I think of her as a very quiet and unobtrusive person. A good person: she and her family do a lot of admirable work getting people fed in this city. But not a person who *talks* much."

"Really?" Jo laughed, relieved to hear there was not some other sort of friendship between the two of them. "We can hardly get her to shut up, normally. In any case, did you really make this? All these pieces, by hand?"

Emily smiled and nodded, looking pleased as she picked up one of the pawns and turned the bottom to Jo, revealing *EC1883* carved into the smooth cherrywood. "I don't often finish a whole set, but when I do, I like to sell them off and put the money toward charity. Mrs. Wickersham gave a very good sum for this one, but I admit, I'm happier to see it here. I assume it gets more use than it would have done at her home. Did you know she's *married*? With children? And it's not a home well-suited to chess, I suppose. I agreed to sell her the set because she enjoys the game, but her children are still young and her husband is a bit…well, let's just say, I've met him. Once again, I have only the greatest of admiration for his character, but suspect that a game with him might be brief and unsatisfying."

Jo nodded knowingly. "Yeah. She's said something to that effect about him before."

"You're terrible," Emily said with a laugh and an unmistakably flirty nudge. Her eyes were looking into Jo's again, calling her. The room grew very quiet, the air rather close. Jo became hyperaware of how the sweep of that long, navy skirt was dusting her own shoes again.

"Anyway," Emily said, voice and chin lowered in a way that was as unmistakable as it was alluring. "What were we talking about? Before the interruption?"

It seemed pretty clear that she remembered what they'd been talking about just fine, but Jo wasn't up to arguing about that. Or about anything. They'd argued enough, probably. Any more would be waste of time that could be much better spent.

"I was asking what sort of indulgences you came here hoping for this evening." Jo brushed a light finger over the rounded head of one of the wooden pawns. "Though, if you made these, I must say, I think you've at least got some mind for art and leisure."

Emily watched Jo caress the pawn with parted lips and wide eyes. She smiled, the expression far from prim and angelic.

"Am I to assume that means you're in less remedial a phase than I previously thought?" Jo asked.

"That depends on what you mean." Emily stepped in even closer, running a single finger down the back of Jo's hand. "You see, I learned all the important anatomical foundations at the women's medical college. But it was quite a perfunctory thing. I fear I am quite remedial indeed when it comes to matters of true indulgence."

Oh, fuck. There really was nothing for it, was there? Any hope of avoiding this was destroyed by the knowledge of these carvings. The fact of more facets to this woman than even Emily seemed to have noticed.

Jo leaned in and Emily leaned up.

"Emily?"

"Yes, Jo?"

"Would a kiss be too indulgent a place to start?"

Emily's breath caught and her eyes shone. "Too indulgent? Not at all, Jo. Not at all."

Jo had imagined kissing Emily more than once by now. She'd assumed it would take a lot of coaxing to soften her lovely lips up. But when Jo finally pressed her own to them, they were not pursed at all, but plush, and perfect, and tasting of port wine punch.

Chapter Thirteen

Emily

It had been so long since Emily was kissed that she'd forgotten what an overwhelming pleasure it was. She gasped at the unexpected heat of Jo's lips and the thrill of a warm hand cupping her cheek. Her mind, usually full to bursting with thoughts, was stunned silent. She pushed into the kiss, her hands feeling antsy by her sides until she rested them on the swell of tweed-covered hips that had haunted her for weeks. It felt like her palms had been carved to fit the spot perfectly.

Jo brought her other hand up, framing Emily's face with unbearable softness, while her mouth grew rougher, licking Emily's bottom lip and nipping at it until the room was spinning.

No sooner had Emily decided she'd found a new calling, that she would be happiest if she could forget all about doctoring and just keep on doing this for the rest of her life, than Jo gave one last little nip, brushed their noses together, and pulled back.

"Indulgent enough?" she asked, breathing a little heavier as she pushed an unruly wave from Emily's forehead.

"Not even close," Emily whispered. Both of them laughed.

"There's more where that came from." Jo ran her thumb over Emily's bottom lip, making her shiver. "But not yet."

"Why not?"

"Supper's ready."

Emily meant to remove her hands from Jo's hips, but her fingers dug in tighter the moment she considered it, like they knew playtime was coming to an end, and were setting themselves up to make a dreadful fuss at the final announcement.

"The others will wonder what we're up to if we don't come down, I suppose," she said.

"Oh, don't worry about that," Jo laughed, looking at the door but not seeming terribly motivated to make a move for it, either. "Let them wonder. They deserve it. No, no, I meant that if I'm going to teach you decadence, we have to do it right. Decadence must be well-fueled. When I've seen people ruined by their appetites—and I've worked down on Bookseller's Row, so I've seen it—I've noticed that it's because they tended to only one of the appetites, rather than a good balance."

"That sounds like poppycock," Emily accused. "I cannot imagine you have any data to back that up."

"Who's the expert in this subject here, eh?" Jo stepped back at last, though she grabbed Emily's fingers on the way down, pulling them in for a kiss. "Trust me, it would be irresponsible to debauch you on nothing more than a few nibbles and a glass of punch. It will unbalance your humors, and you'll be hating me again by morning."

As someone very used to a simple diet and the company of nonconformists who all nonconformed very similarly to one another, the sheer variety of an Orchid and Pearl Society supper was akin to a carnival as far Emily was concerned.

While she hadn't expected the simple repast of her own community, she still figured they were in for a typical London society sit-down supper. But Miss Withers didn't retain a staff the size of her dinner parties, so the usual fashion of multiple courses was forgone in favor of French excess, heaped plates and flowing tureens of everything from the soups to the roast, all available at once on the table. So many fruits and side dishes and even cakes and candies were laid out that Emily might not ever have to decide whether to partake of the meat. She probably wouldn't even get to it before she'd had her fill of everything else.

The company was just as unexpected. It was as ragtag a group as any in creation, with seemingly no set norms regarding dress or manners or mealtime prayers. The dozen or so of them all stacked their own plates with whatever they liked as they carried on conversations with each other, dressed in everything from Tansy Wickersham's woolen sweater, to Miss Cordelia's frothy pink frock, to Quinn's dapper suit and short haircut that made Jo's own low bun and fitted waistcoat seem very soft and polite in comparison.

While Emily and Jo settled themselves at the dining table with Miss Withers, Margot Levin, and some of those others, not all the guests stayed at the table, a few wandering off with their plates for the drawing room or the parlor.

As Emily watched those wanderers go with her glass halfway to her mouth in surprise, Miss Withers put a hand on her shoulder.

"It's all comfort here, not rules," she said, her maternal tone even more of a shock to Emily's nerves than the rest of it. Emily found a kind smile on the woman's face, which became scolding as it refocused on Jo. "Whenever I even try to make rules, they end up broken anyway."

"Excuse me!" said Jo, snatching a roll from the pile in front of her. "I haven't sneaked one of my sodomites through the doors in at least a month."

That word had Emily's hackles up instantly, on alert as she always was for threats to her beloved brother in the one area in which he was so much less free than she was. But Emily got the sense that Jo used the word as David Forester did: with a stubborn pride. She didn't particularly *like* it, but she did, at least, understand it enough to let it go.

Odd of her, really, to let it slide. To let anything slide. It wasn't her usual habit at all. Perhaps it was the punch. Or the small bites of roast she'd had for the first time in ages. Or the way Jo moved their chairs a little bit closer together, not outside the realm of reasonable, but just enough that their arms might brush as they reached for a fork or adjusted a napkin. While Emily spoke with everyone—catching up with Tansy Wickersham and her "real husband," Quinn, taking in Margot's stories of the London art world, listening dutifully to the lists and concerns of a high-society spinster like Miss Withers—not a word went by without a warm awareness of Jo beside her.

She had wondered if Jo might reveal more of herself while in the company of her friends, but if anything, she said less than ever. She sprawled comfortably in her chair, trading in jokes and asking questions about everyone else that led to lovely conversations, but the most anyone got out of her was some surprisingly well-considered opinions on a novel she and Margot had both read recently. It was not necessarily surface-level stuff, but whenever depth was reached, Emily noticed that the spade tended to dig in just to the side of Jo herself.

It made her antsy to get Jo alone again. While she liked the others, that kiss in the parlor had seared itself into her mind, making her body ache for a sort of decadence that not even the richest of Miss Withers's cakes could fill. Maybe, once they were alone again, Jo would sprinkle a few more facts of her soul like sugar over Emily's awareness. Or maybe not. But a certain sort of depth had been hinted at in their letters already, and Emily couldn't wait to see where it led them.

As the eating wound down, the bottles of wine dwindled to their last drops, and the conversation had gone from casual and scattered to more focused and considered, Emily felt Jo bump her knee under the table. She chanced a glance to see that Jo was already looking sideways at her, dark eyes smoldering beneath the glowing light of the chandelier above the table, glinting more stunningly than any of the crystal or silver set before them. She held Emily's gaze for just long enough before nodding along with what Margot was saying.

Heart thumping at the silent suggestion, Emily slid her hand from her own lap to Jo's knee, which she traced with a finger before giving a squeeze. Though still ostensibly talking through the particulars of illustration printing, Jo covered Emily's hand with her own and slid it upward a bit. Not much. Not scandalously. Just enough to have Emily appreciate how much more warmth and softness could be accessed through the single layer of a trouser leg than the usual stack of skirts and petticoats.

"You look tired, Emily," Jo said once a lull had been reached. She released her hold and stretched casually. "Long day of work and travel for you, wasn't it?"

"Oh yes." Emily forced a yawn. "Exhausting. I wish I had the energy to have some more coffee and continue our conversation, but I'm afraid if I try, I'll find myself sleeping in the butter dish in short order."

"Uh-huh," said Margot with a skeptical smile over her coffee cup, even as Miss Withers was making all the appropriate noises of agreement and lack of offense. Emily stood and smoothed her skirts, which felt a bit tight after that supper. "And do you remember the way to your room, Dr. Clarke, or should someone come along to show you the way? Jo, perhaps? If she's not otherwise occupied?"

As Margot waggled her brows, Jo pretended she was going to pitch a dried fig across the table at her. Margot laughed and flinched, spilling a few drops of coffee but otherwise no worse for wear.

"Go on, dears," Miss Withers said as she wiped up the tiny specks of Margot's mess with a very automatic air. "We'll be up chatting for a while yet if you need anything."

Jo led the way up the stairs, playing on the notion that Emily couldn't find her way. It was silly, but Emily went along with it too, keeping close on Jo's heels like she'd get terribly lost if she did not keep track of that lovely cedar scent that hung about her hair and collar.

Though the halls were just as well-lit and even less lonely than before—what with the sound of voices and clinking spoons from downstairs and the laughter and smoke now pouring from the cracked-open door of the parlor—Emily still stepped lightly across the plush runners and winced when Jo's feet fell too heavily, like she was sneaking through an exceptionally strict library to meet someone she should not be meeting, to do something they shouldn't be doing.

It got her heart racing, swelling, her sentiments no less heightened than her senses. There was no way around it: following Jo like this, the tryst on both their minds palpable, pleasurable, and anything but perfunctory, was *romantic*. She'd doubted she would ever feel such a thrill, doubted even whether anyone felt it or if they were just pretending. But she felt it now, with no cheap perfume or silly lights to blame it on. Just raven hair and pinstriped curves and the heat at her own core pulsing and propelling her forward into something she no longer wanted to defend herself against.

When they reached the parlor door, Jo stopped short enough that Emily was faced with the reality of how close she'd been following. She bumped into Jo's back, nose in line with that full and fragrant knot of hair. It was all Emily could do not to bury her face in it, breathe it in and even taste the tresses that had haunted her imagination for a month. All her effort going toward avoiding that, she couldn't take a proper step back. Her chin drifted to rest on Jo's shoulder, a hand wandering down to one of her perfectly formed hips.

Jo peered through the sliver of open doorway into the raucous-sounding parlor. She turned her head so her lips lined up with Emily's ear.

"They're playing with your pieces," she whispered, the indecency of the words solidifying in her smile.

"Excuse me?" said Emily.

Jo nodded toward the gap. Though it required an unfortunate move away from Jo's warmth, Emily peeked inside to see that the chess set, in addition to cigars and brandies, was being put to use. Not very well, it seemed, and rather drunkenly, with players helped along by the whispering advice of the lovers in their laps, but the sight of the game made Emily smile. She shouldn't be charmed by that sort of excess. A critical voice in her mind tried to bat her pleasure down, to remind her that their path to equality was not paved in parlor games and bathed in brandy.

But good heavens, she spent so much time in the company of other doctors who didn't want her there, or patients who eyed her sideways and resented the pain of procedures twice as much as they normally would, that it was lovely to find she'd been providing something so uncomplicated as comradery and joy in this parlor from afar.

She snuggled in a little closer. As she focused on silencing that critical voice in her head, she lacked the resources to keep up the fight with her nose; it nuzzled into the space behind Jo's ear, warm and woodsy and overwhelmingly soft. "Are you going to join them?" she asked quietly. "Or will you escort me the rest of the way to my room?"

Emily heard Jo swallow.

"That depends," she said. "Can you find your way on your own?"

Emily was not practiced in the trade of shrouded questions. But she knew that the one Jo had spoken was not really the question she was asking. It didn't have to be that way; this seemed like a very safe place. Explicit honesty wouldn't hurt anything.

But there was a thrilling thread in Jo's voice, a thickness to the silence that followed her question, and she knew without being told that it was part of the fun. Like their letters. Like their banter. Like the dodgy keeping of mysteries that weren't especially vital. She let that feeling melt into her mind and flow through the rest of her like a warm, rich syrup.

"No, I can't." As she shook her head, her lips brushed the skin of Jo's neck, tickled by downy hairs that were too short to be tamed with the rest. "I shall get terribly lost if I'm left to my own devices."

"You must have an awful sense of direction."

"Yes. I'm afraid I hardly know up from down."

Jo spun around, pressing Emily tight up against the blue-papered wall of the corridor, one of her hands sliding under the cardigan to settle on her waist, the other holding Emily's chin. Not tight enough to be uncomfortable, but with just enough firmness to utterly thrill.

"Must be all that rich food and decadent company," said Jo with a grin too wicked to be allowed. "You were right to avoid it for so long, if you hoped to keep your wits."

Emily panted, tipping her head back against the wall to encourage Jo to come closer, to grip tighter, to continue along this perfect path they'd tiptoed onto at last. "I confess, my humors are all terribly out of alignment now."

Jo nodded with mock grimness as she brought her lips torturously close to Emily's mouth, her ear, her neck, breathing and smiling but not quite touching. She clucked her tongue in a scold that Emily felt all the way in the bottom of her belly.

"I did tell you that you must balance out the indulgence of your appetites, Emily." Her hand slid slowly from Emily's chin down her throat, slipping around the back of her neck. "But don't worry. I'll save you from this path of ruin you've wandered down."

Finally, the kiss. Thank heavens. Emily could not hope to hold back the whimper in her throat as Jo's lips crushed hard against hers. No longer teasing and nipping, this kiss was open and wet, curious and sinful. Emily was absolutely atomized by the sensation of Jo's tongue slipping into her mouth, her entire awareness collapsing like an old star until there was nothing left of her but the velvet-wrapped flame that was the feeling of Jo's body pressed so tight against her own.

By the time they broke apart for a gulp of forgotten air, Emily really did feel like she'd lost track of all directions. But that didn't matter, because Jo took her hand and led her down the hall to the bedroom. It was very dark once the door was shut and locked behind them. The only light now came from the window, which Emily had left open to allow the healthful movement of air. While the moon behind autumn clouds and tall buildings proved as useless as the unlit candles on the dresser, London's mist-shrouded streetlamps on the walkway below saw to it that night never really fell the way it did back home.

Emily gave the darkness no more thought before wrapping her arms around Jo's neck and pulling her in for more kisses. Jo, though, seemed distracted until she'd taken a moment to light a candle and shut the curtains. The warmer glow of the flame danced over her form as she shucked off her jacket and loosened her cuffs and collar, leaving studs on the dresser with a little clacking sound before rolling up her sleeves slowly and sensuously, like she was trying to lure Emily over.

It worked.

A nod from Jo told Emily to conclude her eager journey at the end of the bed, so she sat upon it as directed. Her heart hammered and her body flushed with anticipation as she waited for Jo's approach.

"Is it true what you said earlier?" Jo whispered as she traced the edge of Emily's cardigan where it lay across her shoulder. "About your clothes being a one-woman affair?"

Emily nodded, robbed of speech as Jo's fingers trailed along the hem and indecently over the modest swell of her breast.

"I won't need any help then," Jo said, untying the simple bow that held the sweater together and pushing it off Emily's shoulders. "Glad to hear it."

Emily had ideas about how these things went, and still expected either the practical release of tension she was used to, or else the wild, untamed kissing and rubbing and losing of all sense that she'd dreamed up as being the way of the decadents. But Jo was neither practical, nor out of control. In fact, as she straddled Emily's lap on the end of the bed, deftly handling the buttons of Emily's shirtwaist one-by-one, loosening the drawstring of the chemise below, she seemed exceptionally controlled. *Beautifully* controlled, like she'd been built to bare the breasts of her lover to cool night air and candlelight. Emily felt like putty in comparison as Jo's slightly cold, slightly callused hands cupped and teased her, a little smile of power dancing across her features before that sight was lost in favor of a kiss so deep that Emily's legs started trying to open of their own accord, only to be stopped by the presence of Jo's on either side of them.

Her squirm and groan of frustration seemed to please Jo, who tightened the vise she'd made of her perfectly curved thighs and doubled her attentions on Emily's breasts, the slow, full nature of her touch making it seem like it was the hunger of her own palms and mouth and the tips of her fingers she was satisfying. It made everything that much more intense as Jo moved with that same steady assurance from Emily's lap...

To the floor at her feet.

"What are you doing?" Emily hissed as Jo took one of her boot-clad feet in hand.

Jo looked up sharply from the unlacing she'd started and said, "Hush."

Hush? Normally, there was nothing Emily hated more than being hushed. It was the syllable that men snapped when one too many opinions had been shared at too high a volume for their sensibilities. But Jo was not one of those sorts. She was the sort that unlaced another woman's boots like she was polishing a precious piece of silver before sliding her hands up to find garter fastenings so easily that there might have been magnets in her fingertips.

Emily liked this *hush* in spite of herself. Was tempted to say something else, just to hear it again. But words were difficult to conjure as Jo rolled the stockings down, kissing her way along the skin she exposed and back up again, until her head was vanishing under skirt and petticoat, and Emily was very much *not* hushing in the slightest.

Apparently, Jo had little concern for whether anyone else might hear evidence that its namesake's flower and jewel had been successfully found through the slit in Emily's drawers. No shushing came, perhaps because Jo's mouth was too busy kissing the insides of Emily's thighs while her fingers carefully attempted a few different placements and rhythms until she found a configuration that made Emily gasp and buck up off the bed, grasping at whatever she could reach of Jo's clothes, her hair, the soft curve of her cheek. Apparently encouraged by the response, Jo grew bolder still, moving faster and kissing up, up, until at last she pressed a firm kiss to the apex of Emily's sex, sliding deeper inside as she did so, and Emily became nothing, truly nothing more than the experience of perfect pleasure.

The addition of a single flick of Jo's tongue was all it took to bring the crisis crashing and clenching through her, the blinding heights of it far more intense than anything she'd experienced in the name of easing tension or calming hysteria.

As she returned to earth, she could only pant and stare at the disheveled figure of Jo as she came back around to the proper side of Emily's skirts. Her collar was mussed, a waistcoat button slipped out of place, the heavy fall of her dark hair threatening escape at last. An enthralling vision in the guttering light of the candle, far more captivating than the photograph she'd sent. Less skin, perhaps, but more *sex* by a hundredfold as she wiped her fingers on a handkerchief she procured from her breast pocket, only to tuck it right back where she'd taken it from, a decidedly filthy move that left Emily breathless in addition to speechless.

Jo kissed her deeply, then went to the pitcher in the corner to pour for both of them, since someone had very *cordially* provided two glasses in this room that was ostensibly meant for one.

Emily took a sip, but it didn't cool her in the slightest, her tongue protesting its contact with something so bland when it could be exploring the fascinating person who stood before her.

Jo stroked Emily's face once she'd drained her own glass, kissing her softly and taking her chin in hand again.

"Are you satisfied, sweetheart?" Jo said softly, a teasing lilt to the pet name that left the seriousness of it a bit ambiguous. "Or shall I carry on?"

"I'll do the carrying on," Emily said, stumbling over the words in her eagerness. She must have looked a wanton wreck with her skirts bunched up to the waist and her chemise open wide, but that was alright. It was fitting, in fact, since Jo looked like something out of a pamphlet outlining the depraved dangers one's daughters could face in the streets of London. At last, Emily gave into the impulse she'd had since she first laid eyes on Jo, sliding a hand into her waistcoat to enjoy the heft of that gorgeous bosom. "Lie down, and I'll—"

Though Jo had closed her eyes and sighed in pleasure at Emily's touch, she cut things off with a shake of her head and a move just out of comfortable reach.

"Not tonight," she said.

Though she softened the rejection with a smile, still it stung. Self-conscious now, Emily pulled her shirtwaist back across her exposed chest. "No? But you were... My heavens, it was... It doesn't seem very fair, does it?"

Jo's grin widened. "I don't care about fair."

"But...but fair or not, I want to!"

"Oh, I know you do."

Simultaneously frustrated by this development and growing a bit sleepy and loose-limbed as her body accepted before her mind did that the dalliance was over, she stared up at Jo, wishing she could read that amused yet closed-off look on her face.

"Do you not like it to be done to you?" Emily asked carefully.

Jo laughed now and sat beside her, drawing her own jacket over Emily's shoulders as the reality of the chilly room began to override the warmth of their prior passion.

"I like it done to me," Jo said. "But not tonight."

"If not tonight," Emily whispered, a bit desperately, "when?"

With a little sigh and another smile, she pulled the jacket tighter and kissed the side of Emily's head.

"*Exactly.*"

Chapter Fourteen

Jo

Jo half-hoped for an argument. Though she was happy to bask in the power of bringing pleasure without promise of reciprocation, the fact that Emily Clarke of all people looked so desperate to give it was undoubtedly tempting. The taste of her clung to Jo's lips, the feel of her haunting Jo's hands even as she lit a few more candles to the purpose of hunting down whatever prim, pretty little nightdress Emily had brought along with her. As she walked toward the wardrobe where Emily had hung up her things, Jo was well aware of her own lingering arousal, fairly certainly she'd soaked right through her trousers.

But no argument came. All she got out of Emily was a grumpy, defeated yawn of nearly resentful satisfaction. Jo could live with that. She may not have come herself, but to tame Emily's fiery, bottled-up passions for the moment was good enough for now. She'd fetch Emily's nightdress, and Emily would put herself back together so she did not look so terribly, enticingly debauched over there, half-dressed on the mattress. When she did, the urgency in Jo's body would eventually dissipate.

And then, like the inevitable question at the end of one of

their letters, they'd have something left to answer to. Something to ensure that there was a loose end for them to tie up. For without some dangling, lingering thread, what excuse would someone like Emily and someone like Jo have for ever seeing each other again? Oh, this impulsively arranged evening had been lovely from start to finish, from punch and conversation, to the sharing of a meal with friends, to this rapturous conclusion. But a night was one thing. In the daylight, they had nothing in common. Did not live in the same city. Did not run in the same circles. Once Paul's baby was properly earthside, they would no longer even have that flimsy connection and excuse to see each other.

Emily wanted a brief tour of the decadent, maybe, but she'd given no indication that she was looking to change any of those things that separated them. She seemed to love her family and be loved in return, clueless though they were sometimes. Found satisfaction in her work, even if it was trying and full of stress. Had habits and convictions and communities that seemed likely to last the test of time. She was, perhaps, more suited to the life she already led than most people Jo met.

For just a moment, Jo wondered if Emily could take her on a tour of such grounded acceptance for a day or two, some reversed version of what they'd done for Emily tonight. But try as she might, she couldn't think of how to phrase the suggestion. The idea could not be flipped around so literally.

So instead, she would leave her desires untended in hopes of dragging this out to at least one more meeting, letting those beautiful eyes bore holes into her back as she gave up on the idea and rose to go through the sparse items that Emily had hung up in the wardrobe.

"What are you looking for?" Emily asked.

"Your bed clothes…" Jo stopped when she found a rather unlikely garment shuffled in with the simple petticoats and shirtwaists. She took the hanger out of the wardrobe and stared at the long, dangling arms and legs of a scratchy one-piece undergarment. "It's not this, is it?"

She turned to see Emily looking, no longer debauched and satisfied, but now *mortified* on the bed. She got up hastily, clutching the undone layers of Jo's jacket and her own day clothes to her chest with one hand as she snatched the hanger from Jo's grasp with the other.

"It's the most healthful attire for sleeping," she insisted as Jo began to laugh. "Economical, warm, breathable, and unisex."

"You know what else is economical, warm, breathable, and unisex?"

"If you're going to say 'nothing,' don't bother," said Emily, some of her primness returning, as if she weren't standing there with her tight bun slipping down the back of her head and her clothes practically falling to the floor. "Sleeping naked is *not* warm."

"Well, sure it's not. If you're sleeping alone."

The joke seemed to neither amuse nor offend Emily. Rather, it had her glancing a bit concernedly at the door.

"Speaking of, are you staying tonight?" she asked.

"Must be," Jo said carefully. "It's getting late, and I've already told Miss Withers to put me down for breakfast. There's no getting out of that commitment."

"But are you staying in here?" She clutched the union suit to her chest with the rest of her drooping clothes. "With me?"

"Do you want me to?"

"Yes," she said without any hesitation. "I want that very much."

Should that surprise her as much as it did? While their first meetings had been so tense, once the letters started, Emily had shown nothing more or less than pure interest in pursuing Jo's company. But still. A full night together was an intimacy she had only rarely granted. She strongly preferred to steal away for a smoke and bit of time to herself after a dalliance like this, and had never been fool enough to take up with someone who might demand more.

She hadn't expected Emily to be that demanding woman, but all that standoffishness, that icy independence the doctor emanated…it wasn't the truth of her. Not really. Oh, she could work hard and stand up for herself and all that; her strength wasn't a lie. But it wasn't as tough and spikey a strength as she let on. That affect was something she'd taken on to survive. Useful. Intriguing. But not really Emily.

Who exactly she was beneath that acquired exterior, Jo wasn't entirely sure yet. But she knew one thing to be true, as she examined the lines of that pretty, pointed face, the glow of candles flashing off her light eyes: whoever Emily was underneath wanted Jo to stay with her tonight.

And Jo, whoever exactly she was under almost two decades of shifting identities and ways of being that had thickened and clung to her like layers of different paints, wanted it too.

So, though it was a one-woman job, she helped Emily out of what remained of her clothes and watched with an incredulous smile as Emily buttoned herself into her very silly-looking pajamas with a simple robe on top. They each took their turn at the oh-so-sanitary tap down the hall—Emily sneaking and Jo keeping watch so no one caught her in those bed clothes— and when they returned, Jo let Emily help with her clothes as well, though she did not need it, either, stripping down to her supposedly less healthful but certainly more comfortable linen undervest and long drawers.

She also gave in to Emily's pleas to let her unpin Jo's hair, smooth it with the combs that Miss Withers had stocked the vanity with, and then run her fingers through it.

"Beautiful," Emily whispered as she caressed the dark waves

with something like wonder. "I admit, though, I'm rather surprised you don't cut it short."

Jo shrugged, closing her eyes and letting herself enjoy the feeling of being softly scratched along her scalp. "It's not important to me to pass as a bloke or anything like that," she said, too sleepy and comfortable to care that she probably wouldn't have said that in most other circumstances. "I did try that for a bit when I was younger. Didn't suit much better than the nunnery, to be honest. I'm happy like this."

"Makes sense," said Emily. She sounded like she meant the words, and that easy understanding of something that felt unspeakably complex made Jo shiver more than the caresses. "Shall I braid it for bed?"

"That would be quaint of you."

"Is quaint alright?"

Jo paused. She could not get a primer in security or steady living, maybe, but she'd given quaintness a try here and there for Vanessa's sake. It wasn't something that came naturally to her, but maybe with a little instruction from someone like Emily…

"I'm not sure," Jo said. "Why don't you give it a try and we'll find out?"

As Emily braided her hair down her back with firm, steady hands, Jo decided that yes: quaint was alright. So alright that she couldn't seem to resist this particular reciprocation the way she had the other, running her hand down her own thick braid, which was far tidier and more symmetrical than she usually managed herself, before switching their positions so she could fix the mess she'd made of Emily's tresses. Though, once Emily's hair was entirely freed, it was far frizzier and finer than Jo had suspected, and her unskilled brushing and braiding left a lot more of those frothy flyaways than she suspected would have escaped Emily's own ministrations.

But Emily didn't complain. They lay down together under

the covers on the small bed. It wasn't a roomy fit, but once Emily settled in with her head tucked under Jo's chin like she belonged there, it was comfortable enough. Jo stared at the ceiling for a while, listening as Emily's breathing evened out in slumber.

The last thought she remembered having before she woke up the next morning—alert, refreshed, and with Emily's beautiful, sleep-reddened face smiling at her—was that she was happy to be having this experience, but there was no way in hell she'd get a wink of sleep.

They got their quaintness put away before breakfast, braids swapped for buns, healthful bed clothes folded up in favor of regular attire. Jo always kept some spares over here for the next day if she stayed over, and was very glad to have done so today because when Emily put on the same navy skirt as yesterday with a fresh shirtwaist in pale yellow with little flowers on it and just the barest bit of cotton lace at the collar, Jo knew she'd catch hell if she accompanied such a beauty to breakfast look-ing like a complete beast herself.

The handful who had stayed over took the meal together, including Cordelia, who had fallen asleep in the parlor before adding herself to Miss Withers's list and thus was provided with some scolding along with her kippers (though of course, there were too many of those as it was).

"Are you with us for another day, my dear?" Miss Withers asked Emily once the stakes for an incorrect answer had been established.

"I'm afraid not." Emily was polite and stiff-spined again this morning in the company of others. While Jo had no problem squaring that with the side of her that had become so wan-tonly undone, it was harder to remember that this was the same woman who'd braided Jo's hair and then snuggled up tight to her side all night in silly pajamas. "In fact, delicious as this meal has been, I'm afraid I won't be able to linger over it. I have an appointment with a patient, and then a train to catch."

Though Jo had figured as much, some small part of her was disappointed to hear it said aloud. And was she imagining it, or was there a note of that same reluctance in Emily's voice?

"A shame," said Miss Withers, and Emily seemed taken aback by how sincerely she seemed to mean it. "Well, hopefully *some-one* will escort you to the station when the time comes."

The woman looked meaningfully at Jo.

"I'll take her!" she snapped as she slapped jam onto her toast. "I wasn't trying to be impolite yesterday by not meeting her; I simply didn't know when she was set to arrive."

"I appreciate that practicality, Jo," Emily said with an unde-niable sparkle in her eye. "As I would appreciate your company during my time in the city today, if it's not too much bother."

"You want me to come along with you to see Miss Garcia?" said Jo, surprised and a little panicked about the idea of Emily seeing her home or meeting Paul before they'd even come down from the glow of this meeting...

"I'm to meet her at this address," Emily went on, taking a folded paper covered in very dramatic handwriting and a lot of misspellings from her pocket. "It's where she lives with a few other actresses, as I understand it? I'm not familiar with the neighborhood, so was hoping you could show me the way."

Relief flooded Jo. Though Vanessa often found herself in Jo's home, she did not actually live there yet, in spite of the going assumption that she and her child would wind up there eventually.

"So?" Emily asked. "Is it too much of a bother?"

"It's a bit of a bother," Jo said with a sparkle of her own, one that came with a stupid smile that wasn't missed by the others. "But not too much."

★ ★ ★

When they stepped outside onto Miss Withers's stoop, Jo glared up at the scatter of clouds, trying to determine if rain seemed likely, because rain would be positively miserable in a chill like this. She should have brought her warmer coat...

Her moody musings were interrupted as Emily stepped up beside her, pulling her gloves on and staring out at the residential street that stretched to either side of them, alive with well-dressed foot traffic and a few clopping coaches. Emily took in a deep breath of the autumn air, seeming happy to ignore how tainted it was by coal smoke, horse dung, and that whiff off the Thames that drifted this way when the wind blew just so. In fact, she smiled wider than Jo had seen yet, even as her cheeks went pink from cold.

"To the actresses' house, then," Emily said. "That will make for a lovely constitutional on a day like today, don't you think? We have just enough time for it."

Jo had not been thinking that. In fact, Jo had been thinking of heading out to the main thoroughfare and flagging down a hackney because it looked like rain. But before she could bring herself to be such a damper on Emily's mood, Emily had already taken her by the arm and led her down the stairs to the street below.

It was odd to walk arm in arm like perfectly appropriate lady friends who had only ever undressed one another for a respectable reason like irrationally placed buttons. But Emily didn't seem to think much of it, staying close to Jo as she strode the streets of London in her clacking boots. And it garnered Jo no more odd looks than usual, though she never did get as many of those as she'd once assumed she would. Miss Withers was already known for having "curious sorts always coming and going," and once they got to the busier roads, it was the bloody West End, after all: one couldn't turn their head without finding a dozen fashions more striking, actors more outrageous, or hawked headlines of greater interest than a couple of drably dressed women like themselves, trousers or no.

Jo had been to Vanessa's boarding house only once before, accepting an invitation to further her helpful, sisterly appearance. It was a pretty nice place compared to the other artists' housing arrangements she'd seen over the years, fairly comparable and not too far away from the home she and Paul had first shared when they left their parish neighborhood to start fresh—the biggest difference being the smaller number of books and larger number of women walking round in stockings and chemises.

But as they went up to the door ("Watch that step there, Emily, it wobbles something dreadful") she got the impression that it wasn't a place Emily was thrilled by.

"What is it?" Jo asked, looking around and trying to figure out what had Emily looking so grim all of a sudden. It was a rougher neighborhood than Miss Withers's, but decent enough compared to The Curious Fox.

Emily shook her head politely. "Nothing."

They were let in by one of Vanessa's fellow actresses. Jo happened to know this woman was a real beauty on the stage, but hadn't gotten there yet for the day, her hair in curlers with a scrap of stained fabric tied over it, her slim body wrapped in a dressing gown of similar homeliness.

"Jo, innit?" the woman said. She eyed Emily and her doctoring bag suspiciously. "And 'oo's this?"

"My name is Dr. Emily Clarke," she said. "Here to see Miss Vanessa Garcia. We have an appointment."

"Right." The actress took a cigarette case from where she'd nestled it in her bosom. "Good for you, you know. Doctoring an' all that. And good fer 'Nessa too—she needs it."

"Has she been unwell again?" Emily asked.

The actress got her cigarette out. "Yeah. She's in her room. Come on, I'll take you up."

They went inside the musty foyer with its stained wallpaper nearly overtaken by theatrical posters. Jo put her hands awkwardly in her pockets. "I suppose I'll wait down here,"

Emily nodded, watching with very measured curiosity as the actress lit her vogue and started up the stairs. Emily followed, and smoke cascaded down behind them like they were vanishing into an entirely different world.

After the appointment, Emily rejoined Jo outside. The hint of possible poor weather this morning had fled. After the close, dark atmosphere of the boarding house, the air on the street seemed almost uncannily crisp for this side of London.

"How did it go?" Jo asked.

Emily was quiet as they headed back toward Miss Withers's home. They'd find lunch over there—something suitably decadent to close out the visit—then gather the rest of Emily's things before heading to Waterloo Station.

"I'd say it's mostly good news. In the long run, anyway," Emily said carefully. "She said I could tell you, so I suppose I will: the baby is growing as expected in spite of Miss Garcia's illness, and while she is weak, her vital signs are within a range we can work with. In light of that, along with a few other things perhaps more technical than you need to worry yourself over, I think I've figured out why she's been so ill, and why it has been an on-and-off problem rather than straight through."

Having gotten attached to the woman and her child in spite of herself, Jo's stomach clenched nervously.

"Will she be alright?"

"She will..." Emily glanced back over her shoulder toward the place they'd just left. "So long as she gets out of that house as soon as possible. At the very least, before the baby is expected to breathe in all that mold and smoke. Her symptoms line up with more time spent there, and it's not difficult to see why."

Emily had called it good news, but to Jo, it felt like a lot of pressure to remedy something that Emily probably didn't realize Jo was involved in.

"Are you sure?" Jo asked, silently begging whatever unlucky God was tasked with listening to her that Emily was mistaken. "It's not so different from anywhere people like us might be living in this city. I've lived in places like that for years, no worse for wear."

Emily looked skeptical. "Assuming you're genuinely no worse for wear—which I doubt—you did not live in those places as a first-time mother over forty, working a very physical job and apparently more sensitive to environmental hazards than the average. You may think it was fine for you, but I can tell you with full certainty that it is *not* good for her. And for her child, well…" Emily grew grimmer than ever before. "Did you know one of her housemates had a child last year?"

"She did mention something about her friend taking on childbed tasks when they came up." The chill in Emily's demeanor was contagious, prickling the back of her neck as she realized she'd seen no sign of a child in the house. "Did…did the housemate move out, then?"

Emily shook her head. "No."

The chill deepened nearly to a shiver. Well *fuck.*

"The good news, of course, is that if I'm right, this is easily remedied," Emily said, almost like she was reassuring herself more than Jo. "She's not alone in the world. She has the baby's father, and you, of course. And it sounds as if the two of you moved on to a healthier place. I know that independence is of utmost importance to Miss Garcia, but Jo, you really must encourage her to take my advice and accept better arrangements from you."

Emily said this so straightforwardly that Jo hardly knew what to do with it. Did she really think it was so simple?

Though, even if it wasn't, did Jo have the luxury anymore of making it so complicated?

"I'll see what I can do," she muttered.

The delicious lunch they took was helpful in resetting their spirits, and they left the tea house full-up with delicacies and arm-in-arm like schoolgirls again. Decadence mixed with quaintness; there was something very special and warming about it in the cool breeze that had Jo walking a little slower than she usually would have as they went back to Miss Withers's to collect Emily's luggage.

"Oh, lovely!" Emily squeezed her arm a bit tighter as they passed by yet another newspaper stand. It looked quite the same as all the other newspaper stands they'd been wandering by all day, but apparently not. While nothing about Emily could ever quite be described as *girlish* or *gushingly enthusiastic*, she came close to it as she dragged Jo over to where a few of the West End's more liberal and serious papers had been laid out. "Give me a moment, if you don't mind. I should like to bring a few of these back to my father."

"Really?" Jo asked, surprised.

"He loves this one. And this," said Emily as she perused the selection. "We both do."

"No, I meant… Didn't you come here to get away from him?"

Emily gave her a quizzical look. "I am very irritated with him, and yes, I needed a bit of a break. But everything doesn't have to be perfect for me to bring him a few of his favorite periodicals, does it? Who knows? Maybe it will even pave the way for a conversation we've been putting off."

Jo crossed her arms, trying not to think of the conversation *she'd* been putting off. Or, more accurately, fighting off. She could happily irritate Paul until the end of time, but she could not put Miss Garcia and her baby in danger. There was nothing for it, save for figuring out how to make the situation palatable for everyone.

She watched Emily scan headlines and volley questions at the young seller that he did not know the answers to for a bit, but The Strand offered a lot of distractions, and without the warmth of Emily on her arm, Jo needed them. She wandered over to a girl who was selling little bundles of dried strawflowers, and a nearby cart for some paper cups of coffee. When she brought her purchases back to the newspaper stand, Emily was just gathering her own up. She looked as flushed and shining with her fresh stack of political news as some ladies looked coming out of a hat shop with a particularly beautiful find.

"Thank you for being patient," she said. "I am always stunned by the sheer number of informational sources a single city can put out. It's incredible."

"Not a problem. I kept busy."

Jo held out one of the cups and the strawflowers, taking the papers herself so that Emily was not awkwardly overburdened. Emily pursed her lips again at the rearrangement, though there seemed to be a smile she was pursing them over. She covered her obvious pleasure with the flowers, as if she were trying to breathe in any lingering hint of scent in their crunchy, dried petals.

"Decadent nonsense," she muttered happily.

"I thought it was rather quaint." Jo offered her arm once more. "Either way, there's plenty more where that came from. That is, if you'd like to see me again next time you're here."

Emily took a few quiet steps, seeming satisfyingly lost in flowers and papers and the steam off her hot coffee cup.

"Well, I *will* need to come back soon to check on Miss Garcia, won't I?" she said, losing her fight with that little smile at last. "Not to mention a few other loose ends you and I still need to tie up."

Miss Withers was at her piano again when they arrived. While Emily was upstairs preparing herself for travel and packing her things in a way she assured Jo was "specific and requiring no assistance," Jo stood by with her hands in her pockets and listened.

With the cheerful tune dancing in her ears, she peered around at the well-swept floors, the dust-free surfaces, the prettily papered walls that were clean and dry even up into the shadowy corners. There was no smell of damp in here, and smoking kept strictly to the gents' parlor or God help you. It was a nice place. Sanitary and safe.

"Miss Withers—"

"Joey," she snapped over the sound her music, "if you're going to stand around and do nothing, please turn pages for me."

Jo obliged. After a moment, she raised her voice over the swell of notes again. "Miss Withers, I have a question." Miss Withers did not respond, so she went on. "Are you in a position to take in strays on a semi-permanent basis?"

Through a crescendo, and back down. Miss Withers finally spoke: "Joey, dear, you know any of my girls may consider my home their own."

Jo rolled her eyes at the word *girls* coming from someone who was her elder by less than a decade. But Miss Withers would probably call her own mum a *girl* if the occasion arose. Jo had the impression she'd decided to become an old maid around the age of fifteen, adjusted her speech and dress accordingly, and just never looked back.

"What if she wasn't exactly one of yours?" Jo asked. God, this was a desperate ploy. She felt the shame of it deep in her belly. She had no business doing this, trying to shunt Vanessa off to someone else, just so Jo could hang on to this blissfully ambivalent state for however long she could get away with it.

"Is Dr. Clarke facing difficulties that were not apparent to me?"

"No, not her."

Miss Withers looked up sharply. Jo doubted she knew who Jo meant, but she had certainly sniffed out that Jo was up to no good.

"Society members are welcome to a room anytime," she said. "Should a society member have a special friend in need, I might be able to offer something, if the circumstances were right. So tell me, Jo. Are the circumstances right?"

She was so suspicious and scolding that some old part of Jo that was scared of nuns couldn't help but confess her guilt for even considering this idea: "No, ma'am. They're not."

"That's what I thought." Slowly and with great relish, she finished her piece. In the silence that followed, she added, "But you, dear, are welcome anytime, so long as you give the appropriate notice."

It should have been a comfort, to know she had somewhere else to go in the event she got kicked out onto her arse.

But she wasn't being kicked out onto her arse. As much as she wanted to keep denying it until the end of time, watching Emily pick out newspapers for her father even though they weren't getting along had shifted something in her brain. Something very annoying. Something that forced her to realize that it was her own insistence on seeing her situation as black-and-white that was making all of them miserable.

Emily returned in her soot-gray traveling dress, all her wisps pinned severely up beneath her simple, unadorned hat, the only hint of color coming from the muted petals of the dried bouquet clutched in her hand. When she smiled at Jo from the foot of the stairs, however, she might as well have been decked in crystalline prisms; the sight of her hit Jo's eye like a flash of brilliantly broken light.

"Ready?" Emily asked.

Jo offered her arm and off they went.

"Emily?" she asked when they were nearly at the station.

"Yes?"

"Would you mind if I slipped just one of those flowers out of the bouquet and took it with me?"

"Of course not, there's far too many to begin with," said Emily, absolutely pragmatic as she held it out for Jo to pluck one of the strawflowers from the ribbon that held them together. "What for?"

"As you said, a little something nice might pave the way for conversations one has been putting off."

"Ah, so you have one as well?"

"Seems I do."

"Well, dear Jo," she said with another of those smiles that had Jo wondering how she'd ever thought this woman dull. "Shall we make a pact, then? To have our conversations, and return to each other's arms with a lighter load upon our backs next time?"

Jo felt how her own face was uncomfortably torn between a grin and a grimace. "I see. Now that your tour of decadence is over, you're going back to being responsible, and dragging me along with you."

"Perhaps," she said with a little shrug and a kiss pressed to Jo's cheek that probably looked very respectable to any outsider who could not feel its heat. "If you'll come with me."

And before Jo could work out, yet again, whether that had been a purposeful innuendo, Emily said, "Farewell, Joey. Write to me until next we meet, will you?" then turned in a swish of gray wool and was lost to the crowd.

Chapter Fifteen

Emily

It was just on the edge of too cold to take supper in the garden, but Papa agreed to it anyway. Though all Emily wanted to do was escape to her study, dreaming about the beautiful time she'd shared with Jo and fantasizing about the next, she'd made a deal with her dear new friend. The respite from work, the wickedness, the decadence—they'd strengthened her more than she'd realized was possible. After such an intense instance of connection, it seemed silly to not just get the drudgery of this discussion over with.

Wrapped in blankets against the chill, she and her father sipped soup and buttered bread. Conversation was sparse, to begin with. She updated him on Miss Garcia's condition and asked his opinion on her advice to change living arrangements ("Absolutely. You're spot on, my dear, well done!"). He, on the other hand, updated her on the shift he'd covered for her, mournfully confessing another failed attempt to negotiate better pay from the founders ("They say 'it's fair' no matter how many times I explain otherwise, as if simply saying it over and over makes it true! I swear, if it wasn't lives on the line I'd never step foot in that place when they call on me.")

At last, though, as they were mopping up the last bits of boiled vegetables and onion broth from their bowls, Emily was ready.

Apparently, however, Papa was ready for something too, because they began speaking at the same time:

"Papa, there's something I'd like—"

"I've had a letter from your brother while you were away," he said, voice heavy enough to freeze the rest of the words in Emily's throat. While Papa had probably assumed Emily was staying with Noah, she actually had not seen him at all while she was in London.

"Oh," she said as casually as she could. "When did he send it?"

"Dated before your departure" (*thank God*) "but I wish it had arrived before you left, so we could have discussed it ahead of time."

A different worry ghosted across her mind. "Is he alright?"

"Oh, he's fine," Papa said quickly. "But reasonably disappointed with me, I'm afraid. And he informed me that you know what he's disappointed about."

Emily blinked, incredulous. Did he mean that Noah had actually taken the initiative to confront Papa's lack of equity?

"He…he wrote you? About the…about your…" She didn't know how to say it. *Your gout. Your retirement. Your silence.* Her hands made a motion, vague and uncomfortable.

"He said the two of you discussed it last time you were in town, and that he was extremely shocked to learn I had not shared the same information with you as I had with him. Having not heard from either of us on the subject in several weeks, he wanted to make sure I knew what he'd told you, and his feelings on the matter of my reticence." Papa winced. "His very strong feelings."

Emily drew the blanket tighter around her shoulders, staring over the darkening garden and trying not to smile. So Noah *was* capable of stepping into the void she'd left open. She'd forgone a responsibility, forgone it so thoroughly that she'd been drinking punch and rolling around with a scandal of a woman instead, and somehow the job had gotten done without her.

"I'm sure you had your reasons for keeping it from me," she said at last, trying to make sure Papa didn't notice how pleased she was.

"I did," Papa said. "Admittedly, they were not very good."

"What were they?"

"I wanted to wait," he said carefully, "until you'd built your own foundation. I know medicine has been tricky enough for you as it is, without the added pressure of a looming yet uncertain deadline. I knew that Noah would take the information and begin strategizing, as he should. I feared that you, however—"

"Would panic?" Emily concluded in a tone that showed what she thought of that unfair assumption. "Would break under the pressure? Flail about and make matters worse?"

"Flail about? You?" Papa shook his head and laughed. He poured more chilly tea for both of them. "Certainly not. It's your practicality I feared. I thought that if you looked at your professional circumstances and weighed them against our current security and the future needs of our household, you'd determine that your career wasn't worth building. That you'd let them shunt you into a nurse's role, just to ensure better payment. Or worse, out of the field entirely because you'd say it was the correct choice, that you'd do better financially as a tutor or governess. And when you believe you are correct, there is no arguing with you, is there? I wanted to give you a little more time to change the calculus before you made any over-cautious decisions that could not be unmade."

She'd imagined many reasons for Papa's silence. This was not one of them. And it stung, actually, stung worse than her assumption that it had been a matter of what was owed to a son over a daughter. That was an everyday indignity. But the hard truth that she was always overly quick to act in the most practical fashion possible… It was…well, unfortunately, it was completely true.

"Whatever your reasoning, you still should have told me outright," she said, her voice a match for the cool night air.

"I don't deny it." He looked at her sideways. "But on the other hand, I'm shocked to have not gotten a good scolding already. I knew Noah might mention it to you before I did, and figured that if it happened, you would have laid right into me. But it's been weeks, now, and not a word from you. It concerns me."

"I wanted to see if Noah would bother himself with family matters for once," she said with a detached air she didn't feel. "It was right of him to call you out. I'm very pleased to see that he will do what's right, occasionally."

Papa glanced at Noah's debris-covered chair as if it might let him stare into his son's sitting room. "Is that really the only reason you didn't bring it up? It's not like you give him the opportunity to tackle your many responsibilities. If his lack of help was such a concern, one might think you'd have given him a chance or two before this. Or. You know. *Asked* for help."

The statement fell like an accusation. Was he saying that Noah had never stepped up for her, had never taken responsibility for anything in the household until this moment, simply because she'd never relaxed long enough to give him an opportunity?

"I've had other things on my mind." Emily shrugged, not quite ready to look that possibility full in the face.

"Those letters from London?"

"Perhaps."

He pulled his blanket tighter over his shoulders. "Tell me, Emily, how was your brother these past few days?"

Oh dear. Emily had already lied about this dalliance once. If she did it again, she would be forced to carry that dishonesty further, perhaps further than she wanted to. Jo would become wrapped in secrets and lies that might prove difficult, should their friendship continue to a point where she wanted everyone to meet each other.

Was that silly, to worry about such a thing? Part of her thought it was, but another, more steady and certain part, had a sense that it might come to matter. And an especially hopeful part that had turned out to be romantic after all was already making plans for it.

So, she straightened her shoulders. Though her voice trembled, she managed the truth: "I didn't see him."

Papa nodded like he'd known this from the beginning.

"The letters," he went on. "Are you ready to tell me if they're from anyone of particular significance?"

"They are," she admitted, her face very warm and her hands icy cold where she'd tucked them between her crossed thighs for warmth.

"I hope," Papa went on very tensely, "that your new understanding of our finances isn't pushing you toward an even more desperate move than nursing."

A more desperate move than nursing... Did he mean *marriage*? Is that where he thought she'd been this weekend? Meeting up with some gent she'd been writing to, looking for her future security down that avenue?

God, she was tired. She rubbed her eyes, wishing that the

meaning of Papa's words could have escaped her. "I'm not thinking of marrying anyone, Papa," she said heavily.

He looked relieved. She wondered, not for the first time, if he was the only father on the planet who preferred his children to live as a deviant bachelor at increasing risk of legal trouble and a grim spinster whose future security would always be partially his problem. Of course, it was probably just relief that neither of them would suffer the marital fate that he and Mother did, but his worries had proven convenient in this one way.

Convenient for her, perhaps, but with her heart a bit fuller from her time with Jo and her patience restored by the knowledge that Noah wouldn't actually let everything fall apart in her absence, she found something else under all her resentments and frustrations.

She found sadness for him. And beside it, not a little concern.

"Papa." Emily adjusted her blanket so it fell like an overly thick shawl. "Papa, we can't go on like this. You know we can't."

"What do you mean?"

"I mean…this!" She rattled Noah's chair where it sat beside her. "This. All of this. Noah's chair still sitting in the garden though he's lived in London for years. Mother's sewing basket and all her other things still right where she left them after thirty—"

"Emily," he snapped, looking about as if she'd started a very inappropriate line of discussion. "Please, you don't—"

"Understand? Of course I understand!" Her voice broke into something slightly more laugh than sob, but not by much. "I have lived it my whole life. There is nothing I understand better. I understand that you have a beautiful home, children to be proud of, a noble profession, and a lovely companion in the form of Mme. Baptiste. You have friends, and meaning, and… and guinea pigs!" She waved toward the hutch, where the creatures had retired for the evening as they always did, predictable and sweet as everything else in this life she was describing. "And I know that you haven't enjoyed a minute of it—won't let any of us enjoy a minute of it—because it's not what you hoped it would be.

"Do you really think this obsession with how you wish things were is going to improve when you retire and find yourself here, all day, without the distraction of your work? Money is a concern. Yes. But we're a very resourceful pair who are part of a very generous community. We will find a way to get by. But Papa, the reason Noah does not visit is because there isn't room for him between you and me and all the ghosts you keep. And when you retire, I fear we'll find there isn't room for the two of us, either. As you well know, we must start thinking of that future now, before we are faced with it unprepared."

Emily, of course, wished her mother had lived, had known Emily and loved her and been there through her life as more than someone else's memory. But right now, she wished it for a more generous reason: so her father would not have had to be so alone in his grief.

"I know you wish we could mourn her properly with you, Papa," she said. "But the sight of a dusty sewing basket won't help us know her. We want you to tell us stories of her. Explain the ways we look like her. Let our understanding of who she was grow with us and move with us as we live our lives. As it is, we feel trapped in a past our very existence destroyed—"

"You didn't destroy—"

"Intellectually, I know that," Emily said carefully. "Perhaps Noah does too. But it certainly feels like it, sometimes. Don't you see how we would look around this place and wonder if it would be a better one if we'd never arrived at all?"

He went quiet for a while after that, and she let him. They sipped their cold tea and looked at the moon. She didn't think he would ever respond, had lapsed into either a sadness or anger too thick to extract himself from as the truth—the most paramount of truths she'd ever spoken—continued to echo through the garden on the wings of its owls and the year's last crickets.

Just as she was gathering herself up to bring the tray inside, he said, with quiet kindness, "I want the house to support you and your brother as you are now." He looked up at her, his round, familiar face looking exceptionally tired and lined in the moonlight. "But Emily, my dear, I don't really know how. The script for my situation was to find a new wife. That's what a man does, and maybe I should have done it. But I could not bear it, and the longer I avoided it, the harder it got. I have no guidance for what to do in this situation. How to fix what I've done. To all of us."

He sounded a touch hopeless, but Emily was not.

"We are very resourceful," she said again, gathering up the tea tray and smiling softly. "I do think we will figure it out, if we dedicate ourselves to the task."

Chapter Sixteen

Jo

Princess Emily,

I apologize for the delay in this letter. I wanted to start it the second I returned home from walking you to the station, but didn't have anything to say yet. Being your tutor in decadence was such a joy and an honor that I wanted to have something to show for it when I wrote you. Proof that I too might have learned something from your company. Now that I've got it (and a sheaf of my preferred paper at last), I can share it with you.

I have had the conversation I was putting off, due entirely to you. It was regarding Miss Garcia's living situation, and your expert opinion on the matter of her environment left no more room for argument. I'm happy to tell you (assuming she hasn't yet) that she will make the switch when the run of her latest show concludes. With her condition growing noticeable, she won't be able to secure another role at that point anyway, and will be in a good position for a change. Meanwhile, my husband is preparing the home for this next phase of his life.

All that aside for a moment, will you be in London again soon, for an appointment or one of those bluestocking talks? They're not *my usual entertainment, but I'd happily bore myself senseless if it meant a little decadence with you once we'd left the coffee house.*

With affection and the strawflower I owe you,
Jo

Jo finished up her letter upon an uncannily tidy oak desk. She folded the crumbling strawflower she'd borrowed into the envelope. Then she carefully tucked the lot into the envelope and sealed the parcel with warmed wax. While investigation of the desk had revealed two metal emblems to personalize the seal, Jo opted to leave the red blob as it was. These initials belonged to Miss Withers and the society house. It didn't seem appropriate to claim the insignia, since she was no more or less than *one of the girls*, taking up a room and a space at the dinner table.

It didn't seem right to keep the flower, either. The quaint novelty of it had indeed smoothed the beginning of her conversation with Paul, but once she told him she didn't feel there was room for all of them, and that she'd be getting out of their way at last, he didn't think the flower was particularly funny anymore.

So yeah. Jo didn't need the flower. And with Paul furious that Jo was acting like a prat, Vanessa's fate still uncertain, and Miss Withers's looks of pity all weighing on her, she wanted to give any spare flower—indeed, flowers she couldn't spare; flowers she'd grown or gone broke buying; flowers she'd stolen from rich wankers' gardens; every bloody flower in England—to the beautiful woman who'd asked her to write letters until next they met.

Chapter Seventeen

Emily

The months that followed were lovely for Emily.

Not perfect, of course. The hospital was unchanged, the founders as hypocritically out of touch as usual and the troublesome nurse more vindictive than ever when she heard Emily had been taken seriously enough to secure a private patient.

But home was something else entirely. Emily and her father cleaned the place from top to bottom. Not too quickly. Not too drastically. But really scrubbing out some of the lingering dust balls, making Noah's bedroom fit for more generic company, and finding more dignified places to display or store Mother's things.

"To be honest," Papa said with a guilty sigh as he picked up the old sewing basket that had driven Noah to the edge of his patience, "she wouldn't have left it there."

"Really?" Emily blurted, shocked. "I thought that was its dedicated place!"

"No, she was like you. An exceptionally tidy woman through most of her life. She kept this in the cupboard next to the piano so it would be nearby, but not unsightly. It was just that carrying twins made her charmingly lazy those last weeks of it, and she didn't want to bother with even the few steps back and forth."

Working on the place at last, Papa proved to be full of these sweet little stories. It seemed to do him good to speak them at last, and it certainly did Emily good to hear them.

In the evenings, she spent a lot of time writing letters. Some were to her brother, updating him on the progress they'd made and the stories she'd heard. He seemed to like them too, and had dropped a few hints that he might consider a visit, to see if what she said about the state of their cottage was true.

The other letters, of course, were to the increasingly dear Miss Jo.

As time went on, that small and hopeful voice within her proved to be a wise one indeed. Their letters continued to sparkle and soothe, punctuated by several more visits to London, occasionally even at times when she did not have an appointment with her patient or plans with her community. When she could spare the time, she went just for Jo, just to see her for lunch or a walk, to be decadent together, and quaint together, before their lives called them back.

With both these aspects of her life growing so wonderfully full, she was struck by a strong desire to combine them at last. As her father had been so generous with his speech now that it was not weighed down with despair, she too had become more open, admitting to him the nature of her companion. She was not worried about his reaction being negative, but it was actually far more positive than she'd dared to dream.

And so, well…she found herself daring to dream a little more.

November fell more freezing than bracing, and with it came the London Society for Spiritual Freedom's talk on criticisms of the nativity narrative. Papa had been so looking forward to this one that not even the effect of the chill on his joints could keep him home this time.

While Emily doubted that talks on biblical criticism were the holiday festivities that Jo would choose for herself, it promised to be a lighter lecture than most of the others and therefore her best opportunity to see these two lights of her life—her family and her lover—meet and be joined in friendship at last.

Jo agreed. The acceptance was so thrilling that Emily was eager to the point of ridiculous when the time came to catch the train. She hurried Papa along all morning until they arrived at the station dreadfully early.

"I'm so sorry," she said as they watched the slow progress of the clock behind the station counter, not obstructed by the movements of too many passengers, since Godalming Station had only one line and no one with any sense was here for their departure yet.

Papa smiled and shook his head. "It's just good to know that there's somewhere you wish to be so eagerly."

Even Rochelle Baptiste came along, unable to resist Emily's insistence that everyone even close to being a member of the family be together for this holiday event. She joined them at the station at a more reasonable time, though, closer to when the rest of the passengers were showing up with valises, trunks, and children in tow. Rochelle kissed their cheeks and settled her comparatively excessive luggage with the attendants. Aggressively *French* as she always appeared, as if afraid Farncombe's very *English* nonconformist community might forget who she really was, her traveling clothes were lacier, lighter, and much harder to beat soot out of than they ought to have been. It made Emily smile, and think suddenly of Miss Garcia. There were some charming similarities between the two. Rochelle had been a close companion of her father for many years now—around at the holidays and even permitted to use Noah's chair when she visited. She had never married into the Clarke family but was certainly part of it. Likewise, Miss Garcia, with her strange and uncomfortable connection with Mr. Smith, was not technically Jo's family but still held a certain place in the extended part of it. She liked the thought that Jo would finally meet the more showy, ostentatious little corner of her community after Emily had spent so much time with Jo's actress.

Emily boarded the train with her mind full of these sentimental dreams: of the happier but still quiet cottage suddenly filled with all manner of odd, unofficial relations, sipping lemonade in the garden and telling Papa to give his talk of greens and guinea pigs a rest.

The idea was almost unbearably exciting, so Emily tried to distract herself with a decidedly decadent gift Jo had sent along recently—a morally and intellectually useless adventure story that she'd rebound to look like it was a philosophical treatise.

The train chugged to a stop at Waterloo Station, so much more packed and cavernous than the humble one they'd come from. Once they'd made it off the platform with their luggage cart, Emily scanned the crowd. Though they weren't the most outlandish pair she'd seen in a London train station, Jo and Noah still weren't hard to spot, standing near a coffee cart in their daring clothes, passing a cigarette between them and laughing at some shared joke like the friends Emily sometimes forgot they were.

She felt a ruffle of jealousy, but it didn't last long. She and Jo actually had jokes of their own now, didn't they? Cordial meetings. Women's medical college. The rebound novel. Something more than mere excitement was growing in Emily's chest. It had her footsteps close to scurrying as she pushed the cart toward them.

As soon as Jo spotted her, she dropped the cigarette and stamped on it while Noah gaped like she'd crushed a small animal beneath her boot. Jo didn't notice his dismay; her dark eyes and happy smile were all Emily's. Emily wanted to leave the cart in the middle of everything, sprint the remaining distance, and throw herself into a swoony embrace worthy of the rebound dime novel in her bag. She did not do that, because she did not really do those sorts of things, but she had her own version: steering the cart too fast for Papa and Rochelle to keep up, nudging it into Noah's care, and indulging in a deliciously soft embrace that warmed through the chill of the platform as it warmed her dreams. When Jo kissed her, quick and without shame like a European, Emily flushed with all the secret meanings that such a seemingly innocent gesture really meant between them.

Jo reluctantly released Emily, and shoved her gloved hands into the spacious pockets of her gentleman's coat. "Glad you're here."

Emily grinned. "Even though I'm dragging you to a talk on biblical criticism?"

"The Bible criticizes me enough." Jo shrugged. "It's well past time I settled the score."

"Oh, *dio mio*," said Noah as he adjusted the askew luggage. "*This* is going to be an interesting weekend, isn't it?"

"Is David joining us tomorrow?" Emily asked.

"We'll see. He's been…well, you know, he's been very tired. It's been a difficult week. We'll see if he's feeling up to it."

She drew breath to scold Noah for his characteristic selfishness, still putting off the country respite that David needed just because he preferred to be in the city. But she stopped herself. His recent letters indicated that he was softening on that, now that changes had been made to the house he'd grown up in. If she did not scold or put undue pressure on him, would he do as he did before? Would he step up and take care of something practical and familial, even if it took him a little longer than Emily would have liked?

"I'm very sorry to hear that," said Emily simply. "If it's of any help, please tell him that I treasure his place in our family, and would be happy to help in whatever way I can to ensure he is up to coming along."

Noah looked stunned, gaping for words he couldn't find. The appearance of Papa and Rochelle saved him. Emily, a bit guilty over having left the older pair chasing her dust across the crowded platform, let Noah alone to process her words while she tended to the thing she'd been looking forward to for weeks now:

Introductions.

"Jo, my dear Jo," she said, unable to keep the excitement from her voice as she took the other woman's hand. "I am so pleased to introduce you to my father, Dr. Phillip Clarke," she said, grinning a little wildly. "And this is my family friend, and my father's—"

"My dear traveling companion, Madame Rochelle Baptiste," Papa interrupted as pleasantly as possible, as if he didn't trust his children not to sneak their own opinions into the introduction.

Emily didn't appreciate the lack of decorum, but Jo seemed buoyed by it, forgoing politeness to extend her hand and say, "Miss Jo Smith. A pleasure, Dr. Clarke. Madame Baptiste."

Though it rankled Emily a bit that everyone had gone off-script, Papa and Rochelle looked duly impressed by Jo's lack of conformity, and Jo seemed satisfied by theirs as well. And as the odd-looking group of them left the station in search of a carriage, Emily felt like her train-station daydreams were coming true before her eyes. Rochelle and Jo's presence thickened the Clarkes' familial bonds like a hearty starch added to fresh ointment. She felt that if only they could get David to come along tomorrow, their mother's ghost could put her feet up and relax at last, content that the rest of them would hold together well enough on their own.

★ ★ ★

While Papa and Rochelle were staying at their usual inn near the West End's Unitarian meeting house, Emily put her name down with great finality at Miss Withers's for two nights and several meals. Her valise was feeling *awfully* heavy, so she had Jo help her get it into her room, made up all tidy and perfect once again with two cups beside the water pitcher.

"No escape now, is there?" said Jo, once she'd tossed the valise on the bed and pinned Emily up tight against the blue-papered wall. She kissed her deeply and indulgently for just long enough to chase the chill of the streets from both their bodies. Their lunches and walks had been so lovely, but it had been far too long since they'd had this. Emily's head spun. Her hands traced and grabbed and slid into back pockets as Jo's lips moved down her jaw, Jo's fingers pushing at the high neck of her blouse, looking for more skin to nip and nose at. "You've told Miss Withers you'll be here for at least three separate meals. You're contracted into my clutches, now."

Jo's clutches were nothing to complain about, so Emily accepted them quite willingly, kissing, caressing, and downright reveling in the hot physicality, deliciously human after weeks of nothing but the touch of her paper and ink.

Jo was just getting down to the one-woman job that was the removal of Emily's traveling clothes, when the chime of the grandfather clock downstairs made Emily start.

"Oh heavens," she gasped, stealing her buttons back from Jo's eager fingers and putting them to rights. "Stop it. I've got an appointment with Miss Garcia coming up first on the agenda today, and you're going to make me late."

"She and I were late meeting you the first time." Jo went for the bottom button of Emily's jacket instead, efficiently undoing Emily's rebuttoning as it occurred. "It's only fair."

Emily swatted her hands away in a giggling battle that ended in Jo grabbing her chin again in that delightfully rough way and planting a kiss to Emily's mouth. Emily pulled away more slowly than she should have. "I don't care about fair. I care about correct. A little anticipation will make it all the more pleasurable when we get back to it. There's scholarship on this, you know."

Jo cocked a dark brow. "Really?"

"Oh yes. A month or so in between dalliances is actually recommended for the greatest delight in the long run. We might even benefit from a longer hiatus, since we don't have the pressure of populating the Earth while we're at it."

It seemed to take Jo a second to realize Emily was kidding, but when she did, she grabbed Emily's chin again and gave her a smiling, aggressive kiss that made Emily agree that even one more night was probably too long a wait.

"Alright," Emily said. "Let's go."

Jo blinked. "Let's? You mean both of us?"

"Well, of course," Emily said. "It's your house we're going to, isn't it? She's finally moved in, and thank goodness for that!"

"Um, Emily…" Jo scratched the back of her neck awkwardly. "Look, I don't think—"

"Is there a problem?"

Jo seemed to think that over for a bit, glancing around the room until her eyes settled on the fine little clock that was hung beside the wardrobe. "N-no, actually. It's fine. I'll escort you there, to make sure you can find the place, and we'll make it quick."

"Make it quick? Why?"

Jo tugged gently at the hem of her jacket, the concern on her face returning to a devious smile. "I think you know why, Princess."

They made their way up the slightly-too-treacherous staircase to Jo and Mr. Smith's rooms.

"Will Mr. Smith be here?"

"I think not," Jo said with an odd note in her voice. "No. It's not the right time."

Well, that was a shame. After how beautifully the introduction with her father had gone, it would be nice to get a similar introduction to Mr. Smith sometime soon. Bit odd, of course, that a husband should be the family to meet, but such was their circumstance. Emily was too busy bubbling with happy nerves to care about this detail.

Still, she tried to keep her head on. She was here in just as much a professional capacity as a personal one. She took out her pad of paper, jotting down a note on the state of the stairs—the handrail could use some tightening, if it was to be safe enough for a mother-to-be…

"Are you writing notes already?" Jo asked, turning around on the staircase. Emily peered up at her, only a few steps behind.

"I should hate to forget." Emily went on writing and stair-climbing. When she got second-from-the-top, just behind Jo, she leaned her chin on Jo's shoulder for a brief and smiling moment before the door opened and she pecked the most rapid of kisses against her coat collar.

When Miss Garcia opened the door, she was looking distinctly rounder than the last time Emily had seen her, though her skirts had been adjusted so that there was some deniability as to whether it was her love of layered dresses or love of men's company that caused the change. She greeted them with her customary queenly decorum, and led Emily and Jo into a small apartment filled with some of the most outlandish décor Emily had ever seen in a private home. Her brother's dramatic Arts and Crafts aesthetic seemed suddenly quite tame compared to Persian rugs, gilded statuary, and a bare-breasted mermaid positioned near the doorway to hold the coats.

It was horrible in all the best ways, and decidedly appropriate for Jo. While Jo put on a show of ambivalence about her living situation, it was probably a place she liked very much.

Jo grinned and began to say something about the mermaid, but a man's voice from the room's far end made her stop dead in her tracks.

"Darling," he said, crossing the floor on gangly legs to help ease Miss Garcia into one of the ostentatious chairs by the fire-place. "I could have let them in. There's no need for you to sprint around doing everything."

"For heaven's sake, Paul. Quit fussing," Miss Garcia said, though she looked distinctly pleased by the fussing. "Thanks to Dr. Clarke, I have regained so much of my old energy."

Mr. Smith managed to tear his eyes away from his love long enough to find Emily and Jo at the threshold. When he did, he froze as completely as Jo had, twin statues across the room from each other.

"Jo?" he said. "What are you doing here? I thought you wanted—"

"I'm simply the escort," Jo said sharply. "It's a little tricky getting here from the station. I wanted to make sure she found her way."

Mr. Smith shook his head like he was trying to shake a fly out of his ear. "How did that fall to you, exactly?"

Jo stuffed her hands in her pockets. "We're friends."

His confusion lessoned Emily's buoyancy. Had Jo not even mentioned they'd struck up so much as a friendship?

Well, that was alright, she supposed. She straightened her spine. Perhaps she'd thought it best to explain that to him now, while they were all together.

Content enough with that notion, Emily eyed the fellow curiously. He was excessively dandified with his slick blond hair and mustache, his garishly patterned jacket and purple snakeskin boots. But though he had marked himself so clearly a decadent, a pornographer, and the entirely *wrong* sort of nonconformist, there was something unexpectedly gentle in the way he tucked a shawl around Miss Garcia's shoulders and passed her a mug of tea that was perfectly within reach on the table before her.

"I know her glowing, maternal beauty is distracting," said Jo dryly, "but I'm afraid you must tear your eyes away at least long enough to meet Dr. Clarke."

Emily's head snapped in Jo's direction. It had been a long time indeed since Jo had called her that, and it was unpleasantly jarring.

Paul Smith looked at Emily as if he'd just noticed her—though of course that was nonsense. Still, he went along with his own act, putting a hand to his chest and pretending to sweep a nonexistent hat off his head as he fell into an extravagant, courtly bow.

"Dr. Clarke!" He stood upright and came over to shake her hand in both of his, firm and without hesitation, like equals. "I should kiss your boots if I thought it appropriate. I am grateful beyond all respectable reactions that you stepped outside your usual specialty for the sake of Miss Garcia's health. I know she's doing the best she can with payment, but since it's—" his eyes drifted briefly to Jo and back again "—since it's *my* house that you're visiting now, I'll see to it that you're paid as is more fitting for your extensive experience and education."

Emily just nodded, quite taken aback. While everything about this man should repel her, she found herself at ease with him. He had not looked her up and down in suspicion (or, heaven forbid, something more untoward). He was not questioning her credentials like husbands and fathers invariably did at the village hospital. He was not trying to get unnecessary charity work out of her, figuring her sex meant she did not want to be paid. And while there was an air of absurdity to him, he seemed sincere.

That was…unusual.

It was refreshing.

Most shockingly, she thought she might actually grow to like the man.

If, of course, Jo would quit standing there and introduce them properly.

Emily cleared her throat. Jo did not respond, so she did it again, nudging her slightly with the doctor bag. Jo looked confused, and Emily's face grew hot.

"Aren't you going to introduce us?" Emily whispered in as friendly a manner as possible.

Jo cocked a brow. "Didn't I?"

"Not really, no," Emily snapped.

Jo rolled her eyes, as if Emily was insisting on this for the sake of decorum alone.

"In that case," she sighed, a little amused and annoyed. "Dr. Clarke, this is Paul Smith, Miss Garcia's paramour and father of the child in question. Paul, this is Dr. Clarke, who's been seeing and corresponding with Miss Garcia as her physician."

Clearly, this was all Jo intended to say. After all their letters, after all their time together, after a day spent with Emily's own family as if she were part of it.

That feeling of wholeness Emily had felt at the station was crushed by this reality like the cigarette under Jo's very real, very solid, very earthy-dynamic-sapphic-mysterious-right-in-the-thick-of-life-itself boot.

Jo was not some magical missing piece of Emily's family. And Emily was not destined to be part of Jo's. If Jo were thinking that way, she wouldn't have placed herself solidly outside the connection between Emily and Mr. Smith. Jo obviously had no inclination to bring Emily into her own little fold. This husband. This woman. This baby. These friends like Noah and

Miss Withers and the rest who were so much more like her, who lived just as intensely as she did.

While Emily was just…well, she was Dr. Clarke, as Jo had introduced her to this important person in her life. She was a failing physician from "Farm-Brush" who minded her duties and lived with her father. And no glass of punch, rebound dime novel, or even scandalous postcard could really change that. That Emily had even invited a person like this to attend a lecture and service with her family tomorrow, like they were something beyond a bit of novelty, suddenly seemed so absurd she wanted to cry in embarrassment.

"Oh dear," she heard Mr. Smith say out of the corner of his mouth to Jo. "I've shocked her. I'm sorry, I am trying my very best not to be shocking…"

Jo's hand on Emily's shoulder made her jump. "Dr. Clarke? Is everything alright?"

Dr. Clarke again. The second they left the fantasy world and came into the reality of Jo's day-to-day, she was Dr. Clarke. That it was so technically polite for her to use that name in the presence of people she would never be friendly with made it all the more painful.

But heavens, there was no time to dwell in this. She was, apparently, here to minister to a patient. Nothing more or less than that. So, she straightened her spine and grasped her bag.

"No problem, Mrs. Smith." She caught the way Jo's eyes narrowed when the honorific slipped out. She chose to look away from that, toward Miss Garcia—her patient, the one person in this room she knew how to deal with right now—and said, "Let's get started, then, shall we?"

Chapter Eighteen

Jo

If it weren't obvious all through the appointment, Jo knew for sure that Emily was upset when she agreed to take a hackney to Miss Withers's instead of arguing the benefits of a bracing walk through town.

"What happened in there, exactly?" Jo asked as they clopped and jostled along through traffic. She'd have liked to use the excuse to settle an arm around Emily's shoulders and whisper about the indulgences they could get up to once they made their required appearance at Miss Withers's dinner table. But that steely, sharp quality had returned to the edges of Emily's posture, and the distinctly untouchable air around her was back in full force. It was hard to believe she'd been snuggling up and kissing the back of Jo's neck on the staircase not minutes before it all went sour. "Can you tell me?"

Emily did not look away from the window's view of the passing street. "What happened in the appointment, you mean? When I took Miss Garcia into the room for her exam? Everything went fine."

"That's not what I mean," Jo said, unsure whether Emily was being obtuse on purpose. "You seem pissed off."

The impolite word got her attention at least, if only for a moment before she looked back out the window.

"That," Emily said, "is not the name of a state that I'm familiar with personally."

Jo wasn't sure she even knew what that meant. "Will you tell me what—?"

But she was cut off as the carriage jerked to a stop on Miss Withers's street, and Emily grasped the doorhandle like a convict who's spotted her chance to make a getaway.

Jo all but chased Emily up the steps to the Society House, where they were let in before she could make any headway in the confusing situation. What had she done wrong? And if whatever she'd done was so bad, why didn't Emily just give the full force of her considerable wrath? Jo could take that well enough, but this? Emily speed-walking through the halls, giving clipped greetings to Miss Withers and the staff, heading for the staircase as if Jo were not behind her at all? This was confusing as hell, and Jo didn't know what to do with it.

Emily's steps were clipped and efficient as ever. By the time she got to the drawing room, Jo couldn't bring herself to keep chasing. She did, at least, keep from shouting something along the lines of *well, go on and fuck off then!* which was a small victory that Miss Withers came to celebrate with her a moment later.

"Was it The Beast?" Miss Withers asked with a knowingly cocked brow, using the nickname that Jo gave for Paul to her friends who did not know him.

Jo's mind raced back. Emily had gone quiet right around the time she was introduced to Paul. Sure, the unexpected encounter was awkward, but not outside of what she'd probably expect from a husband and wife who'd taken other lovers. They hadn't argued or discussed anything personal, and against all odds he hadn't said anything scandalous. In fact, he was as friendly as ever and far less scandalous than usual. He'd long been able to treat a woman as an equal, and hadn't said anything that seemed to question Emily's capabilities as a doctor. Absolutely on his best behavior, really, as he'd been more often than not since he'd found out he would be a father.

"Yeah, but he didn't say anything iffy," Jo said, putting her hat on the rack and giving it an anxious spin on its hook. "It's not what I planned on, but it wasn't a disaster, either. Or so I thought."

Miss Withers looked at Jo as if she'd suggested inviting the bloke to dinner (and Miss Withers *really* didn't like having blokes over for dinner).

"What?" Jo asked defensively.

"He didn't have to *say* anything in particular," Miss Withers said as if it were the most obvious thing in the world. "In fact, if he was less beastly than anticipated it might have made it worse."

"What are you talking about?"

"Did you tell her what is going on between the two of you?" Miss Withers's eyes widened at the way Jo's nose wrinkled. "Jo, have you even told her you aren't living there right now?"

"Well, not *exactly*," Jo admitted.

Miss Withers shook her head grimly. She sat Jo down on the chaise, then went to pour some of the Irish whiskey she kept on the liquor cart mostly for Jo's benefit. She handed it to Jo and sat down, waiting until Jo had taken a mystified sip of the burning liquid before speaking.

She patted Jo's leg in a bracing way and said, "You've really bungled it, dear."

While Miss Withers felt that Jo could use the fortification before she went upstairs ("and perhaps a bit of food in your belly as well?"), the last thing Jo needed right now was to stop for a snacking session and then go up smelling of *strong spirits*. With a frustrated sigh, she climbed the staircase.

It was so tempting not to right this wrong she'd done. To take Emily's bad reaction—which Jo thought was overblown, in spite of Miss Withers's opinion—as proof that this whole thing was doomed anyway.

She found the door to Emily's room still open a crack, like she'd been too frustrated to bother closing it properly. Jo nudged it another inch and peeked inside. Emily was brushing off her traveling dress like it had done her grievous wrong. The rest of her things were tidily—almost militaristically—laid out on the bed beside her open valise.

Maybe if Emily had been sitting and moping up here, Jo would have continued to think it wasn't worth sorting this out. But Emily's bottled-up energy, so fascinating and beautiful in its way, hissed out with every smack of bristles on wool, her hair frizzing like steam around her ears and forehead. The sight of it filled Jo with affection like nothing she'd ever experienced.

She couldn't just let Emily walk away. She had to try.

Jo opened the door and leaned against the frame. "Going somewhere?"

Emily kept her eyes trained on her task. "I've had second thoughts about my continued presence here." All that tight, buttoned-up-ness returned to her voice, like the delighted laughs and wanton gasps had all been some absinthe-fueled dream of Jo's. "I should have stayed with my brother from the beginning. I apologize for my presumptuousness."

"Emily, will you please talk to me about this?"

"About what?" Such crisp words, emphasized by harsh strokes of the brush.

"About how you're panicking after meeting Paul?"

The poor dress took a swatting worthy of a flogging brothel. "I am not panicking after meeting Mr. Smith."

"Oh," Jo snapped, crossing her arms as her patience wore very thin. "Then I'll just go then. Leave you to it. Never see you again."

"Alright. Farewell."

Jo groaned, hating to have her bluff called. "Emily!"

At last, Emily looked up, face closed off, but eyes shining. "I am not panicking after meeting 'Paul,' Jo, because I was never introduced to him in the first place."

Jo blinked that in for a moment, anger starting to flare in her own chest. "Why are you being so rigid about these manners all of a sudden?"

"Manners aren't the problem."

"Then what the devil is the problem?"

"You!" she snarled, beating at the dress again. "You are the problem."

"I don't—"

"You let me make a *complete*" she smacked the skirt "*bloody*" another whack "*fool* of myself this morning."

Jo had no idea what she was talking about. "A fool?"

"Threatening to drag you around to my silly events that you don't care about," she snapped. "Making you talk to my father like it mattered whether you got along. Imagining the lot of us traipsing about town like a family when you are clearly not interested in reciprocating."

"Reciprocating?" said Jo. "And how exactly am I supposed to do that? I don't have a family."

"Then what, pray tell, do you call an entire bloody husband?"

"As I've told you before, I call him a technicality."

"No, you don't!"

Jealousy. Was that the thing spurring all this on? Bollocks, of course it was. That was why Jo preferred never to mention her husband at all, let alone let a lover meet him. She'd bungled it indeed.

"I have never, not for one day of my life, loved him like I—"
Jo cut herself off, biting down hard on words that had obviously not come from her brain. "He doesn't *matter*, Emily—"

"Since when, exactly, has that sort of love determined the value of a marriage?" Emily asked. "Of course he matters. If he didn't matter, you'd either be lying to him like Tansy Wickersham or you'd have deserted him properly and run off on your own. Especially now that he's got a baby on the way. Why on earth would you continue inserting yourself into the fate of his paramour and child if he didn't matter to you?"

"I'm not even living there anymore," Jo snapped, pointing toward the door, down the hall to the room she'd taken, where a small assortment of her things was still sitting in crates that Miss Withers covered with silk scarves to make them less of an eyesore. "I'm staying here."

Emily's face grew concerned. "Did they force you to leave?"

"No."

"They implied it would be best, though?"

Jo squeezed her eyes shut guiltily. "No."

"I know you enjoy a foray into the quaint these days, Joey. But your own home seems a lot better suited to you." She glanced around at the flowery, frilly décor of the Orchid and Pearl bedroom. "I was thinking the moment I walked in how perfect that house was for you. Why leave?"

Why? Paul had asked her that too, the night she'd done it. Pointing round at the life they'd built, the shelves they'd filled, the safety and comfort they'd secured after so many years of struggle. She hadn't been able to answer him, when he'd asked.

But when it came from Emily, it seemed, she couldn't do anything but blurt it out fully:

"Because I don't know what else to do," she said, voice almost pleading. "You have to understand. I have been forced to start my life fresh over and over again. It's all I know. Vanessa and this baby…they're a new chapter. And…and the fact is… I'm not a good writer, Emily."

The silliness of the words was reflected on Emily's incredulous face. "I didn't realize you wanted to be a writer."

"That's not what I mean. I just…" She laughed at herself. "I'm a bookseller. Bookbinder. Printer. I read a lot. I know a good story. I know that good stories don't close every single chapter in one place, only to open the next in a whole other country, with whole other characters, and a new name for the hero while they're at it. But that's what I've done. I don't want to leave the life I've made this time. I fucking love the shop. I'm comfortable in our house for now, and if I was going to leave it, I'd rather it be because I'd found something better, than because I had to run. And yes, I'm content with my marriage for what it is, even if it makes things complicated sometimes. I suppose that's why I haven't fully done it yet, why I can't bring myself to actually move everything out and find a real room for myself. But I don't know what else to do. That's why…it's why when he didn't end up kicking me out; I had to do the job myself, alright? It's stupid. It's ridiculous. But I couldn't seem to help it."

"What do you think will happen?" Emily asked. "If you stay and see how it goes, for as long as it seems to be working for you?"

"I'm afraid… I don't know." All of this felt foolish now that she was saying it aloud, but Emily looked so earnest and kind that she couldn't help but go on. "It feels like whatever our life had been before would just…stick around, somehow, make it awkward, or—"

"Haunt you?" Emily provided. "Like the ghost of your old life would still be there?"

Jo brightened slightly at the aptness of her simile. "Exactly! Maybe you have more of a future in literature than I do."

Based on the way her nose wrinkled, that was a little too decadent for poor Emily to even consider.

"And these ghosts of old lives," she went on when she'd recovered from the notion. "Do they really not follow you? When you pack up and leave? Are you as free of them as you'd like to be?"

Jo shook her head. "No," she admitted. "I'm stuck with them anyway. I just feel a bit better about them."

"Can you tell me about them?"

"Why?" Jo asked rather sharply. The harshness of it might have scared someone else off, but not Emily.

"Because, Jo. It's like I said." She smoothed the wrinkles out of the union suit she'd been preparing for her suitcase a moment ago. "I want to expand our interactions beyond the page and our walks and the society house. Let you see something about how I am in the day-to-day matters. It is certainly a step in that direction, to spend a Sunday with your companion's family. I thought you might want that too, but now I... I'm not sure if there's room for me, among all your ghosts."

Well, that made sense, didn't it? No wonder Emily was disturbed to have been introduced to Jo's husband—her family, in all its technical, uncommon glory—like it was nothing. Jo had treated the situation like there was nothing profound going on at all, while Emily was actively trying to make a real connection between her flight of fancy with Jo and the structures of her normal life. The problem wasn't jealousy over Paul, or even their odd, convenient companionship; it was the way Jo had let her temporary anger with him cause her to introduce Emily like a professional outsider. A doctor. A person to work with and look up to.

Not at all like someone who mattered, being introduced to one of the most important people in Jo's life.

Jo gently took the folded garment out of Emily's hands and

put it into the valise. Then she put the whole thing on the floor so she'd have room to sit on the end of the bed. She patted the quilt beside her. Emily looked a bit skeptical, so Jo moved the rest of the unfolded clothes to the floor as well, clearing the bed entirely before she patted it again.

"Come on, Emily. There's room for you," she said, hoping it was clear she didn't just mean space on the mattress. "I admit, we haven't been at this long enough to know if it would be a comfortable fit. I don't know if this is where you really want to be. But I do know there's room. Plenty of room. An enormous empty space in my life, actually," she added, so rapidly and unplanned that the uncomfortable words surprised even herself. "That's what this baby is showing me. There's an empty space. While Paul never occupied it, his shadow was at least near enough to obscure it, until he wandered a bit too far to the side in search of his own happiness, and couldn't hide it from me any longer."

Emily paused, then sat reluctantly next to Jo with her arms crossed and her gaze trained on the carpet. "That's very poetic."

"Like I said. I read a lot." Jo shrugged. "Be careful with that, or next thing you know you're thinking in metaphors and analyzing innocent people's handwriting."

"You never did tell me what you really saw in my handwriting," Emily muttered to the rug. "I knew you were lying, at the time."

"The real answer was inappropriate. I had to lie."

"Not anymore," Emily said. "Nothing you can say would be more inappropriate than the things we've done now."

Sentiments like that could be poisoned with regret, but not this time. Emily's voice was full of clear reverence for what they'd "done."

"Low descenders indicate an amorous fixation," Jo said quietly. "High ascenders, on the other hand, indicate a mental one."

"What if someone has both?"

"That indicates to me that they're probably pretty tired."

Emily pursed her lips, not in irritation, but like she was trying to keep a smile off her face.

"What's the situation with him, Jo?" she asked at last. "You say you're happy enough, living with him."

"Yes," admitted Jo. "It's a habit by now, though to be honest, it's not something we've reassessed the joy of very recently. You can tell by the state of the shelves that we haven't changed anything in a while. I lost that book I mentioned to you, the one with the remedies, because it's been so long since we went through anything that I can't seem to figure out where it wound up."

"You're certain you lost it, then?"

"I'm hoping it's still on the shelves somewhere, and it's just that neither of us has been able to spot it yet. They're a mess, totally disorganized, as you might expect from bookmakers who never bothered getting any aspect of their lives sorted out properly." She smiled sadly. "I'm not holding out a lot of hope, though. It wouldn't be the first thing I'd managed to lose in life."

"How'd you meet him?"

Irritation that they'd gotten back on the real subject coasted through Jo. She hated talking about this. There was something embarrassing about the fact that she'd married, that she'd not been as introspective and independent as someone like Miss Withers or even Emily herself in that regard. It was the image she cultivated, but that was really just a lie to cover up a truth that seemed inappropriate within the life she wanted to live.

But Emily wasn't demanding that she destroy what she'd

built simply because it wasn't perfect. All she was asking for was a bit of space within it.

No one had ever shown any interest in taking Jo as she was. She'd never let a woman close for fear she'd find out about Paul, and the few who'd slipped past her defenses had let her know in no uncertain terms that she had to make a decision. And yet here was perhaps the first woman she'd ever met who seemed worth throwing it all away for, and she wasn't demanding that.

She deserved the truth.

"Well," Jo started slowly, trying to decide where to begin. *Fuck it. Begin at the beginning, you bloody coward.* "I got here, to London, when I was seventeen."

"Why'd you come?"

"Ran away," said Jo as lightly as possible. "I was a bit of a hellion, as you might be able to imagine, and after my gran passed, my parents came to the conclusion that I was possessed by bad spirits. They'd never been what you'd call gentle sorts, but once that idea took hold, they turned on me. They'd see me cured of my demons whatever it took, and let's just say the treatments suggested by the priest and some of the old women in town weren't things I was terribly keen on."

She let it fall like a joke, though of course, it wasn't. Not at all. Emily seemed to understand that, because she did not laugh.

"So I ran off. I had big ideas about what London would be like, but discovered pretty quickly that my fantasy of working in some swanky city restaurant or theater was delusional. London was nowhere near the refuge I'd built it up to be; the spots I could afford were filthy, unwelcoming, and honestly frightening. I had no choice but to find the nearest Irish neighborhood and Catholic mission church. I tried the nun thing on. Didn't work out so well; too many bad spirits still lingering within me, I suppose. Left and did what you do when you aren't keen to make a living on your back in that situation: mended clothes badly for people fool enough to let me, sold some of the cosmetics from Gran's book to the parish wives. But I had no bloody family. I had some helpers and boarders, but no friends. It was hell, but I couldn't afford to get back home and undo my mistake—if it even was a mistake; it's so hard to know for sure—so I was fucking stuck here, like it or not.

"And then I met a nice fellow—bit bookish, bit eccentric, bit older than me but not by too much—who printed all the church's brochures and shit. He had a real trade that could support a family, he seemed intelligent, he treated me kindly and could make me laugh while he was at it, and you know what, Emily? You aren't the only one who's ever looked at her circumstances and seen one option looking a hell of a lot better than the rest."

Emily continued staring at the floor, still quite slumped in comparison to her usual posture. "That all makes sense enough," she admitted. "I'm curious to know how it became so significantly different from any other marriage."

"Oh, fuck. I mean, we're right out of one of those treatises on why women ought to stick to women's work," Jo said. "I asked him to train me on typesetting, and it's been a slow descent into Satan's clutches ever since."

"Oh, stop it." Emily snorted out a laugh, putting her fingers to her mouth like she resented her mirth very much.

"You think I'm kidding." Jo moved the tiniest bit closer to Emily on the mattress. "I started working with him on the printing. I liked it so much, I decided I didn't want any children, so I could keep doing it. I kept that from him for a couple years, until he finally caught on that I was doing whatever was necessary to keep it from happening. He had the legal right to absolutely ruin my life, divorce me, sue me, see me jailed. And he's always wanted a child, so you'd think... But he agreed that if I wasn't suited to motherhood, then it was for the best. He said we'd go on making books instead of babies, so long as I promised not to go behind his back like that again."

She broke off, trying to assess Emily's response—you really never knew with a bluestocking which way they'd go on all that. She didn't look thrilled, but it was more pity than disapproval. Either way, she wasn't running for the hills or launching into a lecture, which Jo counted as positive enough to keep going.

"The idea was such a massive deviation from all we'd ever known that it was hard not to question everything after that. It took a few years before we found ourselves throwing in with the literal decadents, but the fact is, we're both fairly unconventional in our cores. It's not like he seduced me into some wanton lifestyle; he was respectable when we married, and frankly, he had better intentions for the union than I did. We fell into our current life hand-in-hand."

Emily nodded. "So he *is* like family, then."

"Yeah, I guess," Jo sighed, reluctant to admit it, but unable to deny it. "And not bad family, either, if I'm being honest. Do you remember, when you first came here, we discussed the missteps your father and brother make, even in spite of their convictions of equality?"

"I do, yes."

"Well, I… I'm afraid I let you believe we were in the same boat when we weren't. Paul's never let his convictions blind him to the reality of my circumstance. The deck *is* stacked against me. Sure, there's some higher truth that says it shouldn't be like that, but the on-the-ground truth has its effect. He's never taken advantage of that, or conveniently forgotten it. He's been good to me. So, hard as it is right now, I do see him as my family, and by extension, Vanessa and their baby too. And I should have introduced you to him with the proper gravity of that. I just…"

She broke off, distressed by the direction of her thoughts.

After a moment, she felt a soft nudge from beside her as Emily put her hand between them on the mattress, palm up. Still a bit nervous, Jo put hers on top, lacing their fingers.

"Just what?"

"I don't know if they feel the same way about me now," Jo admitted in a whisper. "I feel like I'm about to be out on my arse again when this baby comes. He won't divorce me, maybe. Won't see trouble brought against me. He's proven that before, and it was shitty of me to assume the worst of him now. But that doesn't mean he'll want to stay friends. Or business partners. Or let me and my odd little posse hold his baby when it comes." She chuckled, thinking of Charlie, who asked about the situation every time she saw him. "I'm afraid it will change him. It wasn't you I was trying to distance myself from in that introduction, Emily. It was him. As I said, if I'm going to have to start over again, I'd rather do it on my own terms."

Emily gave her a bracing squeeze, her grip always so much stronger and more comforting than the delicate structure of her hand suggested. "They didn't seem keen to cut you out of their lives when I was there today. And even if I'm wrong about that, you're not a helpless runaway now, are you? Obviously, you're already perfectly capable of living independently. In terms of company and support, you have your friends here at The Orchid and Pearl. Noah and the others at David's club. Me."

The last word was quiet and sweet, trying its best to touch something very soft and vulnerable in Jo's core. Something she couldn't quite unguard enough yet, but wished she could. Wondered if maybe, with enough effort, it would be possible.

"Do I really?" Jo asked. She knew she wouldn't fully believe it, even if it was said again. But still. She wanted to hear it.

"You do, yes," Emily said, leaning in to murmur the words in Jo's ear, so close and warm that it sent an instant shiver through her. "While I doubt the loneliness will be as severe as you suspect, I am happily here to do any number of things that might ease it."

God, how could someone so put together be so relentlessly alluring? Jo turned her head to press a hungry kiss to those oft-pursed lips, letting the responsive softness of them start easing things already. There was something about kissing Emily Clarke that was unlike anything else she'd experienced. She was clearly not practiced in the art, but she didn't let that stop her from bringing obvious passion to it, and she took silent direction very, very well. Jo had never been to a fancy ball where couples partook in fashionable dances, but she imagined that kissing Emily was like leading a dance with the most beautiful woman in the room, who paid such close, intimate attention to the poses and pressures of her partner that no one watching would ever guess she knew only half the steps.

Having undoubtedly bungled things, Jo was exquisitely grateful to get the chance to do this again, to lower Emily to the bed, lying atop her to kiss and undress and find all sorts of lovely frictions in the places they collided. As her terribly reasonable number of layers found their way to the floor, the intoxicating scent of her strengthened, lavender water and crisp cotton and the swirling perfume of feminine passion.

While there was heat in the power of keeping her clothes on while another woman's knickers and camisoles were unceremoniously discarded, Jo was in no state to resist when Emily began to unwrap her as well. The world of velvet softness their bodies would make of this bed with covers atop and nothing between them was too sweet a temptation to pass up. Every unnatural scrap that covered them, from stockings and garters to hairpins, was left forgotten on the cold floor as they nestled into that perfect cocoon of comfort and pleasure.

Finally, Jo was able to do what she'd taken to dreaming of when she read Emily's letters. She took her time touching her unlikely lover, not just with her hungry hands but with the slide of intertwined legs, the crush of bared breasts, the explorations of her tongue as she vanished into the searing space under the covers to spread Emily wide and taste her properly.

Emily gasped and squirmed like a perfectly naughty dream, her hands tangling and tugging at Jo's unbound hair, hips lifting in time with Jo's mouth. She wasn't a talkative one, but she communicated in her way, through moans and movements and ever-increasing slickness that let Jo know what was to her liking. The lovemaking was peaceful and focused, and when she finally cried out in her crisis, clutching Jo's head lovingly tight, it was like there was no world at all outside these deliciously suffocating blankets.

Jo might have refused reciprocation again, still a bit worried this might all fizzle to nothing at any moment, but with Emily's taste on her lips and the sound of her pleasure echoing through her mind, she didn't have the strength for it. Emily dragged her back up toward the pillows, kissing her mouth, worshiping at her curves, stroking between her legs with obvious enthusiasm. Jo was too tightly wound do to anything but encourage it, helping Emily get the pressure and angles right until she was writhing against Emily's fingers, chasing down her release to this madness…

At last, Emily spoke in words, a delicious whisper felt as much as heard: "That's it. That's it, Joey, come for me, will you?"

It was the only thing there was to do at that point. Jo's pleasure peaked and she clenched around Emily over and over, hard and tight like her body intended to never let this poor woman go free.

That notion, of course, was the madness of pleasure talking. But as the cuddly haze of their satisfaction waned, their bodies finally aware once more of things like the chill of the room and their lateness at the dinner table, there remained a greediness in Jo's limbs. She wanted to hold Emily here for another few minutes, hours, days. To remain in this blissful feeling of warmth and oneness with this delightful person she should never even have met in the first place.

And she managed, for a while, kissing and caressing until Jo's own stomach growled too loud to be ignored.

"Come on then," said Emily sweetly, kissing Jo between her eyes. "You know we must make sure to evenly indulge our appetites, isn't that right?"

With a reluctant sigh, Jo reached over the bed for her undervest, the intimacy of that private joke softening the disappointment of having to move.

"You're right," she said, slipping the vest over her head. "But you'd best eat a lot, in that case. Because if you think I'm finished with you tonight, my love, you are sorely mistaken."

The next morning, Jo awoke to small, steady hands shaking her into consciousness. It confused her, this wakeful state. It didn't seem indicated by the weakness of the sun behind the curtains.

"Come on," said Emily. As Jo opened her bleary eyes, she saw that Emily was no longer under the covers with her, but standing at the bedside in her navy skirt and jacket set that did wonders for the color of her eyes. "We can't dally much longer if we're going to have time this morning."

"Time for what?" Jo croaked, pulling the quilt over her head.

Emily tugged the linens down, gave her a practical peck on the head, and said, "Time enough for me to check those disorganized shelves you mentioned myself. For your grandmother's book. It's likely I have a sharper eye than you or Mr. Smith. I think I ought to take a look before you give up hope entirely." Content that Jo was awake enough to be getting on with, she turned to the vanity and began undoing the braid Jo had put in for her the night before, briefly crowned with that beautiful, haloish tumble of hair before she started twisting it up into its usual knot. She met Jo's eyes in the mirror. "While we're there, perhaps you could try again with our introduction? And also, perhaps, it would be a good time for you to begin healing the rift that's grown between the two of you?"

It was kind of Emily to give Jo another chance, more so that she gave two shits whether Jo and Paul resolved their differences. It might even have been saintly if it had come a little later in the day.

"At this hour?" said Jo on the cusp of a yawn. "I guarantee you Paul won't be awake yet."

"We'll stop and get him a bun or something to soften the blow," Emily said, poking pins against the top of her head. "One early morning won't kill anyone, not even a decadent."

She paused in the brutal arrangement of her hair when she caught Jo's groggy smile in the mirror. She turned around, a quirked brow questioning.

"Thank you," Jo said. "It's kind of you to give me a second chance, even if you're going about it a bit aggressively."

Emily turned back to the mirror and pushed in the last of her pins. "You did the same for me, didn't you? I think it's as good a time as any for *all* necessary reciprocation to be honored."

Chapter Nineteen

Emily

Jo brought them up those narrow stairs with their wobbly railing once again. This time, Emily noticed, someone had left
mud on the steps, dry now, but thick enough to cause a slip to
a woman whose center of gravity was changing on a weekly
basis. Once this introduction was done properly, she'd be giving Mr. Smith a hearty lecture on keeping his home up to snuff
for an expectant mother, that was certain.

"Shall we knock loudly?" Emily asked. "So as to wake him
up?"

"Fuck no," Jo laughed. "He'll think we're the bobbies if we
do that. I've got a key."

"Do you need help getting it out?"

"I can—" Jo paused, a sly grin and a hint of a flush spreading over her face. "Would you mind?"

As they got to the top of the staircase, Emily reached into
Jo's pocket, taking her time and swirling her fingers in a bra-
zen way that she had mostly certainly not indulged in last time
this happened. She didn't linger too long, but by the time she'd
gotten the keys out, Jo was biting her lip and eyeing the hall

behind them a little guiltily, though of course, who would ever find anything odd about a bit of helpful affection between lady friends anyway?

She was smiling to herself as they went down the hall to the door they'd gone through yesterday, the one with the little wooden plaque that said *Smith.*

Once they got there, though, they found that that plaque was dangling sideways from one of its corners by a single nail.

Emily selected the next key on the ring, but Jo put an arm out to block her way. She'd gone very still as she looked at the disrupted sign, the mud on the floor, finally bending a bit to inspect the heavy black knob, which, now that Emily was look- ing, also didn't look quite right. Some of the wood had come away from the doorjamb, a shower of splinters on the floor below it, and the knob was clearly loose. Jo whispered a curse, then peered back down the staircase, as if trying to ascertain whether there was anyone at home behind the other two apart- ment doors.

After a moment, she gestured for Emily to take a few steps down the hall.

Out of the way.

"Jo—"

But Jo shook her head, waved her a few steps farther off, then tried the door, which had been left unlocked and swung open easily, given the state of the jamb.

Emily disregarded Jo's warnings and followed her across the threshold.

The first thing she saw was books. Books everywhere. They'd been impressive on their towering shelves, but now, they appeared almost infinite. Some were still standing on the spread of shelves, but a good deal more had been unceremo- niously removed from their places, thrown and scattered and heaped on the muddy carpets with no concern for whether bindings broke or pages went fluttering off. Once she'd gotten over the books, she spotted other troubles: smashed, painted glass that had been a pitcher yesterday; a bright piece of artwork she'd begrudgingly admired ripped from the wall, frame now smashed around it; and at their feet across the rug, as if it had been put there to trip someone, the mermaid coatrack, swimming in jackets and scarves that had escaped her grasp, one of her curving hooks cocked at very final-looking angle.

Stomach knotted with confusion and fear, Emily looked to Jo for some indication of what was going on, how to respond. She'd seen plenty of terrible things at the hospital, things that were certainly more urgent than this. And yet there was something more frightening about this gutted bookshelf. She knew the meaning of blood and fever and screams of pain. They were terrible, but they came with clear causes and protocols. But this…she had no idea what any of *this* meant.

Jo was pale and shaky. She had a hand to her mouth, which she moved just long enough to call, "Paul?" in a trembling voice. "Paul, are you here? Vanessa?"

There was no answer. No flutter of pages. No sign of life in the decimated rooms.

At last, Emily found enough footing to go to Jo and put a hand on her back. She still wasn't sure what was happening, but it was an emergency of some sort, and she was far from useless in those.

"Was he robbed?" she said quietly.

Jo shook her head. "Raided."

It didn't shake Emily to hear the word quite as much as it shook Jo to speak it, but it still wasn't one she was especially keen on. Emily led Jo to one of the fine, squashy armchairs near the cold fireplace and sat her down.

"What does that mean? Not the raid itself; I know what *that* is," she added at Jo's sharp look, a shudder threatening her own stability. She'd never had occasion to deal with a police raid, but between Noah, David, and some of her rowdier suffragist companions, she'd heard enough secondhand stories to have a good sense of dread around the topic. "What does it mean for him?"

Jo put her head in her hands. "Means either he wasn't here, he got away, or he got *taken* away."

"How are you going to find out which it is?"

"I don't know."

Jo looked lost, nearly helpless in her distress. Though a doctor had to cull every shred of such a response from their own dispositions, she could still recognize in others that frozen feeling, that feeling of doom, that of the brain frosting over with indecision even when a decision was of utmost importance.

If Emily had ever found Noah's rooms in similar disarray, she'd be halfway to the police station already to demand answers. Somewhere in Jo was her ability to act, to move, to know what was next. Clearly, though, she was going to need some help to find it.

Emily stooped down before Jo's chair, grateful for the ease of movement her simple skirt and bodice allowed for. "Shall I come along with you to Scotland Yard? I'm sure you have some right to know what's happened. We can...we can rule out the worst, that way."

She took one of Jo's hands in hers. When she got very little response, she drew it gently to her lips. That at least got Jo looking at her, her dark eyes swimming with frightened tears. She squeezed Emily's hand gratefully.

"Not yet," Jo said. As she looked at their twined fingers, she seemed to breathe a little easier, looking up and around like she was awakening somewhat. "No, we...we meet at the bookshop if we run into shit." She did not simply say it, but recited it. "Bookshop first. Then the printers'... No. No, if they were here, they've certainly already been there. Book-shop first, then…"

She faltered and Emily stood, tugging her to her feet.

"Then we make our decisions based on what we find there," Emily said, allowing what was good and useful in her practical nature to have its way. While crises wore on one's spirit, she had become very good in them, and for the first time in a while, she was grateful for that. Jo seemed bewildered to have access to a steady hand to help her through this, and the impact it clearly made on her mindset made Emily feel very strong. She stepped in close and put one comforting hand on Jo's cheek, warm and wet with the tears that had escaped. "We need not plan for the worst, my darling. Only for what comes next."

She was shocked to hear the word *darling* come out of her mouth. She'd thought it quite a lot when she received the let-ters, but hadn't considered it a word she might ever actually speak. But Jo responded well to it, nodding and leaning in so their foreheads touched for a moment. She took a deep, shud-dering breath, and when she pulled back, she looked more up-right and able to handle what was happening.

"Thank you," Jo said. "Does that mean you're coming with me? It's not far, but I wouldn't blame you if you wanted to go back to Miss Withers's instead, or get a start on meeting up with your family."

"There's plenty of time for that," Emily assured her, smooth-ing a bit of hair behind Jo's ear. "I'll stay with you."

Carefully, they started making their way through the mess of books. While Jo was clearly eager to check up on her hus-band, too eager to stay here and clean things up thoroughly, she also didn't seem quite capable of leaving the most distressed-looking of the books to languish. She picked a few of them up with a delicacy that Emily might have reserved for injured puppies, patting their covers gently, tucking in any pages that had come out of place, and setting them on whatever surface was closest at hand. There was a distinct air of *I'll be back for you* in her movements.

It slowed their progress to the door substantially, but Emily joined her in the task anyway. She found a tall volume sprawled open near the mermaid, the pages slanted and out of place, with a muddy boot print marring the top ones. It was a sad-looking artifact, made especially so when Emily picked it up to find that the words within it were not printed, but hand-written very tidily...

Carefully, since the binding was already in such a fragile state, she flipped to the front, where she discovered a simple inscription in the corner of the first page. The spelling was irregular, but not so odd that she could not make out that it was *from the kitchen of Catriona Creagh, for her granddaughters' use.*

Jo had finally made it almost to the door. Emily called her back, rushing to meet her in the middle with the damaged book outstretched.

Goodness, it was hard to witness tears spilling over the edges of such devious, shining eyes. It nearly inspired the same in Emily's own. Jo ran her palm down that front cover, examining the damaged spine, the twisted, spoiled pages, the stain of an officer's uncaring boot.

"I'm so sorry," Emily whispered.

"Sorry?" Jo sniffed and wiped her face on the back of her sleeve, hiccupping. "Don't be sorry. You found it. You fucking *found* it!" She was laughing and crying, and carefully turning the pages like she couldn't quite believe it was real.

"I only meant that it's in such dreadful shape."

"Yeah, I guess." Another finger down the spine, a sharp eye looking over all the injuries with a look not unlike what Emily had seen in her fellow physicians. "But I'm a very good hand with restoration. We might lose a page or two, but if I can make out enough of the letters, I bet I could rewrite them myself. I'd rather have it in hand like this, than perfect and lost forever."

She hugged the precious book to her chest, and then pulled Emily in as well, pressing kisses to the side of her head as Emily started to really wonder how freeing it might be, to be loved by someone who went about the business of loving with an attitude like that.

Chapter Twenty

Jo

Maybe she'd been spending too much time with Emily. Though it was near to freezing, Jo didn't even consider catching a ride to the bookshop. Her feet moved toward their destination automatically, pounding out their path on the familiar segment of earth beneath them.

"We ought to get a coach," she muttered, not really to anyone in particular, but since she was clutching Emily's arm like it was the only thing tethering her to her senses, it was Emily who took responsibility for it.

"Don't be silly," she said, that clipped, professional tone she'd taken in the flat returning. The first time Jo had heard that tone, she'd despised it. Now? Under these circumstances? It was comforting beyond all reason: firm, assured, and kind, like a good hand with a frightened horse. "It's not much farther, and it doesn't sound to me like speed is the thing that matters. He will be there, or he won't. You must prepare yourself for either eventuality with a stretch of the legs and a few good breaths of…well, whatever it is we're breathing here in London."

Jo appreciated Emily's understated levity, even if she couldn't quite bring herself to laugh.

"Jo, may I ask you a question?"

"Anything," Jo said, happy to be distracted.

"Are you likely to see trouble over this? Legal trouble?"

Jo thought about it, but came up short. Strange. Obsessed as she'd been for months now over her own legal fate, she hadn't thought about herself once regarding this raid. "There are too many possible factors," she said, shaking her head. "I don't know. Like everything else, much of it is in his hands. My name's not on anything official. That's the downside of a wifely position, but a benefit too, under circumstances like this. Scotland Yard won't be overly interested in me unless he says they ought to be."

"Before we arrive at the shop, then, are you certain you shouldn't give this whole thing a bit of space? Just in case?"

"In case what?"

"In case he says they ought to be."

Jo's feet paused their incessant movement. She drifted with Emily out of the way of the foot traffic, near the overhang of a bakery that smelled temptingly of the morning's bake, a very wholesome, safe smell, at odds with the circumstances.

"Are you nervous to come along with me?" Jo asked. "In case it goes bad? I've appreciated your presence this morning, Emily, but you have a point. This might be on the dangerous side for someone who needs their reputation. I'd hate to cause you trouble in the other areas of your life."

Emily glanced down the street, where the Morgan & Murray's sign was finally in view. She took Jo's hand and gave it a squeeze.

"I am not nervous if you aren't," she said. "If you believe he wouldn't bring you trouble, that he really is the friend you think he is, then I trust your judgement. But if you're at all nervous,

I do hope you will..." She drew her eyes from the road ahead and met Jo's at last. "If you're at all nervous, dear Jo, I hope you will extend our bracing morning walk past the bookshop entirely and straight along to the train station. My father and I have grown quite used to entertaining outlaws, you know. You'd be comfortable with us until this all blows over."

For a moment, Jo didn't know what to do with an offer like that. It seemed so immense, so profound, so unreasonably kind, that it fell almost like another language to her ear.

"What?" she said, unable to summon anything else.

"You can stay with me for a little while," Emily repeated. "In Farncombe. To wait things out until you know it's safe to return to London."

Jo looked down at their clasped hands, filled with the sweetness of the offer. This was it, wasn't it? The escape hatch from this life she'd built. She might never have to find out whether Paul would betray her in this legal situation. Or even if he'd shun or betray her later, when his baby came. She could scarper, flee into the suburbs to start the newest phase of her fragmented life. Become a Unitarian. Live a proper "spinster" life with a lovely woman and her dotty old father, setting type for one of Farncombe's liberal-minded newspapers, and maybe even giving one of those rational skirt sets a go when she went into town. They didn't seem so dreadful, honestly.

She could see it clearly. See it like she'd read it in a novel— not an adventuresome one, of course, but one of those more domestic tales. It was a happy enough ending, really...

But it wasn't what she wanted. She didn't want to start again, *yet again*. She'd built up a life here. Not an average one. Not even a particularly good one. But it was hers. She'd made it, scraped it together from the scraps she'd been granted.

And while she was absolutely enamored of the notion that Emily Clarke was now part of that life's future, the sort of lover she'd never dared dream of, there was still a quirky old git knit into the fabric of that life, and she didn't want to cut him out for good. Not if she could avoid it.

At last, she shook her head, managing a half-smile for Emily. "I appreciate that more than you know," she said. "But I don't really believe he's going to betray me. Others have, so I've been readying myself for it. But he hasn't. And I won't do it to him, either." She held her arm back out for Emily to take. "You were right. He's my family, and it's well past time you met him properly. I don't want to start a new life, Emily. I want to bring you into mine, as you've brought me into yours."

Emily took the offered arm with a smile. "That sounds very lovely, Jo."

"It does, doesn't it?" said Jo. They started walking, the clip quicker as urgency returned to her movements. "If, you know, he's actually *at* the bookshop and not sniveling in a cell somewhere, yeah? I may not think he'll turn on me, but that doesn't mean he's not in a fucking barrel of trouble himself."

Though the remainder of the walk to Morgan & Murray's bookshop was brief, hurried, and fueled by Jo's barely contained fear, they did find her bugger of a husband hiding in plain sight behind the counter. Face a bit pale. Eyes a bit bloodshot. Tie askew and jacket wrinkled. But decidedly on the right side of the bars.

"You fucker, you scared me to death!" Jo hugged him a bit violently until he ducked out of her grasp and clasped his hands together as if in prayer.

"Joey," he said, meeting her eyes with a glowing desperation. "I must thank you *profusely* for being so disorganized." He gave an obnoxiously low bow before hugging her amicably one more time. "If you hadn't made me realize what a damned disaster those shelves were, I would be good and fucked, no question."

"Why?" Jo demanded. "What happened?"

"Well. Let's set the stage, shall we?" He spread his hands in front of him like he was literally drawing a performance space with them. It was Paul all over, familiar as an irritating but nostalgic folksong, the sort that families sang drunk around the fire.

"All set. Now—" As he completed this bout of theatricality, he finally noticed Emily hovering near the door. He smiled and pretended to doff a hat that he was not wearing. "Oh. Well, hello, there, Doctor! To what do we owe this oddly timed pleasure?"

The circumstances were, admittedly, bizarre, but Jo was determined to do this right. She'd gotten another chance, not just to do right by Emily, but by Paul as well. She took Emily by the arm and led her across the shop to where Paul stood, his head still tilted with curiosity.

"I wasn't just an escort yesterday, Paul. Dr. Emily Clarke is formally here, in the city, to visit with me," said Jo with a note of pride. "She was with me at your place, when we found it all fucked. And I'm glad she was, because I could hardly think straight, worrying about you."

"Why, exactly did you bring her to my place at this horrifically godly hour?"

"To reintroduce you properly." Jo took Emily's hand and pulled her forward. "Emily, this is my good companion and business partner, Paul Smith. Friends call him Smithy, so you should too. And Paul, this is Emily Clarke. You call her whatever the fuck she wants to be called, but she's not just Vanessa's doctor; she's my very dear friend, here for a visit with her family and me in addition to yesterday's appointment."

It was the first time Jo had ever witnessed her lover shake hands with her husband, firm, friendly, and smiling on both sides. It was one of the most beautiful things she'd ever seen, and she would be thankful to Emily forever for being willing—no, eager—to give Jo this gift.

"Your dear friend," said Paul, looking very pleased. "Isn't that interesting?"

"No more questions—that's the limit of what's your business," Jo said. "Now what's happened to you?"

"I shall begin with a beautiful, shining, vital prologue," he declared like some royal herald or minstrel. "In which the misplacement of your grandmother's book made me realize that I really did need to finish getting those shelves cleaned up, and sooner rather than later. That day when I brought your things out to the shop for a stunt, I also handled the *choicer* volumes, which I brought to the print house, where they're supposed to be kept anyway. Over the course of looking for the book and getting a handle on the mess, I've made a few more trips like that in the interim.

"Now, if you'd asked me about the situation yesterday morning, I might have had different feelings about the timing of all this, because that's when the prologue ends and the story begins—when the police bust down the doors at the print house."

"They raided the print house yesterday?" Jo repeated, aghast. "Why didn't you tell me?"

"Well, you weren't here, were you? And given how well our conversations have been going lately, I figured you didn't want me barging in at your clubs, looking for you. You weren't in danger, so I just made sure there was nothing for them here that could tie you back to the print house raid and decided to try again today." He grinned winningly. "And here we are! No harm done."

"No harm? You prat, our bloody house has been ransacked!"

"*Our* house?" he said with unfortunately reasonable irritation. "Weren't you just insisting it was only *my* house?"

"Oh, fuck off, you know I didn't mean any of that."

A heavy pause fell between them as Jo realized what she'd just said.

"Didn't you?" he asked, as if genuinely unsure.

Jo crossed her arms against an onslaught of regret over how she'd handled all this. "No, Paul. I didn't. I'm just a wanker, alright?"

There was another of those suspended moments, the sort that could go either way.

And this time, Paul chose to smile. "You really are."

She felt doubly so, now that she was being forgiven so easily. But she'd take it, and hopefully, remember this moment the next time she considered the path of the wanker.

"So what happened?" Jo prodded. "Tell me everything."

"Well, apparently, during that first raid, they got a couple of the dissenters who were actively using the press at the time. I hadn't realized anyone had actually been arrested, because I was chatting with one of my authors in my office, and we managed to sneak out the back no worse for wear."

"Not Reginald Cox, I hope?"

"No, thank God." Paul laughed darkly at the notion of his most paranoid author being present when the bobbies showed up. "I'd never get another word out of him if it had been. Nah, it was just Tipton, funnily enough." He turned to Emily, ensuring she wasn't left out. "Tipton doesn't even write anything bothersome, unless one despises lofty literary musings on the human condition, which would not surprise me in this political climate, to be honest." Back to Jo. "Anyway, I felt like an idiot for moving all that inventory from home, because the police took it all, along with a few other stacks that hadn't made it to the cellar yet, which is a damned shame, but it means that when they most unexpectedly busted through *our own* door at the crack of dawn today, there was nothing for them to find."

"How'd they find you?" Jo asked.

"The blokes who were arrested talked," he said. "No hard feelings, though. We use the same machines, but it's not as if we're old chums. I imagine it was either talk or take responsibility for the politics *and* the porn. I probably would have done the same, so it's only fair, really.

"Anyway, I played it off as being properly offended by the police harassment, denied any knowledge of the books, the printer, the radicals, any of it, and since there was nothing left in the house to contradict me, they eventually accepted the idea that they'd gotten the wrong Smith." He turned to Emily once more with a conspiratorial smile. "It's a decent enough name to possess in a crisis, don't you think?"

Emily looked stunned, eyes wide and lips parted in indignation. "Good heavens!" she said, looking like she was about to tell Paul off for having printed such indecent material in the first place. But then she said, some of that beautiful fire escaping as she did: "If they believed they had the wrong man, why would the police leave your sitting room in such a horrific state?"

Paul and Jo shared a look. He gave a sweet smile. "Joey, how on earth did *you* cross paths with such an uncynical soul?"

"She let me into her house for that first appointment with Vanessa, remember?"

"My dear doctor," he said to Emily with overblown concern. "Hasn't anyone ever told you not to let the vampires in? They can't cross thresholds without an invitation, you know."

Emily's nose wrinkled. "Excuse me?"

"Don't worry about it." Jo rolled her eyes. "He just thinks he's funny."

"On the other hand," he went on, "I must congratulate you, Joey, on making a friend who could possibly believe that London's police care if they leave an innocent man with a mess to clean up." He turned to Emily. "Not that I am an innocent man, of course. I absolutely deserve my mess, the trouble it will be to fix it, and the fact that my landlady's given me one week to clear the hell out after that debacle. But the officers who trashed everything don't know that, do they?"

One week to clear out?

After all the fear of this morning, all the fury that came with police invasion of her spaces, somehow, it was the landlady's words that got Jo's legs shaking again. Any insistence she'd made that the flat was not her home evaporated. She was starting over after all, and it hadn't even come down to her original worries. It wasn't Paul and Vanessa forcing her out. It wasn't that their baby was taking up too much room. It didn't even stem from the desperate itch that had always lived within her that said she had to run.

She should have known better. It wasn't friendship, love, little ones, or any of the other lovely things in life that kept forcing her out of her circumstances. It was police and landladies. Priests and parents. Power grabs and the fearful demands of people who saw her as an object for their own ends, too wrapped up in their own safety and self-image to give two fucks about hers.

A gentle grip on her upper arm brought her out of the swirling fog of helplessness. Emily. Emily's grip, Emily's clipped insistence that Jo allow herself to be led to the stool behind the counter. Emily's fingers brushing a stray bit of hair off her forehead and tucking it securely into one of her pins.

"She looks like she could use a drink," said Paul.

"Of tea," Emily said like the hiss of cold water over hot coals, harsh but warm and satisfying. "Is there somewhere here I can fix one, or should I go across the street?"

"Upstairs," Paul told her. "The other shopkeep, Miss Merriweather, lives up there, and she's got Vanessa with her. They'll help you find the fixings. She takes—"

"Sugar and extra cream, I know."

"Would you like me to go instead?" Paul offered. "You stay with her?"

"That is very polite, but no thank you," said Emily, unsmiling and a bit stiff. "I assume the two of you might like a moment to talk without me anyway."

Paul waved the notion off. "If Jo's brought you here, then I don't think that's necessarily true."

"I could stand to check in on Miss Garcia," she said. "I'm sure this morning has been a terrible shock to her nerves."

"You just think I'm going to slip whiskey in her tea if I'm left to my own devices, don't you?"

Emily pursed her lips so tight that Jo couldn't help but fix her own into half a smile.

"Well," Emily said, "you will, won't you?"

"Absolutely."

She took a moment to secure Jo's pin one more time before fixing her gaze on the staircase. "I'll handle it, then."

As she left, posture perfect as ever, Jo watched her, thinking that while she'd rather not have to start again, if whatever came next involved exchanges like that one, maybe it would be worth the trouble after all.

Chapter Twenty-One

Emily

Emily had entered that practical mode again, but it didn't trouble her. It was of such obvious comfort to Jo that it spurred her on with a purposeful righteousness she hadn't felt since the first days she'd spent shadowing her father through his appointments. In those days, she'd handed him instruments and medicines with a sense that even the most mundane actions she took mattered. She couldn't put her finger on when that feeling had fled, but when she went to fetch her suffering lover a healthful cup of tea, it was with the same sense of pride she'd had the first few times she'd fetched the bandages that might save a life.

She put her hand on the rail and peered up an even more treacherous stair than the one she'd encountered at Jo's home and nearly screamed when she saw a shadowy figure moving at the top of it. As her eyes adjusted to the dimness, she realized she knew the specter.

"Miss Garcia?" said Emily.

The woman seemed just as startled by the words as Emily had been of the sight. Miss Garcia stood up fast but unbalanced, like the new distribution of her own body weight had surprised her. She put one hand on her belly and the other on the rail to steady herself, even as Emily reached out in a panicked and unthinking notion of catching her in a fall.

Miss Garcia's painted smile seemed to spread in spite of herself as her balance was restored.

"I thank you for the generous impulse to catch me," she said in her clear voice. "Though I confess, I'm glad we didn't have to find out how effective it would have been."

"I could not agree with you more."

"Would you like to come upstairs?" Miss Garcia asked, clutching again at the roundness that disrupted the fall of her skirts.

"If it's not too much trouble," said Emily. "I'm in pursuit of tea for Jo. This morning has been a shock to her, as I'm sure it's been to you, as well. Were you there? When the police came?"

Miss Garcia shrugged dramatically with one of her hands drifting toward the ceiling, sending the silk fringe and rattling beads of her shawl into a tizzy.

"I was. But I'm trying to think of the whole thing as an *adventure*. A bit of *insight* into the deep range of emotions and experiences we can have as humans," she insisted. "You told me that lowered anxiety and a positive outlook would make all the difference for my little one, so here I am, doing my best."

While Emily appreciated how seriously her patient had taken the advice, she thought reframing a literal police raid as an adventure was taking things above and beyond.

She followed Miss Garcia up the stairs and into a small apartment. It was not especially modern, probably boasting nothing so nice as a tap nor possibly even a gas line. Still, it was well-kept for what it was, filled with worn but sturdy furniture, accented here and there with things like flouncy curtains, flowery china figures, and organized bookcases. Emily had a sense that she was not the only one occupied with keeping ghosts at bay; the place had the distinct air of somewhere that had once been haunted.

The other woman, the shopkeep Miss Merriweather, sat in a chair by the fireplace with some exceptionally lumpy knitting on her lap. The wrapper she wore was much finer than the rest of her home, and the way her face instantly shifted from a smile for Miss Garcia into a more polite and dignified nod of curiosity when she spotted a stranger gave the impression of a very different history than the performers and tradespeople she was in the midst of.

"Dr. Clarke!" the woman said, setting her knitting down so carelessly that one of the stitches slipped unnoticed from the end of a needle. She stood with both her hands outstretched for an enthusiastic shake. "It's so lovely to meet you at last! Goodness, you are beautiful, aren't you?"

Emily was shocked by such a strange, nearly schoolgirlish greeting. "Excuse me?"

"It *is* you Joey's been writing, isn't it?"

A blush crept across Emily's cheeks. "Did she tell you that?"

"Of course not, she never tells anyone anything." Miss Merriweather waved a hand. "But she's not as sneaky as she thinks she is. I figured it out ages ago."

"Dr. Clarke is seeking a cup of tea for our favorite sneak," said Miss Garcia, putting her hands on Emily's shoulders, a decided sign that whatever she'd overheard of Jo's new introduction had elevated Emily out of the mere doctor role. "Might we fix one?"

"Oh, let's make a whole bloody pot, shall we?" said Miss Merriweather, heading to her cupboards. "Let's make two, in fact. We could all use some fortification after the morning we've had."

As Miss Merriweather bustled about, busy with tea, Miss Garcia sat heavily in one of the chairs. She seemed to attempt her usual regal posture, but she looked a bit slumped and glassy-eyed again, the recently renewed color in her cheeks having fled once more.

"Are you alright, Miss Garcia?"

"Oh, I'm just a bit tired," she whispered to the floor. "Adventures do take a lot out of you sometimes, don't they?"

If everyone hadn't been so welcoming, Emily might have felt like an interloper in this near-miss with disaster. As it was, though, she felt comfortable taking the other seat, the part of her mind that was Dr. Clarke assessing Miss Garcia's pallor while the part that was Jo Smith's lover creased her brow with concern over a dear friend.

"Are you eating alright today?" she asked Miss Garcia gently. "Even with the…adventurous insights that filled your morning?"

Miss Garcia nodded and looked up to spare half a smile. "Admittedly, I became a bit queasy again, but I went back to the lemon water and ginger like you suggested, and managed to have a bit of breakfast. A soup Jo recommended."

"And I, of course, am taking impeccable care of her too!" Miss Merriweather chirped merrily as she stoked the coals beneath her kettle.

"She is," Miss Garcia agreed. "Between the three of you, I must be the best-tended actress in London."

And you need it, don't you? Emily thought. All the makeup and artistic excuses in the world could not hide how this woman had been rattled to the core. Given the fact that her health—while improving—was still precarious, it made Emily very nervous.

"And is the little one feeling as well-tended today?" she asked as lightly as she could. The last thing she wanted to do was induce more panic, but… "Moving about as usual?"

"I think he's been in hiding since the adventure." Miss Garcia put a hand to her belly without nearly as much concern as her words spurred in Emily. "It was a bit loud."

All that professional calmness Emily had cultivated over her years in the hospital threatened to run off into the streets of London, never to be seen again. She hardly dared speak, terrified that her sudden fear would show up as a quiver in her voice. In fact, she considered saying nothing at all. It was probably fine. Probably her own imagination running away with her as she envisioned the various chains of disaster that could cascade from a babe who wasn't moving as usual. No sense panicking everyone else over her own madness...

As she attempted to get her worries under control, the kettle began to boil in earnest. Miss Merriweather, humming to herself, gathered it up and went to pour water over the leaves in the pot.

Mere moments ago, that silly old cup of tea she was brewing had instilled Emily with an old confidence she'd lost. But satisfying as those helpful, comforting tasks had been, if they were everything Emily wanted, she could have much more easily become a nurse.

It was easy to forget, addled as she was by the unequal treatment she received. But she liked to use her very specialized skills to be of help in dire circumstances. It was only when caring for someone felt meaningless and unappreciated that she wondered why she bothered. But when there was conviction or... or love, she supposed...behind it, that was something different.

That was everything.

Jo cared about this woman. By extension, so did Emily.

She could handle this case. Not just because she was professionally equipped, but because she bloody *cared*.

"Miss Garcia—may...may I call you Vanessa, actually?"

The woman's sly eyes lit up. "Oh, of course! I love that. But only if I may call you Dr. Emily."

"That...yes, I think that would be alright," Emily agreed.

"Vanessa, may I take a quick assessment? After such an adventure, I simply wouldn't feel right without checking on things."

She remained impressively calm, though Vanessa—ever aware of people's attitudes and energies—seemed to sense her nerves. She nodded quietly and said very little as Emily checked her pulse and the color of her nailbeds, palpating her abdomen gently in hopes of waking the babe up, if indeed it was just napping.

"Is everything alright?" Vanessa asked.

"Let's have a bit of that tea," Emily said. "Miss Merriweather? Could you—"

"Got it!" said Miss Merriweather, pouring generously.

"Add a good heap of sugar," Emily instructed.

"I thought I was to take less sugar and more lemon," said Vanessa.

Emily felt bad about the suggestion now that she'd become a bit more accepting of the positives of pleasure. "That's true most of the time, but I have to admit that even sugar has its uses. A good lump of it can sometimes give a sleepy babe a wake-up call," she said. "And... I suppose a bit here and there is alright. Might even give him a sweeter disposition."

Vanessa, to her credit, seemed to get the joke immediately, in spite of the dryness of Emily's delivery. Jo was not, it seemed, the only person in the world who could spot her humor, and there was something very nice about that.

The tea was sweetened. Vanessa drank it all with her feet up and a cool cloth over her forehead while Miss Merriweather brushed her hair and Emily tried not to stare too worriedly for too long a stretch.

Just when Emily thought she couldn't take another moment, Vanessa sat bolt upright so fast the cloth fell into her teacup.

"Oh, there he is!" she laughed, hand back to her belly. "Yes, rolling all round now. Goodness."

Emily and Miss Merriweather let out matching held breaths and smiled, each taking a turn to feel the proof of nothing-to-worry-about.

Yet.

The thought of leaving this woman here, where she was about to be displaced from yet another home, possibly at risk for more devastating shocks like the one this morning, struck Emily suddenly as untenable. What if there was another scare like this? And Emily at least an hour away, even once word reached Farncombe? She'd planned to stay with Noah for the last six weeks of the confinement, but that didn't sound like enough under these circumstances.

They needed to be close.

And Miss Garcia needed to be somewhere safe. Secure. A place with plenty of fresh air and healthful food and room to move about.

"Vanessa," said Emily, righteous purpose building high in her again. "How would you like to spend the rest of your confinement with me in Surrey? You saw that there is more than enough room for you to move about quite comfortably. And as for sleeping… Well, my brother's old room is unoccupied nearly all the time, and as it happens, I've just cleaned it out and made it suitable for company. Having someone in it would keep the dust balls from collecting so quickly."

"Goodness, Dr. Emily!" Vanessa exclaimed, clutching her chest. "That is almost absurdly generous. I couldn't impose like that."

"Don't think of it as an imposition," Emily reasoned. "I'm your doctor. If I recommend a cleaner, less-stressful atmosphere than your own corner of London, then wouldn't it be reasonable for me to provide what I have recommended?"

"Opening your own home is beyond the scope of a doctor's responsibility."

"What if I didn't offer as your doctor, then?" she said in a rush, thinking so fondly of the woman downstairs still waiting on that cuppa that her voice nearly broke with affection. "What if I offered as a friend of the family who just so happens to have extra space for a guest in need?"

"Of the family?"

"Yes. I'm Jo's friend," she said, feeling assured in it now. "And she's something of a family member to you, isn't she? Not a namable one, or a proper one, but something?"

Emily stood up, smoothing her skirts and wondering how she could possibly feel so calm, inviting a woman to have her baby in the same home that had witnessed her own mother's tragic end. But she did. More than calm, she felt convicted. She felt love. She felt it was right in a way she could not quite explain to herself just yet.

"Do think about it," she said. "Talk it over with Mr. Smith. With Jo. With whoever else you have in your life that you talk things over with. And send word as to whether I ought to prepare you a room of your own."

Emily finally managed to get that cup of tea for Jo, then went back downstairs to let her and Smithy know that they ought to encourage Vanessa to take the offer, if she ended up asking their opinion.

"Her staying with you?" Jo clarified over her steaming cup. She seemed improved after some further talk with Smithy, and even more so upon seeing Emily.

"Yes," said Emily.

"Instead of you coming here?"

"Given the circumstances, I think it's the best option," Emily said in the most authority-laced doctor voice she could manage while watching Jo warm her lovely hands on the hot cup. "I know you will both miss her, but I shudder to think what might happen if she finds herself in the thick of another fright. It's my professional opinion that she should leave the city until the child is born and she's through the first few weeks of lying in." She let her voice soften as she looked at Jo. "And it is my personal opinion that if I had room enough to offer you shelter a mere half-hour ago, then I have room enough for one of your friends. Admittedly, she takes up a bit more space than you at this time, but it's not enough to make the difference."

Jo chuckled a little, but then locked eyes with Smithy. They were both wincing slightly, like they had something on their minds.

"What is it?" Emily said. "I hope you don't think to argue with me."

"Quite the contrary, Doctor," said Smithy with that ironic, sun-in-your-eyes brightness he seemed to enjoy exuding. "We'd come to a similar conclusion in your absence."

"Oh, really? Well, that's lovely then, isn't it!"

Jo turned back to Emily, still wincing. "He said *similar*."

"Alright," said Emily slowly. "What's dissimilar about it, then?"

"I was wondering, um." Jo looked into her tea, up at the ceiling, anywhere but at Emily. "You see, it looks like, at least temporarily, a bit of a new life is necessary again for me. We've lost the home already, but we might be able to avoid the same fate with the shop if we're careful. I'm going to stay away until we're in the clear, just to make very sure they don't find a wanted man's wife running the place. Alma and some of our friends are more than capable of running it—and running it clean—while I'm away. So… I suppose I'm doing something different for a while. Not forever, hopefully, but…a while."

"Oh no!" Emily was hardly one for a show of affection in front of another person, even a person who wouldn't mind, but she could not resist extending Jo the comfort of a hand on her shoulder. "That's quite the opposite of what you wanted."

"It is. But...it wouldn't be so bad if, I think, if that new start included...well...you."

"What are you saying?"

"Vanessa and her babe come first," Jo said carefully. "But if there's room enough for me, I might like to take you up on your original offer after all."

Emily's gentle strokes turned into a squeeze. The circumstances of it were such a shame that she hated to be thrilled, but there was no other word to describe her response. "Of course there's room!" she said, a smile spreading across her face and right on down the path to Jo's as well. "Plenty of room."

"That's wonderful," said Jo. She looked happy, but that half-a-wince was still there. "In that case I have one more question."

"Anything."

"Is there room enough for this git?"

She nodded toward Paul Smith.

The question shocked her enough that she didn't answer right away, and it seemed she wasn't the only one surprised. Smithy himself looked at Jo like she'd grown about six heads.

"Joey," he hissed, like he was trying to be subtle even as the sound bounced off every spine in the bookshop. "You can't just ask her that."

"Seems I did."

"Why?"

"So I can reset my status as a wanker, Paul!" she all-but-shouted, the silly verbiage eaten up by a genuine note of regret. "I have been a complete shit, while you go on smiling and joking and giving me more chances than I have ever deserved. I owe you back for the way you've waited for me to come to my senses. And so I will ask her, even though it is inappropriate and awkward and far too much to ask of a person." She turned her perfect, impassioned face back toward Emily. "Can you give him a place too, just for a bit?"

"If you say no," said Smithy very politely, "I will not hold it against you. And I will talk Jo out of holding it against you as well."

But Emily was nodding before the decision had even been fully made, as if her body, her very bones, knew the answer before her mind could catch up.

"Of course I'll make room," Emily said. "If you are that important to Jo, you are that important to me."

Chapter Twenty-Two

Jo

And after all that, it was time for some biblical criticism with the Clarke family.

Emily said it would be alright if everyone started getting themselves together to leave the city sooner rather than later, but while some distance from the shop might save it in the end, such a talk was the very last place anyone with any sense would ever go looking for Mrs. Jo Smith anyway. There was hardly a more anonymous place for her in world.

"If you'll take my irritating husband into your own damn home," Jo reasoned, "then I'd be a right prick to refuse a few hours with your perfectly nice family, half of which happen to be my own friends already."

"I haven't heard yet whether David will be joining us—"

"Oh," Jo said with certainty, thinking how pleased he'd be to know what exactly had come of the disastrous match he'd hoped to make of them. "Once you tell him I'm coming and why, he'll be there."

It wasn't exactly a double shot of whiskey and a game of cards with her friends, but it wasn't the worst way to unwind after such a bizarre morning. Jo sat on a hard bench in a simple meeting house that did not feel like a church to her at all. The few odd glances she got seemed more to do with her status as a stranger, rather than the strangeness of her attire. The service, if one wanted to call it that, was brief, pleasant, and didn't involve communion or anything she needed to figure out how and whether to participate in.

The talk afterward about nativity criticisms or whatever it was was dull, frankly, but seated between Noah and Emily, she spent it getting last night's club gossip on one side and further context about the lecture subject on the other. While that context was unnecessary—Jo wasn't exactly set on taking this knowledge out with her and doing anything with it—Emily leaned in shiveringly close to whisper into Jo's ear, and Jo was so charmed and pleased by it that she decided she'd happily come back to criticize the Pentecost too, if they could do it just like this.

She wasn't quite as keen to go to the coffee house afterward, between the possibility of seeing the Bradigan family and intrusive questions from the obviously curious Dr. Phillip Clarke and Mme. Baptiste. But Jo's attempts to excuse herself from the social meeting were disrupted by David, who did not voice his motivations for thwarting her escape, but he didn't need to. Clearly, they lay somewhere between *if I have to go, you have to go* and *as your matchmaker, I cannot let you bungle things with this woman again.* They were both reasonable enough arguments, even if he didn't speak them directly, and so she tipped her hat over her face until she'd passed by the Bradigans and settled upstairs, preparing to tolerate the barrage of questions that inevitably came her way.

Notably, Emily did not tell her father about her invitation for Jo and the rest to take up shelter with them just yet. But it went well, otherwise.

By the time Jo and Emily returned to Miss Withers's Orchid and Pearl Society House for the Sunday supper they'd irrevocably committed to, Jo was somehow both dead tired and wound so tight with both stress and affection that she worried she might never sleep again.

"Miss Withers," she heard Emily say as she loaded plates for both of them from the excessive spread in the dining room. "Would it be too much trouble if we took this upstairs?"

"All comfort, dear," Miss Withers said in her usual way. "Not rules."

"Save for the one about committing to meals ahead of time."

"Well, that's not a rule. It's simple manners."

This time, Emily led the way, and Jo's feet were happy to have someone else making the decisions for once. She clutched Gran's book—which she'd carried along through the day's events—under her arm and followed along.

God, Emily really should have run for the hills the second she saw Paul's wrecked rooms. Jo'd had some questionable times with lovely women, but this one really took the cake. Yet Emily, who should have been even more disturbed than the average, had handled it like a dream. For a day that had begun with a police raid, it had been a surprisingly good one, all things considered.

They sat together in the parlor, just the two of them, eating their supper while Emily tried to encourage Jo to have opinions on the talk. When that didn't get them further than teasing (which led, perhaps, to a bit of kissing here or there), they set their plates aside, curled up together on the small couch, and began to properly examine the damage to Gran's book.

"This could be a lot worse," Jo assured Emily as they flipped through, finding all the crimped pages, the muddy boot prints, the jagged rips through recipes handwritten in Gran's heavy, left-slanting script. As they carefully turned pages, Jo was filled with a warmth that not even the damage could compete with.

"Oh, God this soup was always the best. I never did get it right myself, but if you could ever manage, you'd be in for a treat… This is the rouge I used to sell to the women in the parish, like I told you. Not that any of us were really *supposed* to be using it, but you could hardly tell that the pink was fake, so they paid well for the stuff… And fuck, *this* bugger. It's a good medicine for a head cold, assuming the taste doesn't kill you first…

"Nothing seems to be entirely illegible… Except… Oh, well fuck!"

Jo stared at the page she'd come to, smeared, with some of the page missing entirely. She laughed. Not happily, of course, but what else was there to do when she found that the only page not in salvageable order was the one titled Button Stitches.

"What was it?" Emily asked, running her hand over what was left of the page.

"It's what I was looking for in the first place, of course." Jo laughed again. If she didn't, she knew she'd cry instead. She'd been a twat to misplace the book. To forget the stitch in the first place. She'd refused to look back one too many times, it seemed, and this was to be her punishment. Loose buttons for eternity. "My stupid waistcoat buttons keep coming loose."

"I wonder why?" Emily mused, tracing the row of them down the center of Jo's chest all the way to her stomach—a ticklish, pleasant action—and then across the page to what was left of the sketch Gran had done of her stitch. "What's this then? Looks like a simple thread shank—"

"That's what it's called!" Jo exclaimed, pointing at what was left of the picture. "Is that something you've heard of, then?"

Emily cocked her head to the side like she thought Jo might

be kidding. "It's a fairly standard sort of thing. Don't you already sew them on with a shank?"

"I don't know," Jo admitted, a little smirk ghosting over her face. "I sew them the way I sew them. Why don't you take a look and see what I did?"

"I suppose I could try to diagnose the problem," Emily said with a dramatic, world-weary sort of sigh as she settled herself on Jo's lap, facing and straddling her.

"God, this rational dress is just relentlessly convenient," Jo said, settling her hands on Emily's hips, and tipping her head back to allow Emily to undo, caress, and very closely examine Jo's most desperately strained buttons. "Between ease of removal and ease of movement, I can do without seeing the extra frills. You're more than pretty enough without all that anyway."

With a final nudge to the button with her nose, Emily raised her head. "You're obviously not using a pin or a toothpick to hold your threads when you stitch the holes," she said. "It's not leaving enough of a shank, and it's straining the threads until they snap. You could stand to wax the thread too, if you're not already. I could do it for you, if there are some supplies."

Jo couldn't believe how it all came back to her as soon as Emily said it. All at once, she could remember her gran pulling a pin out of her own hair and using it to hold threads in place, to ensure the tension fell in the right spot in the end.

She squeezed Emily's bottom in a show of thanks. "How did you know that? Noah?"

Emily scoffed so vehemently that Jo laughed. "I hardly need a Milan-trained tailor to get a button on properly. Did you never bother asking anyone for help?"

"Who would I have asked? Gran's gone. My mum and aunts are—"

"Why didn't you ask Miss Withers? Miss Merriweather? Even Noah—though he might have pretended it really *was* some tricky thing he learned from someone important instead of a rather basic life skill."

Jo was bewildered by how silly the whole thing sounded now. "I remembered it being so complicated. Something I wouldn't find anywhere else. Her own trick..."

"It goes that way sometimes, doesn't it?" Emily sighed, pushing a bit of Jo's hair behind her ear gently. "I find ghosts are very prone to complicating matters like that."

"You believe in ghosts?" Jo snorted.

"Of course not—" Emily broke off, thinking about it for a moment. "Well. Actually. I suppose I must. It's not rational, and I would very much prefer not to, but...one in particular has been complicating my life since the beginning. To deny her presence has only ever led to trouble."

Something a bit chilling occurred to Jo, then. "Emily, are you sure you should invite Vanessa to have her baby at your house?" she asked, concerned that she'd accidentally pushed Emily into offering something that she really shouldn't have. "It's one thing to risk a pigeonholing, Em, but if it's more than your mind can handle—"

Emily smiled. "Honestly, Jo, I think it will be the best thing either I or my father has done for our minds in ages. Our house has felt empty, tragic, frozen in time for as long as I can remember. I understand why Noah wanted to run from it."

"I thought it was because he didn't want to be a doctor."

"Oh, he says that. Might even actually believe it, for all I know. I myself believed it was David's influence that drew him away for an embarrassingly long time. But even now that all those rifts are healed? He's still avoiding the house, leaving me alone to take care of a father who is going to need a lot more care much sooner than I anticipated. And it's because the damned house still feels so... I truly don't know what else to call it other than haunted."

Jo nodded. "You think it might make Noah more willing to come help you? If you can chase that feeling out with a successful birth?"

"No," Emily said immediately. "There's no guarantee this will be successful, and I would never be so foolish as to bet on such a thing. But standing still and refusing to participate fully in our own lives, in our relationships to other people, is not keeping the past at bay. It's giving it all the room in the world to thrive at our own expense. I want Vanessa to come stay with us just as much as I want you to come. As I want your very silly and surprisingly likable husband to come. I want everyone to come, because I cannot stand another year somewhere empty and frozen. There must be life in our house, Jo. Like there's life in the place you sometimes share with Smithy. Or in your clubs. Or Miss Merriweather's little flat above the shop. People making tea and pouring champagne for each other, playing chess, passing questionable novels around, giving each other flowers. Those things aren't decadence. They're life. And there's a chance I'm bringing more death to our doorstep. I understand that. But that's the risk you take, isn't it?

"And maybe it won't convince Noah to do right by me. Maybe it won't wake my father out of his stupor. But I will enjoy every bloody minute of every bloody day. Because it is something in this world of nothing I've been moving through." She paused at last, putting her small but strong hands on either side of Jo's face. "And because you will be there. And being there is the most wonderful thing that anyone has ever done for me."

"Just being there?" Jo repeated with a nervous chuckle at the notion. "Emily, darling, I hope to do that and a whole lot more for you in the future."

Kisses were inevitable then, lovely ones. Soft with just a touch of heated hunger until Emily pulled back, breathing heavy but clearly determined to speak.

"Well, there's one thing I'd like to do for you as well, before we go."

"What's that?" Jo asked. "I'd have thought hiding my husband's stupid arse from the police would have been more than enough…"

"Where can I find some thread around here?" Emily spun her finger around the worst of Jo's waistcoat buttons, then slipped her hands under the fabric like she might find sewing supplies conveniently hidden beneath the fall of Jo's breasts. "That one's a little loose already; I'll show you how it's done, and we can rewrite the page together, to replace the ruined one when you rebind the book."

Jo arched her back into the touch, closing her eyes, grasping at Emily's skirts, and letting the feeling of hands and then kisses carry her off a bit.

"But which of us should write it?" she mused, voice going rasped and floaty as Emily handled shirtwaist buttons just as dexterously as she had the outer ones. "Your script being so lusty and mine so cramped and closed off, it won't look right."

Emily's next kiss was curved into a devious smile.

Jo pulled back, suspicious. "What?"

"There's something I haven't told you."

"You? Keeping a mystery from *me*?"

She leaned in and whispered in Jo's ear, "I know how to forge people's handwriting."

"*What?*"

"Well, you can't blame me," Emily huffed. "It's society's fault. If everyone took documentation and follow-up instructions as seriously from me as they do from my father, I wouldn't have to. But I've been writing up notes to look like they came from him for years. Otherwise, the patients won't listen, and that sort of closemindedness can be dangerous. Look, I'm not saying my skills will get past the sharp eye of an expert like yourself." She tapped a single finger against Jo's bottom lip. "But I can probably do well enough that your dear old grand-mother won't look like as decadent and lusty a writer as I am."

As the joke landed, just as dryly delivered as all her best ones were, Jo was lit with a pure and uncomplicated happiness.

"I love the way you do that," she said with a grin. "I love the way you are, Emily. I…"

Emily smiled back, blinking a few times in encouragement. "Yes?"

"I love you very much," Jo said, a certain reverence in her voice that she herself hardly recognized. "I can't believe I'm say-ing that to someone. Particularly someone who doesn't drink whiskey."

"Strange for me too," said Emily. "To love someone enough that I'd go on kissing her even if she reeked of the stuff."

Chapter Twenty-Three

Emily

Farncombe, Surrey

It was another week or so of letters before Emily saw Jo again, though this time, there were presents involved, as Christmas drew nearer and Jo cleared various possessions from her home and shop.

She sent a few more rebound dime romances, artfully swathed as if they'd been penned by none other than Mary Wollstonecraft, along with a famous horror story that was not rebound but had genuinely been written by that great thinker's own daughter. She also promised that there was still one lingering volume that was not ready yet.

Emily would just have to check back in for it later. Nothing for it.

As for Emily, she sent the first piece of the chess set she'd designed especially for Jo. Unable to bear parting the two co-ordinating queens on her desk to complete that set, she'd created a new one in which the bases looked like cubes of type whose letters coordinated with their names. It was a new and blocky style, and she was conveniently slower at making them.

Jo would simply have to stick around long enough to receive the complete set piece by piece.

With those lingering, unfinished promises, they had no choice but to plan for the time they'd spend together during the last months of Vanessa's confinement.

Emily knew that Jo hated to leave her work behind, hard-won as it was. Idleness and dependency weren't her way. So Emily asked around at the local papers and print houses until she'd secured Jo and Smithy some regular work setting newspaper composites for the *Godalming Times* that would last the length of their stay. Meanwhile, Vanessa would help tend to the animals and learn from Jo, Emily, and Betsy some of the life-things like soup-making and child-tending that actresses weren't expected to know, but that working-class parents needed at least a basic understanding of. When she returned to London, it would be well-rested and prepared for whatever came next.

It was all arranged fairly well, actually.

Except for the fact that Emily hadn't told Papa yet.

She'd told him friends were coming to stay, since Betsy insisted she could not prepare for arrival without it impacting the household accounts enough for Papa to notice. So, he had to be told that Emily's friends from London—including whom he called "that delightful Miss Jo"—would be riding out the end of winter here.

What she hadn't told him yet was that a baby was set to be born within these walls and under the care of this odd, broken family and all of its ghosts.

She considered pretending that Vanessa planned to leave before the birth itself and acting surprised when it came "early." But Betsy didn't like that one, either.

"What you're doing for this woman is an act of charity and

generosity that will reflect beautifully on this entire household for years to come," Betsy said. "Don't you even think of hiding your light, Miss Emily. You tell him what you're doing, and if he complains about having a daughter so inclined to goodness, you tell him to take those complaints and..." She broke off, blushing like she'd been about to make a rather rude suggestion indeed. "Tell him to, er...take them to the chaplain. That's right. See what *he* has to say on the matter."

With that rather scolding encouragement echoing in her head, she...well, unfortunately she proceeded to just let the words go on echoing while she put the conversation off even further, avoiding every opportunity until the very day the company was set to arrive.

There was a quiet knock on her study door as she rocked in her chair, working on a rook perched securely upon its letter *R* for Jo's chess set.

"Yes?" she called, certain she knew whom it was and knowing she could put it off no longer. "Come in, Papa."

He opened the door and stepped tentatively inside, his eyes flicking around the room as they always did on the rare occasion he came into this place, like he couldn't quite believe it was no longer the sewing room it had been for so long.

"Your friends are set to arrive soon, aren't they?" he asked. "Are you ready for them?"

"Oh yes," said Emily, still rocking and carving. "But I'm not planning to sit around waiting, what with the train always being so late coming in from London. They'll arrive when they arrive. In the meantime, I'll enjoy this bit of quiet while it lasts."

Papa smiled. "Wise of you. I'll leave you to it, then."

"Papa, wait."

He turned back as Emily let her carving things fall into the nest her apron made across her lap.

"You need to know something," she went on, "about this visit."

Much to her surprise, Papa smiled widely. "Oh, my dear. I do know that you and Miss Jo are a very special sort of companions, and you should know by now that I would never stand in the way of love in any form. She is as welcome in this house as David is, and our family will be all the better for her presence in our lives."

Well, that was so sugary sweet and unlike her father that she felt dreadful following it up with the real news she had to give.

"That's very lovely, Papa, and I thank you for that sentiment. Really." She cleared her throat and picked at a woodshaving. "But you ought to know that while she's partly coming to grace us with that presence, she is also coming to accompany Miss Garcia, our other friend, who required a comfortable place to wait out the end of her maternal confinement, and a safe place and skilled attendant to see her through the child's delivery."

To his credit, the panic that crossed her father's face was kept very quiet and very close. He waited the span of a few calming breaths before responding in a voice that was almost convincingly practical.

"I thought you were concerned about being trapped in that specialty. While you could possibly obscure the details from London, once the village hears you've brought a patient like this into your home…"

"You're not wrong," Emily said, rocking and staring at the beautiful rows of brown, black, white, and tan chess pieces that lined her shelves, the useless, decadent items of beauty and leisure that she created and surrounded herself with in the quiet hours. "That was my fear. But I don't fear it anymore."

"You've accepted the inevitability?"

"Not exactly." She met his eye, and for once, was able to keep her face and voice soft. She'd been thinking on this for weeks, now. What it meant for her to have done this. What paths it might force. Or cut her off from. But how little that mattered, in the end. "I don't think the success or failure of my life will be measured by the perfect, sensible line of my career path, any more than it might have been defined by a husband. My life is my own to live. To support us, I'll do the work that makes sense for me. For the moment, it makes sense to help Miss Garcia. Perhaps after, it will make sense to take on a few more patients like her. Or not. Perhaps it will make more sense to demand that the hospital start paying me properly if it wants me to act as both doctor and nurse for such long, trying hours. Maybe I'll learn something new. Something ridiculous. Like printing." She smiled to herself. "I hear that having a loving companion teach you printing can lead to a very interesting life indeed."

Papa had not recovered from his stunned silence until the bell rang from the front door, and Betsy's shuffle started toward the entryway below them.

Emily put her carving things on her desk, right at the feet of the two swirling queens, who stood surrounded by dried flowers and stacks of letters atop the stately stage of Shelley's *Frankenstein*, an artifact she liked very much even if she wasn't sure she wanted to read it. She adjusted the queens slightly, then went over to kiss her father's cheek and squeezed one of his hands, hoping they were not in any pain today.

"I don't know what comes next, exactly," she admitted. "But I know I am surrounded by you, and Miss Jo, and Noah and David, and so many people who I would do anything for, and who would do much for me. Whatever the next phase brings will work out well enough, under circumstances like that."

And Papa, for all he still looked nervous about the prospect, squeezed her hand back, smiled, and expressed that he'd like to hear more about these insights over coffee tonight.

"With Jo along to share her own thoughts on the matter,

I hope," he added. "She strikes me as a very interesting person, with many interesting ideas, if you can get her talking. Or writing. She seems to have an awful lot to say in that particular format."

She followed Papa out into the hall. She hesitated on the threshold, realizing she'd forgotten to sweep. But the dust and ghosts would keep, she supposed. She had a long-awaited guest to greet first. A living one. But before she could go downstairs to see if she could help anyone with their luggage, she heard boots on the staircase, and watched as a dark-haired head appeared over the railing.

Jo all but stumbled to a stop when she got to the upstairs landing, grinning in a windswept sort of way as she spotted Emily. Papa got himself out of the way and down the stairs quickly, as Jo came and crushed Emily up into the sort of chilly, sooty embrace that came after a morning's travel.

"Sorry," she said sheepishly, stepping back and holding out a fresh handful of dried flowers wrapped in ribbon, lavender this time. They would be a beautiful addition to the queenly décor on Emily's desk. "I couldn't wait. Your housekeeper told me where to find you."

"She's always been a very helpful woman," said Emily as she accepted another embrace. "I'm so glad you're here."

"Me too."

"Really?" Emily teased. "Glad to be stuck in Farm-Brush for months at a time with some drab old spinster and her guinea pigs?"

"Well, when you put it that way…" Jo made a face for a moment, then grabbed Emily by the hand, pulled her in like they were about to start the most unlikely of dances right there in the upstairs hallway. After a quick and pleasantly unnecessary glance to make sure there was no one looking on from the staircase, she kissed Emily full and smiling on the mouth. "Yes. Yes, Emily, I am bloody thrilled to be here."

Epilogue

"I can assure you, little fellow, you've got the very best uncle in all the world." The blond baby in Charlie Price's arms gave a skeptical coo. "Don't believe me? Well, I have sparkling references. I just watched my niece write a very nice one up for me right on the nursery wall in pink chalk: 'Uncle Charlie is great.' Her parents weren't thrilled, but her enthusiasm really couldn't be confined to paper…"

Jo watched him with reluctant respect from her spot on the counter. It was getting on evening and the shop—back in her hands and safe at last—had just closed for the day, but it was more full of life than she could ever remember. Paul and Vanessa had brought baby Peter over from their new—very safe, very anonymous—place in Victoria to properly meet a couple members of his odd, not-so-little-anymore family: the shopkeep Alma Merriweather; the gruff Miles Montague, one of Paul's writers and friends; and Jo's very dear, very baby-loving old chum Charlie, who had been more excited about this development than anyone but Paul and Vanessa themselves.

There was still someone missing, though not for long, Jo hoped. Someone she suspected might be as happily greeted by the little one as she would be by Jo herself. Jo loved Emily, and that was profound in itself, but to Peter Whittaker—Jo got to keep the Smith, though the others had not—Emily was the first pair of hands to hold him, the one who'd revived his mum when things looked grim, who'd been the keeper of his first home and a face he'd seen daily until he and Vanessa were strong and safe enough to return to London, where they'd started their life…well…not anew, but afresh.

"Are you ever going to give him back to his mum?" Jo asked Charlie, pretending she wasn't straining her eyes and her ears as she spoke, hoping to catch the sight of a particularly straight spine among the foot traffic outside, or the severe clack of a harsh heel on the threshold.

"Oh yes, I'll give him back!" Charlie rubbed his nose against Peter's tiny one until he'd gotten a smile. "Just as soon as he cries or soils himself or does anything remotely unpleasant, she'll have him back straightaway, I promise."

"You always say that's the fun of being an uncle," Miles muttered, half mocking, half affectionate.

"Exactly," said Charlie. "Here, you try!"

Charlie pushed the little one into his lover's arms. Miles looked stunned for a moment, but seemed to settle into the situation surprisingly quickly for such a large, rumpled fellow. Within moments, he was walking the lad around the shop, showing him the new books and the old newspaper clippings on the wall that held the place's history.

Jo shook her head, pinching a bite off one of the Bradigan raisin cakes Alma had brought over along with an assortment of proper supper foods. They all chatted and ate and passed the baby around until Jo nearly found herself tempted to complain

about the lateness of the trains these days like some old cur-
mudgeon...

That curmudgeonliness was cut short, thankfully, by the
sound of knocking on the locked shop door.

"*Bello!*" Noah shouted through the keyhole. "Your lover and
darling sisters have arrived!"

Alma let them in, Noah first, sweeping around the room to
pester everyone with European kisses while Emily and David
came in behind him with Emily's trunk. Paul tried to take Emily's side of it, an act of chivalry that was met with a glare until
Paul nodded across the room to where Jo was just slipping down
off the counter to greet her properly. Emily conceded her half
of the trunk so she could scramble into Jo's arms.

"Couple more bags out there," David said with a grunt as
they dropped the trunk at the foot of the stairs. "Not much,
though. She packs light."

"Light?" said Paul, eyeing the luggage. "How long is she
staying for?"

Emily turned, still clutching Jo's waist with one arm. "I'm
irrevocably confirmed with Miss Withers through the summer, at least. Hopefully, the hospital will want me that long."

"Don't be modest," Jo scolded. "The Soho Women's Hospital
asked for her specially. And she was good enough to say yes."

"For now," Emily said very deliberately. "I am going to give
it a go. They'll be paying me, at least, and seeing as I have a
most *cordial* old friend to keep me company in the city—"

"As all the best female physicians do," said Noah with a little wink.

"Stop that, it's presumptuous and impolite," Emily scolded.
"Anyway, I have a cordial old friend here, so I'm going to see
whether it's a good fit. No harm in it. If it doesn't suit, I suppose I'll either head home or..." She smiled and fiddled with
one of the more innocently located and solidly stitched of Jo's

waistcoat buttons. "Or maybe I'll start mixing up rouges and sell them as a witch in the streets of London. Who's to say?"

"What of your dear old father?" said Vanessa with a warm concerned look. "All on his own in that house. Will he be alright?"

Emily caught Noah's eye across the room. Her brother did not look entirely happy about what he was going to say next, but he took a breath and managed:

"David and I will be spending the summer with him," he said. "It's close enough that I can get to London when I need to, and it's clear that David could use a little fresh air. So off to the quiet hills and streets we go, while Warren and the rest have their fun running the club into the ground without us."

David patted him on the back. "He's very excited, as you can see."

"It's well past time I took my turn for a bit."

"And after?" Vanessa asked a bit sharply. She and Phillip had become good friends while she was recovering at the Clarke cottage and she had clearly become a little protective.

David's eye gave that sort of horrible twinkle that came before a good matchmaking. "Don't you worry about that. I'll make sure he has suitable company in the form of a particular Frenchwoman well before we come back to London. After all, seems I can set anyone up."

He was eyeing Jo and Emily like he'd done all the real work of bringing this about in the first place.

Jo met Emily's eye. She rolled hers, clearly thinking along the same lines as Jo: that David's impact had been minimal, but that they ought to let him have it.

After a bit more chatter and hellos, Emily turned to coo at little Peter, who did seem to recognize her from his earliest weeks of life. Then she came back to Jo, her now-familiar smile so beautiful that it was almost hard to think about how such an expression had once seemed impossible on her lovely face.

"Either way, I've decided that the next phase of my life—our lives—" Emily added, with a sweet nudge "—will be carried out right here. Together."

★ ★ ★ ★ ★

Acknowledgments

I would have loved to write Jo and Emily's book in some perfect little cabin in the woods with nothing to do but pen their story. Unfortunately, that was very much not the case this time around, and so I am especially grateful to everyone who supported me through the writing and production process. We did it!

As always, thanks to my husband and best friend, Michael, for being able to spot the soul in my earliest, messiest drafts, and reminding me of it on the days I think everything is terrible.

Many, many thanks to my amazing team at Carina Press, who kept everything moving forward no matter what came our way: Stephanie Doig, Kerri Buckley, Katixa Espinoza, Stephanie Tzogas. Not to mention all the other awesome people in art and design, marketing, audio, and the wider Harlequin and HarperCollins world who I don't work with quite so directly, but who are making things happen behind the scenes every day.

And of course, thank you to my agent, Laura Zats, for just... everything you do. Keeping me sane, handling details and awkwardness, brainstorming ideas. All the things!

Last but not least, I want to sincerely thank my incredible

readers. Your enthusiasm for this series, and your contagious joy and kindness, kept me motivated and excited to sit down and face the page every day. You are truly the best!